A Change in Entropy
John Bacon

Chapter 1 – Alpha and Omega

Peter Turnus

One enemy remained; two if you counted God. They lasted longer than expected, but the Great Nations always won in the end. Peter almost felt sorry for them. But, orders were orders. Peter's ears rang with mortar fire. His lungs burned with soot and smoke. His vision blurred light and dark, clashing in an endless rage. Peter pressed forward. Even if his senses failed, Peter knew he could always trust Sinon.

"Get down!" Sinon pulled Peter to the earth. A deafening blast of black light screamed over the boys' heads followed by a barrage of dirt and shrapnel. Peter groaned. Religious wars were the worst.

"What are you waiting for?" Sinon shouted. "Get a barrier up!" Peter channeled his numen. Soft white light flowed from Peter's body, enveloping him in a warm cloak. He scrambled to his feet and focused the numen to his outstretched palm. Energy surged through his arms, powerful and invigorating. Ahead, a storm of limestone and shattered tanks hurtled towards them. Peter's face paled.

"I can't do this!" Peter turned to Sinon, frantic.

"Yes you can!" Sinon pressed his back against Peter's to act as a brace. "Trust me." Peter's arm trembled. He glanced towards the incoming debris.

"Now?"

"No." Sinon clamped his eyes shut. Peter's breaths shortened. He concentrated on the numen surging into his palm. It wasn't enough. The shockwave was too big and too fast. Peter opened his mouth to speak. "You can do this," Sinon whispered. "I know you can. Trust me." Peter closed his eyes.

Sinon was the only reason they were still alive. Most of their classmates were already dead. No matter how bad things got, he always made the right decisions. Now, Sinon trusted Peter with both their lives. Sinon knew he could do this. Peter knew he could do this.

"Now!" Sinon shouted. Peter released his numen. A transparent barrier leapt from his hand. Peter's ears rang with deafening shrieks of screeching metal. He covered his face, waiting for the shockwave to carry them away.

The screeching stopped.

Peter opened his eyes: darkness. The air thickened brown with dust. Peter coughed. His nostrils stung with the rancid stench of smoldering carbon. Peter waved his hands in front of his face. Dust remained.

"Sinon." Peter choked. "Sinon!" Peter turned, but his legs were trapped knee-deep in dirt. "Where are you? Sinon!" Peter's panicked arms sifted through the rubble. At last, he felt the calming touch of a human hand. "Sinon!" Peter pulled. The arm had been severed.

"Peter!" Sinon's voice cut through the smoke. "I'm here." Peter turned towards the noise. Through the dust, he saw Sinon's faint silhouette. "Your barrier held!" Sinon nodded. "Great job!" Peter looked. Sure enough, his barrier remained, light dim and fading.

"Thank God." Tears welled in Peter's eyes.

"Don't thank him too soon." Sinon laughed. "We may fight him soon enough."

"I didn't mean **that** God." Peter snapped, but it felt reassuring to hear Sinon laugh.

"Come on." Sinon pointed upwards. "We need to get out of here before the walls collapse." Peter squinted towards the sky. Sinon was right. They were trapped in a crater of dirt and shrapnel.

"Race you?" Peter offered, encircling his body with numen. The barrier left him drained, but Peter had enough energy for a simple footrace.

"You're on!" Sinon flashed Peter a familiar grin. Both boys were exhausted, but neither wanted to admit it. "Ready. Go!"

Peter sprinted up the hill creating small numen barriers under his feet. Sinon was usually faster, but Peter's ability was better suited for the lack of traction. He reached the top in ten seconds. Sinon finished in thirteen.

"You cheated." Sinon smiled. Peter grabbed Sinon's hand and helped him over the ridge.

"I prefer to call it strategy." Peter expected another comeback, but Sinon dropped the playful attitude.

"We're winning." Sinon surveyed the devastation with a solemn frown.

"And the casualties?" Peter's eyes darkened.

"Too many." Sinon shook his head. "On both sides. This war will end today."

"I see." Peter sighed. "And then the real work begins."

"You're serious about that?" Sinon cast him a sideways glance. "Peace will not be easy to achieve."

"I know." Peter glared at his hands, stained with unknown blood. "But after this, we have to try." Sinon nodded in agreement. He sat against a shattered tank and withdrew an Accretion Bar from his pocket.

"The battle moved away from us." Sinon watched the verdant peaks of Mount Malum where flashes of mortar fire illuminated the coming night.

"Is that bad?" Peter pressed.

"Depends." Sinon broke the bar, tossing the dark chocolate half to Peter and keeping the white chocolate side for himself. "I can't read his mind this far away, but…" Sinon trailed off.

"But what?" Peter eagerly devoured the candy. The bitter succulence of dark chocolate washed down his throat.

"But…" Sinon twiddled the white chocolate half between his thumb and forefinger. "If we move closer, he will fight back."

"We have no choice." Peter spoke through a mouthful of chocolate. "Caerule is counting on us. The world is counting on us."

"We always have a choice, Peter." Sinon sighed. He ate the chocolate slowly, watching the Great Nations' forces advance. "Alright." Sinon rose to his feet. "Follow me." They ran towards the foothills of Mount Malum, weaving between divisions of Ardorean rocket artillery.

"Right!" Sinon changed course. Tendrils of black numen obliterated the center hill, annihilating the artillery.

"Left!" Sinon shifted again. Metal and limestone blasted across the plain, crushing divisions of robotic tanks from Nemo and legions of Aquillan infantry. Beyond the crumbling hills, Peter saw the offshore devastation. His heart sank. Caerule's flagship aircraft carrier was cleaved in half. From the deck, South Alaman engineers fired a nuclear laser at an unknown enemy. The vessel sank into the dark sea, taking the laser and crew with it.

"Faster!" Sinon sprinted towards the mountains. Peter struggled to keep pace. Black light shot into the sky. Smoldering shards of Borean fighter jets and helicopters crashed to earth.

"We'll follow them!" Sinon pointed towards a herd of velociraptors surging between the jagged cliff-face. Peter hated the nation of Ferox and their genetically engineered war animals, but running with the raptors would be better than charging over the hills unprotected. Sinon was right. This was their best option.

Sinon surrounded himself with numen. Peter followed his lead. They were inside the herd. The sounds of scraping claws and pounding feet thundered around them. Raptors charged through the gap like water through rapids. To them, Sinon and Peter were invisible. The raptors pursued a different prey, an unseen enemy, The Pale Raven.

"I see him!" Sinon reached the end of the ravine. He pointed to a dark spot moving in the distance. The scattered remnants of coalition forces lay strewn across the valley. The only lights emanated from surviving numen users. These faded one by one. The dark spot remained.

"Where is God?" Peter cast a nervous glance towards Sinon.

"Up there." Sinon pointed towards the sprawling peaks of Mount Malum. "They're fighting for the high ground."

"How much closer do we need to be?" Peter stared at the black spot. Sinon's breaths shortened. "What is it Sinon? Sinon!"

"We're too late." Sinon's face paled as he stared into the night sky. His eyes shone both shock and despair. A red streak arced across the horizon, calm, bright and beautiful.

"No." Peter's eyes widened with realization and fear. This light was not hope. This light was darkness. An atomic bomb. No escape. BOOM!

The valley vanished in a blinding flash. Peter clamped his eyes shut, waiting for the shockwave. The shockwave never came.

"Peter!" He heard Sinon's voice. "Peter!" Peter's eyes snapped open.

"How are we alive?" Peter asked.

"I don't know." Sinon bit his lip, trembling. Peter never saw him so confused.

"And the radiation." Peter pressed. "What happened to the radiation?"

"I don't know!" For first time, Peter saw fear in Sinon's eyes. "I have a bad feeling about this." Sure enough, the earth shuddered beneath their feet. The valley writhed like an animal in pain. Pillars of blackness erupted from the scorched terrain, disintegrating everything.

"Sinon!" Peter yelled. Sinon did not respond. "We have to get out of here!" The black pillars encircled them in walls of nothingness. Sinon fell to his knees. "Sinon!" Peter rushed to his side. Sinon's eyes widened in terror. They were surrounded by darkness.

"I guess you're the last of them." Peter heard a voice. It was not angry or vengeful. Instead, it felt tired and sad. The darkness receded to reveal a small boy who could not be more than twelve or thirteen years old. His hair and clothes were pitch-black, but his skin was sickly pale. There was no mistaking it. This boy was Raven.

Peter leapt in front of Sinon. He focused his remaining numen, creating a barrier between them and the boy. "You know that won't work." Raven stopped. Peter strained to increase his numen. "You'll kill yourself at that rate." Raven shook his head. Peter's barrier flickered and faded. He collapsed, face-planting into the dust. "I promise I will make this quick." Raven coated his hand in black numen resembling a blade.

"Please," Peter begged, barely managing a whisper. "Don't hurt Sinon." Raven paused. His eyes were calm, maybe even apologetic. He stared at Peter, as if considering the request. Then, he shook his head and proceeded towards Sinon, hand raised.

Peter could not move. His numen was depleted and his body weighed with exhaustion. Peter glanced towards his fallen friend. Sinon had already lost consciousness. There was nothing Peter could do. There was nothing anyone could do. Peter prayed for a miracle. It was at that moment he first saw God.

Before the dark-haired boy could plunge the blade through Sinon's heart, a violent tremor shook the battlefield. Through the smog, Peter saw three silhouettes, battling at the peak of Mount Malum. Holding his ground at the top of the mountain was Dr. Eli Ulysses Septem, the man otherwise known as God. His body radiated an immense shroud of golden numen which bathed the battlefield in a soft glow.

Of the seven Grand Masters, two remained. On Septem's right, Peter recognized Rex Newton, wielding the Warhammer of Aquilla. On the left, Peter was relieved to see Marius Sulla of

Caerule deflecting Septem's attacks with his strong but weakening numen.

The battle was more vicious and elegant than any Peter could have imagined. Despite the intensity of each strike, the orchards covering the mountainside remained undisturbed. Blows were delivered and countered with such efficiency the fight seemed nothing more than a well-practiced dance. The battle could last forever.

Then, Peter remembered the tremor. Someone made a mistake. Someone was getting tired. No sooner had the thought crossed Peter's mind; Master Newton missed another swing with his hammer. The valley shook with unrelenting force, splitting the mountain in half. The hammer spiraled out of Newton's grip and the Grand Master fell to the ground.

Dr. Septem seized the opportunity and lunged towards Marius to strike the final blow. The numen in his fist raged so intense the wind and waves twisted in opposite directions. Marius remained firm. Septem had underestimated Marius. It was a fatal mistake.

Abandoning all defenses, Marius focused his remaining numen in his left hand. He dodged Septem's attack and delivered a devastating punch of his own. Marius collapsed as the remaining numen left his body. Septem stumbled backwards, falling to his knees.

"No!" the dark haired boy screamed. He understood what was about to happen even before Peter. Behind Septem, Master Newton retrieved his hammer and swung the final blow.

CRACK!

The sound of a crunching skull echoed through the valley. The golden light of Septem's numen vanished, leaving the battlefield in darkness. For a brief moment, everything stood still. Then, God's lifeless body tumbled into the crevasse of Mount Malum.

"No," the dark-haired boy cried, tears streaming down his face. Rain fell across the battlefield, washing away the dust. The shattered remains of tanks, planes and fallen soldiers were cleansed by the falling water, flowing towards an endless sea. The boy stared at the broken mountain in absolute silence.

"Take care of your friend," Raven spoke after a long pause. He walked alone through the war-torn landscape and his footsteps faded in the falling rain.

Chapter 2 – Seven Years Later

Sam Pere

Life works well when it follows a plan. Sam ignored Meg's exasperated stares as he flipped through holograms of charts and stat sheets. Accidents, variables, acts of God: Sam prepared for them all. Everything was a function of numbers and logic. Sam deactivated the hologram projector on his Wrist-Pro, readjusting the touchpad computer screen to sit perfectly symmetrical on his forearm; and watched their Carbot merge into the morning traffic of Aprilis.

Sam loved traffic. Whenever a vehicle merged, everyone accelerated. Carbots soared between voltage planes, propelled by the superconducting plates below. Vehicles weaved past each other with such precision that Sam couldn't help but marvel at the triumph of engineering. He smiled and reached for his Wrist-Pro again.

"You know." Meg glared out the window as another Carbot almost collided with their left capacitor. "In a real fight, you won't be able to prepare like this." Sam raised his eyebrows. Meg was wearing her pristine Caerule-blue dress uniform which delayed their departure by half an hour. Did she not see the irony?

"Sure." Sam resisted the urge to roll his eyes. "But, I'll use the advantage while I have the chance."

Meg shook her head and returned her attention to the ancient Caerulean longsword she examined with white-gloved hands. The words 'Truth, Loyalty, Justice' glistened on the blade. Outside, a clown-faced robot pulled alongside them, flashing a red light in Meg's face. "Ronald's! Ronald's! Ronald's!" The face yelled, blinking and beeping with irregular frequency. "Ronald's! Ronald's! Ronald's!"

"What!" Meg glared at the clown. It was a rookie mistake. The robot scanned Meg's retina and the light turned green.

"Payment accepted." The Carbot's window rolled down. A wrapped hamburger launched from the clown's chest cavity, striking Meg in the face. The contents burst from the wrapper, spilling everywhere.

"Damn it!" Meg covered her eye. The robot sped away.

"Are you going to eat that?" Sam nodded to the lopsided burger.

"Knock yourself out." Meg tossed the burger to Sam, brushing mustard off the longsword with her sleeve.

"Don't worry." Sam reactivated his hologram projector and began to eat. "I packed extra clothes in the back."

"Of course you did." Meg sighed, channeling her numen through the sword. The blade glowed, shrank and shifted until Meg was holding what appeared to be a small pocket knife. "Haven't you memorized those holograms by now?"

"Probably." Sam spoke through a mouthful of hamburger. "But you never can be too prepared." The hot cheese saturated the meat with a heavy, oily juice. Sam felt his stomach rumble with displeasure, but the burger tasted too good.

"What's your strategy for Artemis?"

"Artemis is an augmenter." Sam finished the burger and tossed the wrapper into the Carbot's incinerator. "She strengthens her arrows with numen, but is weakened by firing them. I need to dodge her attacks and engage at close range."

"What about Tom?"

"Tom is an assimilator. He can redirect my attacks, but has less numen than I do. I need to wear him down and focus on endurance."

"And Leah?"

"Leah will be…difficult." Sam looked up, but Meg was no longer paying attention. Two enormous soda cans chased their Carbot across the plateway.

"Those things aren't supposed to be networked." Meg fumed. Sam smirked as the rival-brand robots tried to run each other off the road. "It's not funny! They could kill someone."

"We're almost at the Helena Bridge." Sam nodded to the Carbot's navigation computer. "They can't follow us there." Meg eased into her seat, but continued to watch the sparring soda cans. Their Carbot climbed to a higher voltage plane and the robots receded from view.

"Are you sure you're ready for this?" Meg returned her attention to Sam.

"Why are you so worried?"

"You're my brother. It's my job to worry about you."

"I'll be fine." Sam laughed and patted his Wrist-Pro. "I've planned for everything."

"I hope you're right." Meg sighed.

Sam's heart leapt as they approached the Helena Bridge. He watched ten holodisks about it and visited the museum fifteen times. The structure was a pinnacle of engineering efficiency, connecting the government buildings on Central Island with Caerule's capital city of Aprilis. Carbots streamed in both directions, undisturbed by the constant mist rising from the Atropa River. Through the fog, the bold white pillars of Central gleamed in the rising sun.

"Meg." Sam's eyes glowed with curiosity. "You've been to Ferox, right?"

"Once." Meg gripped the pocket knife with unusual force.

"Is it true they have a bridge twice as long as this?"

"Yes." Meg raised her eyebrows. "But it's made of poison sumac."

"Wow!" Sam breathed.

"That's not supposed to be impressive." Meg shook her head. Sam wanted to press her further, but Meg seemed troubled by something. Their Carbot landed at Central Forum. The door slid open and Sam prepared to leave.

"Sam." Meg's face grew serious. "Do you want to be an agent?"

"Yes!" Sam answered without hesitation. "More than anything." It was such a strange question, today of all days.

"Okay." Meg smiled. "Good luck!" She pointed to the holodisk in Sam's Wrist-Pro. "Leave that here. You shouldn't be reading about numen in public."

"Right." Sam hesitated before ejecting the holodisk. Meg reprogrammed the coordinates of her Carbot and sped in the direction of Central Command.

Sam sprinted across the forum, weaving through mobs of tourists and government officials. Everyone was watching him; scared; angry; curious; some a mix of all three. Sam avoided eye contact and steered clear of the large crowd gawking at the central stage. Sam hated that stage. It reeked of iron and rotting wood and always seemed to be in the way. Fixed in the center of the forum, the loathsome platform was such an eyesore next to the polished marble of Central. Sam wondered if the stage was deliberately ugly.

As he approached the academy, Sam's heart sank. Grand Master Marius Sulla blocked the entryway, his pearl-white robes gleaming in the morning sun. He glared across the thronging crowds spread throughout the forum. Sam dove behind a marble column, desperate to avoid the Grand Master's gaze. Marius's eyes rested on the column. Sam's breaths shortened.

Marius returned his attention to the wooden stage, allowing Sam to dart behind a row of bushes. He began formulating a strategy. The front entrance was too risky. Marius would sense his numen, no question. Sam's best chance was to avoid the Grand Master or distract him somehow. Sam peered through the branches, analyzing the walking patterns.

"Pssst!"

"Ahh!" Sam clutched his chest. He wheeled to see Leah hiding in the bushes. "How long have you been there?"

"Since this morning." Leah whispered. "We were waiting for you."

"That's not creepy at all." Sam masked his anxiety with sarcasm. "Wait. Did you say we?"

"Welcome to the party." Artemis jumped from the branches of a nearby oak tree. "We hoped you'd have a plan for this."

"Of course I have a plan." Sam hissed. "Just not for three people."

"It'll be fine." Leah patted him on the back. "What's the worst that could happen?"

"Err...Right...Well." Sam's heart pounded. The plan could still work. Everything was under control. It would just take a little...improvising, that's all. Sam wiped the sweat from his brow. "Follow me." He led the way to a small breaker box on the outside wall.

"You're not gonna cut the power on them, are you?" Artemis grinned.

"No." Sam's breaths shortened as he began to panic. "Central never uses breaker boxes. I mean they do, but not outside." Sam's hands trembled as he opened the breaker box. Why did spontaneity make him so nervous? "You see what I'm saying. The box is fake. I mean the box is real, but the wall is fake." He continued to ramble, tense and incoherent.

"There's a door behind the wall." Sam channeled numen to his hand, creating feeble arcs of electricity. "A secret door. The box is the access panel, and my numen can-"

"Thanks, Sam." Leah found the hidden door and forced it open with brute strength. Sam severed the alarm's circuit just in time, panting heavy breaths.

"We'll see you at the match." Artemis ran after Leah.

"-help." Sam finished. He stared at the gaping doorway, frightened and alone.

Sam trudged to the changing rooms. Inside, Tom Bell was fastening the final straps of his armguard.

"Tough morning?" Tom smiled as Sam entered. "I haven't seen you this bad since your alarm clock went off five minutes late."

"Not funny." Sam scanned his thumbprint and opened his locker. Each shelf was organized in sections according to form, fit and function. Books were filed alphabetically; clothes were ordered according to the visible color spectrum; and the few food items were arranged by expiration dates.

"Sorry." Tom rummaged through his disorganized locker, tossing several pairs of torn shorts and sweaty t-shirts onto a nearby bench. "It's just, life's random, you know. Sometimes, you just have to roll with it."

"Here." Sam sighed and withdrew an Accretion Bar from a neat stack on the bottom shelf of his locker. "Have one of mine." He tossed the candy bar to Tom.

"Thanks." Tom unwrapped the chocolate and tore a large section with his teeth. "Are you gonna be alright?"

"Yeah." Sam sighed. "Believe it or not, I'm actually feeling good about today."

"That makes one of us." Tom sat on the bench and stared towards the door. "My dad's in town. I want to win this one for him but-" Tom was cut off by the obnoxious five minute warning buzzer. "Don't worry." Tom turned back to Sam. "I'll wait until you're ready."

"I'm ready now." Sam walked towards the door.

"You're fighting in that?" Tom raised his eyebrows.

"What?" Sam shrugged. "Leah fights in shorts all the time."

"Yeah, but she's Leah." Tom rose to his feet. "And you're…well…not."

"Thank you for that great observation." Sam's voice dripped with sarcasm. "Don't worry. I have a plan."

The boys arrived seconds before the bell rang. The stadium was packed. Younger students jammed together in the first five rows. The rear of the auditorium was packed with agents and naval officers. Meg and Tom's father, General Jesse Bell, sat together. Meg flashed Sam a quick thumbs-up. The General beamed at Tom, brushing a joyful tear from his eye. Grand Master Marius loomed behind them, eyes fixed on Sam.

Professor Plummet gave an overenthusiastic wave and motioned Sam and Tom to join him on the stone stage in the center of the auditorium. Leah and Artemis already stood at attention. Sam and Tom raced down the stairs to join them.

"Welcome everyone!" Professor Plummet clapped his hands. His voice was excited and high-pitched as always. "I am Professor Plummet. Before we begin, I would like to give the younger students a brief overview of what they are about to see."

"These." The professor beamed at Sam and the others. "Are four of the greatest students at the academy. They already mastered the basics of numen and have begun developing their own unique abilities. Based on the results of today's examinations, some may even be ready to become agents. They are fantastic students and it has been a privilege teaching them." A glass sphere descended from the ceiling, projecting the image of a seven-pointed-star. The words 'Creation', 'Manipulation', 'Transformation', 'Observation', 'Assimilation', 'Adaptation' and 'Augmentation' appeared clockwise around the star in bright gold letters.

"To start the examination." The professor continued. "Each student will submit a quick numen count. The test will be measured in Wolframs, the amount of numen required to raise one gram of tungsten by one degree Celsius." The center of the stone stage slid open, revealing a small tungsten platform.

"In reverse order of class rank, Artemis Arundo will go first." Professor Plummet explained. Artemis had already started walking. She drew a single arrow from her quiver and loaded it into her bow. Numen flowed from her fingers into the arrow, causing it to glow strong white light. Artemis stood on the tungsten platform, aimed straight down, and fired.

"1856." Professor Plummet shouted the number, brimming with excitement. The number appeared in the center of the glass sphere and the upper left point of the star glowed bright yellow. "Artemis is an Augmenter who strengthens her arrows with numen, often giving them unique properties. She has a natural talent for ranged combat and excels in stealth missions." The professor smiled as he praised Artemis. "Up next is Tom Bell."

Tom and Artemis exchanged high-fives as they passed each other. Tom proceeded to the tungsten platform and began channeling numen to his feet. The platform beneath him dazzled brilliant colors as Tom forced his numen into the metal.

"1795." Professor Plummet read the number with a grin. The bottom left of the star glowed red. "Despite his lower numen count, Tom has the second best one-on-one battle record in his class. Tom is an Assimilator, meaning he can use the numen of others to his advantage. In Tom's case, he can absorb and redirect numen attacks; a powerful ability that is perfectly suited for numen battles." The professor turned to Sam. "Next, we have Sam Pere."

"Good luck." Tom smiled as he passed Sam.

"Thanks." Sam nodded, proceeding to the center platform. He closed his eyes. An enormous swell of energy writhed within him, turbulent and volatile. Numen crackled across his body in a series of electrical discharges. Sam opened his eyes. Directing the surge of electricity to his outstretched finger, Sam pointed at the tungsten platform and fired. Lightning arced from his fingers; striking the metal with a satisfying CRACK! Sam grinned.

"2087!" The professor read the number, shocked. The top center of the star glowed green. "We have a new record." Everyone in the crowd cheered, except for Grand Master Marius who continued to glare at Sam with unsettling scrutiny. "Sam is a Creator who, as you can see, specializes in generating electricity with his numen. His score of 2087 surpasses the previous class record of 2055 set by Sinon Donafer almost ten years ago."

"Congratulations." Leah slapped Sam on the back as he passed.

"Thanks." Sam grinned with satisfaction as he rejoined Tom and Artemis.

"Remind me to bring sunglasses next time." Tom joked, blinking several times.

"Don't you mean welding glasses?" Sam quipped.

"You tell me." Tom smirked.

CLANG!

A loud noise jerked Sam's attention back to the center stage. Leah punched the tungsten platform as soon as she arrived with hardly any preparation. The metal rang like a bell, quivering and shaking as the momentum propagated through it.

"2150!" Professor Plummet read the number, more excited than ever. The left-most point of the star glowed orange. "Another record! Adapters can use numen to alter their physiology. In Leah's case, she increases her strength and stamina well beyond natural limits; a fantastic ability that is versatile in countless situations." The crowd cheered.

"Well, that was short-lived." Tom's face paled. "Did you know she could do that?"

"Of course not." Sam spat, nervous sweat running down his brow. "My whole plan depended on it."

Professor Plummet signaled to someone in the back row. "Colonel Peter Turnus will now explain the rules of the examination."

Sam's heart sank. Peter was by-far the harshest examiner at the academy. He never passed anyone. Last year, Peter failed everyone in graduation tournament, including the winner. No one seemed to meet his criteria.

A dark shadow rose from the rear of the auditorium and approached the stage. Sam squinted into the glaring spotlights. The crowd erupted in confused whispers, but Sam only heard the clip-clip of Peter's boots descending the stairs. The sound was slow, steady and methodical.

At last, Peter's face came into view. Sam's eyes widened. Peter's body was scarred and battle-hardened. Sam expected that. What surprised Sam was the charisma radiating from Peter's eyes. He looked like a soldier, but acted like a politician. Peter proceeded to the center of the stage, smiled at the students and turned to face the crowd.

"Thank you, everyone." Peter's voice boomed across the auditorium, strong and confident. "The rules are simple. The students will compete in a four person single-elimination tournament. If a student is knocked off the stage, that student loses. If I decide a student is no longer able to fight, that student loses. Does everyone understand these rules?"

"Yes, sir." The students shouted in unison.

"Good," Peter continued. "I will now determine your matchups." The image in the glass sphere shifted, projecting a four pronged tournament bracket. Sam's heart sank again. "The matchups will be Leah Penthes vs. Sam Pere followed by Tom Bell vs. Artemis Arundo. Sam and Leah will take the arena now. Tom and Artemis, join me offstage."

Tom and Artemis followed Peter to the side of the arena, leaving Sam and Leah alone. Leah took her position on the blue dot near the edge of the stage. Sam took a deep breath and proceeded to the white dot on the opposite side. Everything would be okay. Sam tried to reassure himself. Just stick to the plan. The glass sphere began the countdown. "Three. Two. One."

Sam converted his numen into electricity and fired a high voltage arc at Leah. Leah intensified her numen and deflected the blast. Sparks showered the stage. Leah clenched her fists and charged. Sam was one step ahead of her. He unleashed a surge of electricity, striking the ground beneath Leah's feet. The tiles shattered into loose grains. The stone gave way.

"Yes!" Sam launched a fury of attacks at Leah's trapped foot. Leah blocked the blasts, but the heat caused the stone to glassify. Leah winced as the grains solidified around her, but Sam knew better than to stop. He fired an arc at Leah's head. Leah punched the ground beneath her feet and rolled away from the blast. Shards of glass protruded from her leg.

"Nice plan." Leah smiled as her numen began healing the wounds. "Too bad it didn't work."

"No worries." Sam grinned. "I have plenty more." He ran along the edge of the stage. Leah charged after him. Sam fired several desperate blasts at her damaged leg, but failed to slow Leah's progress. Within half a lap, she closed the distance. Leah concentrated numen into her fist, preparing for the final blow.

Sam knew the fight would soon be over. All his matches with Leah ended the same way. Sam scored a few good hits. Then, Leah chased him down and ended the fight with one punch. Sam's only hope was to try something different; something new; something unexpected. Sam glanced over his shoulder. Leah finished charging her fist with numen and was about to strike. Sam attacked.

Sam pivoted and dove beneath Leah's incoming punch. He gasped as Leah collided with his outstretched leg. Leah stumbled. Sam crashed head-first into the stage. Leah wheeled to face him.

"Time for plan B!" Sam shut his eyes. He fired a blast of electricity at the glass sphere above their heads. The room erupted in a blinding flash of light. Everywhere, Sam heard shattering glass, confused screams and the crackle of electricity. He opened his eyes just in time to see Leah's fist collide with his abdomen.

The impact rippled through Sam like a shockwave. One second, his feet were on the ground. The next, he was hurtling through space. Sam's heart sank; the weight of defeat magnified by its inevitability. But, even as his helpless body flew through the air, Sam could still see Leah; her eyes clamped shut and feet surrounded by shards of broken glass. She never saw a thing. After all that, it was a lucky punch. The realization enraged Sam. Matching his fury, Sam felt the storm of electrons rampaging around him. All he could think about was directing their ferocity towards Leah. A blast of electricity erupted from Sam's hand, striking Leah in the chest. Sam watched Leah wince in pain; watched her fall backwards; watched her tumble off the stage. Before he could see what happened, Sam crashed head-first into the stadium stairs and fell unconscious.

Chapter 3 – Caerule Attacked

Meg Alumen

History haunts historians more than most. Alex and Esther Alumen shambled around their hospital room, twitching and groaning garbled speech. Meg watched her parents through a one-way mirror, clutching an antique pocket knife.

"You're here again." General Jesse Bell limped towards her, leaning on a wooden cane. "I thought you'd be with Sam."

"He's fine." Meg remained firm. "The doctors said he'll make a full recovery."

"That's not the point." General Bell shook his head. "Right now, Sam needs you more than they do. It's what your parents would have wanted."

"You're right." Meg wanted to cry, but what was the point? "All this time and I still can't help. I don't know why I thought today might be different."

"I'm sorry I couldn't save them." General Bell's eyes darkened.

"Don't apologize." Meg shook her head. "You're the reason they're still alive." Bell did not respond. Meg knew he hadn't forgiven himself, despite her constant insistence. They watched in silence as Esther drew nonsensical scribbles on the other side of the glass.

"I heard you found the sword." General Bell spoke after a long pause. Meg tossed him the pocket knife. Bell bobbled the trinket three times before catching it. He stared at Meg, confused.

"Use your numen." Meg nodded.

"Oh, right." General Bell channeled his numen. The metal glowed, lengthened and shifted until he was holding what appeared to be an ancient katana. The words 'Truth, Loyalty and Justice' glistened on the shining blade.

"The Sword of Caerule." Meg explained. "Takes the form of any blade the wielder desires; a useful trick for swordsmen who don't want to change their fighting style, or someone like me trying to smuggle it out of enemy territory."

"Incredible." General Bell ran his fingers along the blunt edges of the blade. "Your father would be proud."

"I didn't do it for him." Meg's face hardened.

"Maybe not." General Bell nodded. "But he was the last to wield it. I think he'd want you to have it."

"I didn't do it for me." Meg remained firm.

"I see." General Bell paused. "Why did you do it, then?"

"Who knows?" Meg shrugged. "For Caerule I guess." General Bell opened his mouth to respond, but was interrupted by Grand Master Marius slamming the hallway door open, almost striking a frightened nurse.

"Alumen!" The angry Grand Master glared at her. "Sam's awake. Let's go."

"Right." Meg resisted the urge to roll her eyes. "General, I-"

"I understand." General Bell nodded, handing her the sword. "We'll talk another time."

"Thank you." Meg channeled her numen through the sword, transforming it back into a pocket knife. She met Grand Master Marius's gaze, cold, hard and unflinching. "Alright, lead the way."

An uneasy silence permeated the air as Marius stormed through the sprawling hospital wards, Meg following close behind. Doctors, nurses and patients cleared from the Grand Master's path. Meg gave apologetic nods when Marius wasn't looking.

"I'll give you five minutes." Marius snapped when they arrived outside Sam's room. "After that, I'll interrogate him myself."

"Whatever." Meg shook her head, exasperated. She closed the door behind her, dismayed to find it didn't have a lock.

"What happened?" Sam lay in the hospital bed rubbing the back of his head.

"You have a concussion." Meg sat in the chair next to him. "Leah hit you pretty hard."

"Is Leah okay?" Sam bolted upright.

"Better than you are." Meg sighed. "She beat Tom in the second round."

"That's a relief." Sam eased back into the pillow. "I was worried that … For a second I thought. . ." He closed his eyes without completing the sentence.

"Sam." Meg's voice harshened. "Look at me, Sam." Sam turned his head to face her. "Never hold back in a fight. No matter the situation. Never hold back."

"But-" Sam tried to protest.

"Even against your friends." Meg interrupted. "You two were paired together. You have to trust we did that for a reason. Holding back in practice won't make you or Leah stronger for the real threats." Sam gripped the sheets in his fist.

Meg rose from her chair and walked to the window. The city ebbed and flowed without a care in the world. Ships sailed towards the open ocean. Buildings sparkled in the noontime sun. Carbots zipped across the Helena Bridge, weightless and free. Aprilis seemed almost perfect, but Meg knew better. The sky shone shades of Caerule Blue, but dark clouds brewed on the horizon.

"Sam." Meg turned towards him. "Are you sure you want to be an agent?"

"Yes." Sam's face puzzled. "Why do you keep asking?"

"This life isn't for everyone." Meg sighed and stared through the window. Her reflection cast faint shadows on the pane.

"Yes." Sam insisted. His eyes were hard and firm.

"Alright." Meg prepared to leave. "Marius is waiting outside."

"Again?" Sam groaned.

"Unfortunately." Meg nodded. "Then, the doctors want to check on you. Apparently, your numen was interfering with the equipment."

Meg left the room. Marius was listening at the door.

"Well?" The Grand Master demanded.

"Well what?" Meg met his glare.

"Nothing." The Grand Master entered, slamming the door behind him. "I'll find out myself."

A team of doctors and nurses waited in the hall, ready with carts, supplies and various apparatuses. Meg shook her head. Sam's injuries were minor. She did not need a doctor to know that. Still, Marius's obsession was becoming increasingly dangerous. If Sam's condition had been worse, the Grand Master would be interfering with Sam's health. Meg proceeded to the elevator. It was time to pay Peter a visit.

As she walked across the Central campus, a chill ran down Meg's spine. She could feel the bloodthirsty stare of unknown eyes. Meg's heart pounded. Each step felt heavier than the last. The danger was mounting. It was almost here. Meg turned. Nothing.

Meg returned her attention to the path. Had she just imagined it? No. Soft and slow, Meg channeled her numen, adapting the refractive index of her body until it matched the surrounding air. She was completely invisible. Meg continued altering the refractive index around her eyes. Magnifying the light from various angles, she scanned for her pursuer in visible, ultraviolet and infrared. No one was there.

Meg's breaths shortened. This pursuer was skilled and already knew her ability. Meg released her numen, hurried to the command center and took the elevator to the lower levels.

Peter's office was a basement storage closet. Central was weird like that. The higher your rank, the worse your office was. The system was a relic of some long forgotten policy meant to confuse infiltrators. Now, the arrangement remained enshrined by tradition.

Peter's one complaint was his officemate: the building's industrial strength HVAC system. Every five minutes, the thing would whir to life, emitting obnoxious noises and temperatures.

Meg thought about scheduling her office on the tenth floor, but decided against it. This meeting was different. She wanted to catch Peter off-guard.

"Come in! Come in!" Peter smiled, motioning Meg inside. "I was just talking about you, to President Millenavis no less. He's expanding the new section of the Aprilis Museum and wants you to present the Sword of Caerule to him when the exhibit opens."

"Wow...uh." Meg tried to hide her disappointment. "Isn't that a security risk?"

"Admiral Lodon said the same thing." Peter laughed. The HVAC system roared to life. Peter grabbed a role of tape from his desk and began taping additional insulation around the noisy air ducts. "She wanted to lock the sword in our fallout bunker, but you know Millenavis. He'd never waste a good photo-op."

"He's not the only one." Meg muttered under her breath while Peter was distracted.

"Don't worry." Peter returned his attention to Meg. "We'll handle the details. It's a tremendous honor. You've earned it."

"Thank you, sir." Meg's eyes fell. Peter seemed to sense her uncertainty.

"How's Sam?"

"I'm not worried." Meg lied. "He's tougher than he looks."

"I'll say." Peter nodded. "That Leah girl really packs a punch. I'll have my hands full with her."

"You passed a student?" Meg stared at him, stunned.

"Two actually." Peter nodded to an open bottle of champagne sitting on a table next to a large sofa. "General Bell and I were just celebrating. Tom passed too."

"Two in one day." Meg's heart sank. This would be more difficult than she thought. "Wow! That's … Wow."

"I know. I know." Peter grinned. "I never pass anyone. But, Tom was right on the edge. Besides, the General will protect him." For a moment, his eyes wearied with doubt. Then, Peter's face brightened as he returned his attention to Meg. "Anyways, what can I do for you?"

"Well, sir." Meg sighed. "It's about the sword mission. Sylvania Birnam was there."

"I see." Peter's face darkened. "I'm glad you're alright."

"I almost wasn't." Meg pressed. "She's gotten much stronger. I was lucky to get out of there alive. Next time, I don't think I can beat her alone."

"What are you getting at?" Peter's eyes locked with Meg. It was time for the real conversation.

"I want to take a student of my own."

"No."

"You have to give me a better answer than that." Meg pressed.

"Sam is not ready. No."

"He has more numen than I do and he's only fourteen."

"Doesn't matter."

"We both know this is only a formality. I can choose a student at any time. Why won't you give me your blessing?"

"I won't let you go through the same things I did!" Peter shouted. Meg's eyes widened. Peter never raised his voice to her. His face softened and he slumped into his chair. "I'm sorry. You didn't deserve that."

"Do you want to talk about it, sir?" Meg glanced at the blackened dog tag hanging around Peter's neck.

"No." Peter's eyes darkened as he stuffed the tag beneath his shirt. It weighed on him like a millstone, constant and heavy. The HVAC system whirred to life and shook the room with loud creaking sounds. "Look," Peter continued after the noise subsided. "I've known the pain of losing a student. With you and Sam being family, that pain would be tenfold." His eyes were unwavering and his voice was stern. "If you want my blessing to train Sam, I will give it to you only when I'm certain he can protect you and you can protect him."

"I understand." Meg sighed. The decision was disappointing, but fair. "Thank you, sir." She turned to leave, but stopped before reaching the door. Peter shot Meg a quizzical look. Then, his eyes widened. Peter sensed it too. Someone was watching them.

Meg channeled numen to her eyes. Her vision shifted to the infrared. Peter's heat signature shone through the darkness, but it was not alone. Another faint glow lurked behind him.

"The vent!" Meg pointed to the steel duct that ran across the ceiling to the HVAC system. The metal echoed and pounded as the figure tried to escape. Meg surrounded herself with numen and redirected all incoming light to her right arm. Her body darkened. Her hand brightened. Meg slashed through the air. A white laser surged from Meg's finger, slicing the duct in half. Bolts, cables and corroded copper wiring fell from the ceiling. The duct collapsed and the unwelcome eavesdropper rolled from the metallic channel, panting. It was Sam.

The three stared at each other, dumbfounded. Sam was first to break the silence. "Umm, is anyone going to put that fire out?" He pointed to the wall. The laser incinerated the world map on the far wall and flames were spreading fast.

Peter hesitated, the haunting fire reflected in his eyes. Meg recognized the look immediately: fear. Peter calmed himself and walked towards the burning map. He channeled his numen, creating five small barriers in the shape of an open box. He placed the box over the fire, smothering it in its own smoke. Meg's heart raced. At last, the fire died and Peter returned to his desk. He stared at Sam a long time before speaking.

"How long were you up there?" Peter asked.

"Uhh," Sam replied, confused. "Not long, sir."

"What was the first thing you heard?" Peter pressed again.

"It was." Sam looked down, crestfallen. "'Sam is not ready.'"

"Impressive." Peter grinned and scratched his chin. "You hid your numen from a Colonel and a Major for over five minutes."

"Sir?" Meg asked.

"I tell you what, Meg," Peter continued. "You have my permission to train Sam under one condition. For the next three months, the two of you will only complete missions within Caerule's borders. I will then re-evaluate Sam to see if this arrangement should be made permanent."

"Thank you, sir," Meg stammered. The deal was more than fair; better than she could have hoped. Peter grabbed a folder from his desk and prepared to leave.

"Oh! One more thing." Peter turned before walking through the door.

"Yes, sir!" Meg said. "Anything, sir."

"Could you clean my office before I get back?" Peter flashed a quick smile before leaving. Meg stared at the open door, dumbfounded. Behind her, the enormous HVAC system spewed a cloud of dust and metal shavings through the room.

"I can fix the vent," Sam offered. Meg wheeled, eyes burning like hot coals.

"What the hell were you thinking?" Meg's voice echoed through the room.

"I'm sorry for spying on-"

"I don't care about that!" Meg continued. "You could have been killed." Sam's eyes widened as he looked at the severed steel vent, realizing the severity of his close call. Meg sighed and helped Sam clean the office. He was meticulous as always. Using a broom and dustpan, Sam collected every speck of dirt and metal.

The most challenging task was the duct. After realigning the collapsed section, Sam welded the metal with his numen. Meg adapted the refractive index of her hand and placed it over Sam's eyes to act as a face shield.

When Sam finished, they proceeded to Meg's office. Her phone had fifteen messages from frantic doctors regarding Sam's disappearance. Meg called the hospital and explained the situation.

Chapter 3 – Caerule Attacked

"How did you get out of the hospital anyways?" Meg asked, after finishing her call.

"I kind of jumped out the window." Sam wringed his hands.

"We were on the tenth floor."

"On the street side." Sam shrugged. "I'm kind-of able to fly on the voltage planes."

"Let me get this straight." Meg shook her head. "You have a concussion; the doctors don't know how bad it is; and you think it's a good idea to jump out a ten story window into oncoming traffic?"

"I'm sorry."

"You're sorry?" Meg shook her head. "What you did in your match, today, was reckless. What you did in the hospital, today, was reckless. What you did in Peter's office, today, was reckless. If you keep doing stuff like this you are going to end up like…" Meg trailed off without completing the sentence.

"What, you can't even say it?" Sam challenged. "I'll end up like mom and dad." They turned away from each other. Meg watched the sun setting over the Helena Bridge. Sam glared at the world map hanging on the opposite wall.

"Come on," Meg said after a long pause. "I'll drive you home." Sam nodded. After delivering the map to Peter's office, they proceeded to the charging station where Meg's Carbot was parked. Meg entered the coordinates for Sam's apartment and power rushed to the undercarriage voltage plates. The Carbot navigated past the other parked vehicles and rejoined the flow of traffic. Meg stared out the window, watching the world fly past them. The Helena Bridge basked in the soft glow of twilight, glimmering like a flickering candle over the Atropa River. When they arrived at the apartment building, Meg grabbed a small wooden box from the Carbot's trunk.

"Thanks for the ride." Sam walked to the front door of the building.

"You're not getting rid of me that easy," Meg replied. "The doctors don't know the severity of your concussion. I'm spending the night, just to be safe." Sam nodded and held the door for Meg.

When they arrived at Sam's apartment, Meg heard an excited buzzing from the other side of the wall. Sam sighed and unlocked the door

"Hi, Sam!" A Mercury-1 automated assistant flew around the room. "You didn't tell me we were having company."

"Meg this is Merc." Sam rolled his eyes, introducing the robot. "Merc, Meg"

"Nice to meet you!" Merc hovered in front of Meg's face. "Can I get you something to drink?"

"Err…" Meg replied, bewildered. "Water's fine, thanks." The overenthusiastic robot zipped to the refrigerator. Merc grabbed the handle and strained against the refrigerator door. Its motors struggled and whined, but failed to generate enough lift to open it.

"I've got it." Sam shook his head, opening the door. Merc rushed into the refrigerator and retrieved a water bottle for Meg.

"Thank you." Meg took a sip while Merc continued to dance around her head. Sam had reorganized the apartment since her last visit. Everything was arranged by some strange numerical system that seemed to make logical sense. Food was organized by expiration date. Electronics were strategically placed. The furniture was symmetrical with the floorplan.

"What's in the box?" Sam eyed the package in Meg's hand.

"Oh, that." Meg unpacked the box on a nearby table and removed a square seven by seven game board. "It's called the Septagon Game. Peter and I played it when I was his student. I think you'll like it."

"How does it work?" Sam sat on the opposite side of the table.

"The goal is to get five in a row." Meg began unpacking the pieces. "There are 32 pieces with a unique combination of five attributes: white or black; tall or short; wood or metal; solid or hollow; septagon or seven-pointed star. The player who gets five in a row of any attribute wins the game."

"What about the other spaces?" Sam's eyes glinted with curiosity.

"There are 13 red half-spheres and 4 black boxes." Meg explained. "The half-spheres act as all attributes simultaneously. The boxes are null with no attributes."

"Why wouldn't you just use the universal pieces?" Sam frowned.

"That's the catch." Meg grinned. "You don't choose your piece. Your opponent chooses for you." Meg handed Sam a black, short, solid, wooden star. "Now, place that anywhere on the board and choose a piece for me." Sam placed the piece in the corner and handed Meg a black box. She placed the box in the opposite corner and handed Sam a red half-sphere. Twenty turns later, the game was finished. "All septagons." Meg placed the final piece and pointed to five diagonal pieces.

They cleared the board to start a new game. Sam gave Meg a white, short, hollow, metal, septagon. She placed it in the center.

After twenty-three turns, Sam realized he was trapped. Meg handed him the fourth black block. No matter where he placed it, Meg would have the option of winning with all black pieces across the top or all white pieces through the center. Meg won three more times; once by solids; once by metal; and once by stars. After the fifth game, Sam came to a realization.

"This game is based on numen, isn't it?" Sam grinned.

"Yes and no." Meg smiled, pleased Sam made the connection. "It's based on the concept of numen, but numen is not required to play."

"Well, what is it trying to teach me?" Sam glared at the board, confused.

"If I told you that." Meg laughed. "It would kind-of defeat the purpose."

"Can we play again?"

"Not tonight." Meg stretched and yawned. "We'll have plenty more nights to play and I don't plan on losing anytime soon."

"We'll see about that." Sam accepted the challenge. "There is another bedroom in there." He pointed to the opposite door of the symmetrical living room.

"Thank you," Meg replied. "But I'll wait a bit longer." Sam nodded and retired to his room. Merc halted mid-flight and looked towards Sam's door. The robot seemed confused whether he should follow Sam or stay with the guest. "It's okay, Merc." Meg grinned. "I'm fine."

"Great!" The robot buzzed and beeped with irregular frequency. "I'll go recharge!" Meg rolled her eyes. As if that robot needed more energy.

"Oh Merc," Meg asked. "Is there a Fenestravision in here?"

"Of course!" Merc flew to a small control panel on the wall and hovered like an excited hummingbird.

"Thank you." Meg walked to the panel. Merc zipped around the room in an awkward circle and then whizzed into Sam's room, shutting the door. Meg shook her head and pressed a few buttons.

The lights darkened and the walls, floor and ceiling began to shift. Spreading from the control panel, the city of Aprilis came into focus; projecting live video from one of countless drones spread across the city. Above, the moon and stars glowed in the night's sky. Below, the sounds of Carbots ebbed and flowed. Sam's apartment was not on the top floor, nor was this the tallest building in Aprilis. It did not matter to the Fenestravision. The room floated above the city; weightless; limitless; free.

Meg watched the city in perfect silence, wondering about the future. Could she teach Sam? Could she protect him? The stream of Carbots thinned and faded. The moon reflecting off the Atropa River dimmed with passing clouds. The city was quiet, almost peaceful. Of the remaining lights, the Helena Bridge shone brightest. Even now, Carbots streamed across the voltage planes in both directions. The bridge unified the city. No, it unified the country.

A shooting star streaked across the sky, leaving a trail of fire in its wake. The mass accelerated as the conflagration consumed the weaker elements. Meg's eyes widened in fear.

"No!" Meg screamed. The light struck the Helena Bridge, engulfing the city in impenetrable fog. A ripple of blackouts spread from the impact as vehicles lost power and plummeted to the plates below. "No!" Meg pounded on the wall as the Fenestravision disconnected. The room shook and the world plunged into darkness.

Chapter 4 – Bridge of Death

James Lakon

Detective Lakon never heard the explosion. No one could have heard it. Sound does not propagate at temperatures approaching absolute zero. Instead the splintering beams, crashing vehicles and screaming people had all been silenced by the cold, unmoving air. Withstanding the initial blast, the Helena Bridge remained; enveloped in an eerie mist of sublimating vapor.

It took Lakon four hours to arrive at the scene. The deactivated plates forced responders to stage emergency vehicles ten blocks away. Between the ankle-deep snow and bulky insulator suits, progress was difficult.

"How were we so unprepared?" Lakon watched in horror as a medical team dragged their supplies on a makeshift sled made from a broken Carbot door.

"Lakon!" Sergeant Miles waddled through the snow. Lakon flinched. He had not expected sonic temperatures for at least another hour. The bridge was heating too fast. "Lakon, thank god you're here. No one's examined the scene yet." The Sergeant's voice trembled with a mixture of urgency and apprehension.

"Miles, wait!" Lakon watched the pattern of Miles's awkward shuffling. It was too late. Miles's foot snagged a small gap in the plates. He slipped on the snow and tumbled forward. Lakon managed to catch him.

"Thank you." Miles leaned on Lakon for support. "How did you know that was there?"

"Each plate is fifty meters long. You should know that."

"I guess I never thought about it before." Miles sighed. His face was tired and defeated. "Look, I need you to examine the scene before the bridge collapses. You have a good eye for these things."

"I thought you gave this one to Al?" Lakon masked his excitement with a begrudging growl. He glanced at the bridge's remaining support structure. The nearest suspension tower splintered in two places. Inside the truss, a large pendulum leaned against a broken beam. Lakon suspected it would last five hours.

"Please don't do this." Miles shook his head. "Not today."

"Fine." Lakon turned towards the fog. "But don't take me off it until I find the truth."

"Son." Miles voice cut through the air. Lakon stopped examining the bridge. Miles never referred to their familial relationship at work. "Please be careful." Lakon rolled his eyes.

"Help!" A shout pierced through the thickening fog. "Please, anybody!" Lakon and Miles rushed towards the voice. Lakon leapt over a Carbot that had been sliced in half by a steel beam. "Help!" The voice called. Lakon swatted through the mist. At last, he found the source of the voice. Five men in blue insulator suits knelt next to an overturned Busbot.

"What's wrong?" Lakon sprinted towards the men. Miles struggled to catch his breath.

"My son is trapped." One of the men pointed to the Busbot. "Please, help us." Lakon stared at the five men who were throwing themselves against the vehicle in a futile attempt to free the boy.

"You'll never get him out that way." Lakon examined the Busbot.

"I'm not leaving him!"

"I never said that!" Lakon snapped.

"Well what do you suggest, then?"

"You." Lakon looked at the five men and identified one who was more exhausted than the others. "There's a medical team twenty meters in that direction." Lakon pointed into the fog. "Go!" The man scrambled to his feet and ran in the direction Lakon indicated. "You." Lakon addressed the first man. "What's your name?"

"Ne..Neil," he stammered. "Neil Whitney."

"Ok, Neil," Lakon continued. "We passed a broken steel beam on our way over here. You're going to help us bring it here."

"I already told you," Neil said. "I'm not leaving him."

"Neither am I!" Lakon turned to retrace their steps. "Miles, you come too."

"What?" Miles wheezed. He opened his mouth to protest, then closed it and shook his head. "Okay. Where do you need me?"

"Here!" Lakon lead the way to the crushed Carbot they passed earlier. The fallen beam twisted inside the Carbot's titanium frame. The steel must have struck something. Before Lakon could decide if he wanted to know the truth, his mind already made the connection. Lakon's eyes fell on an oblong snow pile beneath the center of the beam. His heart sank. "Neil, you take the high side. Miles, you're on the low side. I'll take the middle." They were under enough stress. Lakon did not want to add any more.

Neil and Miles assumed their positions. Lakon adjusted the gloves of his insulator suit and slid his protected hands into the snow. Sure enough, Lakon felt the spherical shape of the passenger's head. Lakon closed his eyes and heaved a long, deep breath. Judging by the lack of blood, the man had frozen long before the beam fell. At least his death would help save another life. Lakon reached behind the head and found a handhold. "Three. Two. One. Lift." Struggling, the men pried the beam from the Carbot and pushed it onto the fresh snow. Then, they began the arduous task of sliding the beam to the overturned Busbot. The men and the medical team rushed to help.

"Now what?" one of the men asked.

"It's okay." Neil panted. "I think I know … what he has in mind."

"Lever." Lakon tried to catch his breath. He pointed to small indentation in the snow beneath the Busbot. "We'll use the beam … as a lever." The four men looked at each other, then began maneuvering the beam into position. Lakon turned to the medical team. "When we lift the Busbot, you'll have ten seconds to get him into an insulator suit. Can you do that?" The two looked at each other, and nodded in agreement. Lakon grabbed the end of the beam. "Is everyone ready?"

"Yes!" the team shouted.

"Okay!" Lakon called. "We go on three. One. Two. Three." The men pressed their combined weight onto the beam. The Busbot shuddered and lifted from the ground. Lakon strained against the beam, but feared the roof would fail first. He counted the seconds in his head:

One.

The steel crunched and crackled as ruptures began to propagate.

Two.

A freezing wind shrieked across the bridge, buffeting the men with snowdrift.

Three.

The vehicle lurched forward, teetering on the edge of the beam.

Four.

The team screamed and panicked. Lakon held firm.

Five.

Lakon slid further from the Busbot, increasing leverage and control.

Six.

The cold wind howled a second time.

Seven.

The steel snapped and the Busbot slammed onto the plates. Vapor spewed into the air, enveloping everyone in a dense fog.

"No!" Neil's voice tore through the mist. Lakon stared in disbelief at the fractured beam. He had been wrong by three seconds. Was that all they needed?

"We got em!" Lakon heard from the front of the vehicle. A cold gust of air rushed past him. It was Neil. Lakon proceeded towards the voice. Sure enough, Neil and the medical team huddled around the makeshift sled. Resting on top of the sled were two boys around Lakon's age. He breathed a sigh of relief.

"Great job!" Miles smiled and patted Lakon on the back.

"We'll get them to the hospital right away," One of the rescuers assured Neil. Tears streamed down Neil's face as he knelt over the boys.

"I'm going too." Neil brushed the tears from his eyes.

"No!" Lakon's smile faded.

"Why not?" Neil turned to face Lakon, furious.

"Lakon," Miles said in a warning tone.

"You're Neil Whitney, the lead engineer for section seven-dash-eight of the Helena Bridge." Lakon began to explain.

"Lakon, please," Miles repeated.

"We need you here in case more lives can be saved."

"James!" Miles shouted. Lakon stopped talking. "Go check the crime scene!" Miles turned back to Neil. "I apologize, Mr. Whitney, but we really need your help. I promise they'll get the best care possible. Is the other boy's father here?"

"No." Neil sighed. "He died in the explosion."

"I'm sorry." Miles shook his head. "If you want-"

"No." Neil nodded. "I understand. If I can help, my place is here." Neil turned towards Lakon. "Thank you for saving my son."

"I'll take it from here." Miles placed his hand on Lakon's shoulder. "Go check the scene before…" Miles stopped mid-sentence. His face paled.

"What?" Lakon followed Miles's gaze. He couldn't see through the dense fog. Lakon looked back at Miles, confused. Then, he heard it: the methodical crunch of snow compressing under heavy weight. Lakon never heard the sound before, but knew what it was. His heart raced. Sure enough, a Caerule-blue armored truck emerged from the fog, creeping across the hardened snow on eight decagonal wheels. The vehicle was clearly designed for use on active or inactive plates. Lakon glared at the truck with a mixture of awe and disgust. If this technology had been given to the medical staff, who knows how many lives could have been saved?

"James," Miles whispered. "Please be careful."

"I will." Lakon shrugged Miles's hand off his shoulder. The armored vehicle came to a halt. Lakon wanted to get a better look. He strode into the fog, driven by curiosity. He wanted to know. He needed to know. The cold mist swirled around him. Lakon pressed forward, determined and absolute.

After ten strides, Lakon finally felt the weight Miles's words. It was too late. Lakon turned, hoping to catch a final glimpse. Miles was gone. The mist obscured everything. Lakon stood alone, with nothing but his own thoughts.

"Who's there?" A sharp voice cut through the fog. Lakon wheeled to see a teenage girl and a younger boy.

"James Lakon." Lakon hid his shock and extended his hand. "Detective James Lakon." How had the agents snuck past him?

"Major Alumen." She stared at Lakon a long time before accepting the handshake. "What are you doing here?"

"Investigating the scene." Lakon tried to remain calm. Instead of insulator suits, the agents wore navy blue business suits and tinted sunglasses. Anyone else would have frozen to death. Did these people defy physics?

"Have you found anything?" the boy interrupted the Major who opened her mouth to speak. Major Alumen shook her head in disapproval, but the boy did not seem to notice.

Chapter 4 – Bridge of Death

"Yes, sir." Lakon hid his confusion. How were these agents so young? The Major was about his age and the boy was at least four years younger. Lakon removed a notepad from his pocket and began to read. "At approximately 22:12, an unknown object struck lane 13 of the Helena Bridge. The superfluid Helium-4 vaporized, causing a compressed gas explosion. This triggered an automatic shutoff of all Helium-4 to the damaged pipe." Lakon closed the notepad and stored it in his pocket. "So, that's where we stand. Without Helium-4, the plates will thermally expand creating compressive stresses on all parts the bridge. Since the Helena Bridge is not designed to handle these loads." Lakon shut his eyes and took a deep breath before finishing. "The Helena Bridge will collapse." The agents stared at the nearest suspension tower without speaking. Despite their differences, they were all Caerulean citizens. The loss of the Helena Bridge was difficult to accept.

"Well, then." Major Alumen broke the silence. "We better get moving. Detective Lakon, I would like you to accompany us if you are able."

"Yes, Major," Lakon replied.

"And let's drop the formalities. From now on, it is Meg and Sam."

"Yes, Major; I mean Meg." Lakon heaved a sigh of relief. "Thank you. Everyone calls me Lakon."

"Nice to meet you, Lakon." Sam stifled a laugh.

"Follow me." Meg strode into the mist. Lakon and Sam rushed to catch up to her. She never tripped or stumbled. She never walked into beams or Carbots. She even seemed to know which snowbanks were sturdy enough to hold their combined weight. Sam and Lakon struggled to keep pace. At last, they arrived at a clearing where the mist and snow lessened. "We're here." Meg called.

"Watch out! This section is unstable." Lakon looked around the clearing. Something was wrong.

"Where are the Carbots?" Sam asked. Lakon's eyes widened with realization. The clearing was a circle.

"There!" Meg and Lakon pointed to the center of the clearing. Sure enough, the snow was much thinner than the surroundings. The three of them rushed to the spot. Meg arrived first. Kneeling down, she plunged her hands into the snow.

"Ahh!" She recoiled and clutched her hands, screaming.

"Are you okay?" Sam ran to Meg's side and caught her before she hit the snow. Lakon grabbed her hands. Sure enough, Meg's fingers blistered a sickening shade of red and yellow. It was frostbite.

"Put these on." Lakon pulled an extra pair of insulator gloves from his pocket and slid them onto Meg's hands. "How are your legs?" Lakon pointed to Meg's pants which were covered in a sleet mixture.

"They're fine." Meg breathed heavy. "It's just my hands. Thank you."

"What was that?" Sam's face paled and panicked.

"Don't touch it." Meg closed her eyes. Lakon stared at the spot. Why did Meg suddenly need an insulator suit and why did she only need it for her hands? Lakon did not ask. Instead, he began sifting through the snow.

"What are you doing?" Sam's eyes widened.

"Investigating the scene." Lakon continued to sweep around the spot.

"Didn't you see what happened to Meg?"

"I'm wearing an insulator suit." Lakon met Sam's gaze. "Besides, I'm more expendable than you." Sam did not seem pleased by the answer. As Lakon brushed away the final layers of ice, he felt a sharp pain.

"Oww," Lakon whispered under his breath.

"I told you," Sam shouted. Lakon ignored the boy. He removed his hand from the snow and inspected the glove. A small gash cut through the aerogel lining. The pain was sharp, not cold. Lakon finished clearing the snow. Sure enough, a jagged metal shard protruded from the plate.

"Found it!" Lakon drew a small camera and an evidence bag from his insulator suit. He took several pictures before prying the metal from the hole and sliding it into the bag.

"Are you done?" Sam's voice trembled.

"Yes." Lakon nodded.

"Good." Sam helped Meg to her feet. "Let's get out of here."

BONG!

A loud noise echoed across the bridge like a ringing bell.

"What's that?" Sam yelled. The color drained from Lakon's face.

"The tower." Meg's arm drooped as she pointed towards the truss. "The pendulum."

BONG!

The pendulum swung again.

"We need to get out of here now!" Lakon glanced around the clearing.

"We'll run to the ATV," Sam yelled.

BONG!

"It's not fast enough." Lakon shook his head.

"There's no other way!" Sam eyes darted back and forth like a trapped animal.

BONG!

"We need to find a Carbot with a backup power supply." Lakon pointed to the snow piles on the outer edge of the circle. "But Aprilis stopped using those years ago-"

"We carry one with us." Sam interrupted, looking at Meg.

BONG!

"Wow…uh…Great!" Lakon raised his eyebrows. Power supplies spanned the length of entire Carbots. Where could these agents be hiding one? Lakon ran to the nearest snow pile.

"Not that one." Meg winced. "The one in front of it." Lakon accepted the suggestion without argument and started clearing snow from the buried vehicle. Sam helped Meg to passenger's side door.

BONG!

"Install the power supply. Now!" Lakon took the wheel. The bridge shuddered beneath their feet. They were out of time.

"Already done." Sam jumped in the back seat. Sure enough, as soon as the boy entered, the Carbot roared to life and wobbled into the lowest voltage plane.

BONG!

With the seventh strike, the pendulum broke free from its steel enclosure. The tower crumbled and the bridge shook with tremendous force. Lakon weaved to avoid the falling beams

"You can fly manual?" Meg lay back in her seat, eyes closed.

"Can't you?" Lakon increased the voltage. Sam grit his teeth.

"No." Meg sighed. "I always wanted to learn."

"I tell you what." Lakon spiraled into a desperate corkscrew to avoid a web of snapping cables. "We live through this, I'll teach you myself."

"Great." Meg forced a weak laugh. "Shift left. This lane is about to collapse."

"Fine." Lakon maneuvered to the leftmost lane. "But I don't like backseat drivers, especially with their eyes closed."

"Shut up!" Sam winced. His arms trembled and beads of sweat rolled down his face. "Both of you."

"You're doing great, Sam!" Meg smiled. "We're almost at the end of the bridge."

"Which one?" Sam snapped. Lakon glanced in the rearview mirror. His heart sank. Plates, beams and cables cascaded into the river in a chain reaction that was rapidly gaining on them. Less than fifty meters left.

"We need to risk a higher voltage plane." Lakon gave Sam a quick nod. Lakon couldn't explain it, but somehow it felt necessary to ask the boy.

"Do it." Sam clamped his eyes shut. Lakon pressed the button and the Carbot shuddered upwards.

"Look out!" Meg's shouted. A large hole opened between them and the end of the bridge.

"I see it!" Lakon snapped.

"Well?" Meg's eyes opened. Sam's breaths shortened. "What are you going to do?"

"Leave it." Lakon pressed forward full-throttle. "To fate."

"What?" Meg and Sam shouted in unison; too late. The vehicle lost power at full speed and rocketed across the hole. Their trajectory held for a moment. Then, the Carbot nosedived towards the plates. There was nothing left to do. Lakon braced for impact.

The Carbot slammed into the bridge, skidding across the sleet. Lakon lurched forward, striking his head on the dashboard. The vehicle slid across the end of the bridge. Lakon slumped in his seat. His vision swam and blurred.

"Leave it to fate?" Sam fumed. "Are you kidding me?"

"Are you okay?" Meg placed her hand on Lakon's shoulder.

"Yeah." Lakon took several deep breaths. He expected more pain. "I'm fine."

"You're tougher than you look." Meg patted Lakon on the back. Lakon fumbled with the door latch. He stumbled outside and leaned on the Carbot for support. The last remains of the Helena Bridge sank into the Atropa River. Frozen Carbots floated with the current. Twisted towers protruded from the water like monuments to some long forgotten war.

"We'll get justice." Meg reassured Lakon as the last remnants of the Helena Bridge sank beneath the waves. "Trust me." The fog between Aprilis and Central thickened, obscuring everything.

Chapter 5 – Friends and Enemies

Peter Turnus

Peter hated the war room even more than he hated war. In war, Peter could change the outcome. In the war room, things were far less certain.

"Enough!" Admiral Margaret Lodon slammed her fist on the table, denting the mahogany. "Some of us have a nation to defend." General Jesse Bell and General Patricia Rocklos avoided eye contact with the angry Admiral.

"The President will be here shortly." Grand Master Marius Sulla took a deep breath. A vein twitched in his temple. "If you want to wait outside, I'll send Peter to get you when he arrives."

"He should be waiting on us, not the other way around." Admiral Lodon crossed her arms. "We're missing the perfect opportunity to strike."

"As soon as we find the culprit, you will be the first to know."

"You mean we still don't know?" Admiral Lodon fumed. "A transmission ship was attacked in our national waters!"

"And a bridge was bombed in our capital city." Marius countered. "Or do you care about civilian casualties at all?"

"Spare me your crocodile tears, Marius." Admiral Lodon snarled. "You know how important transmission ships are to our command structure." She spat each word more furious than the last.

"If that wasn't enough, our entire investigation corps was on that ship because our president ordered that damn dedication ceremony."

"Sorry I'm late." President Reginald Millenavis entered the room, a stupid smile on his face. "The press conference ran over." Admiral Lodon rolled her eyes. "Where do we stand?"

"We're ready to strike at any time." Admiral Lodon glared at Marius. "But it seems we don't have a target."

"Is this true?" President Millenavis sat at the head of the table and flipped through his briefing folder. He skipped the words, looking only at the pictures.

"I'm afraid so." Marius sighed. "Major Alumen recovered a munition from the scene. She'll give us full report when she joins our Fenestravision conference."

"Another numen user?" Admiral Lodon raged. "It's bad enough we let Colonel kiss-ass in here." She glared at Peter.

"With all due respect, Admiral." Peter pushed a button on the central console and the Fenestravision whirred to life. "Meg's the best archeologist in Caerule and, right now, she knows more about this case than all of us combined. She deserves to be here."

"Peter." Patricia warned.

"You've got more guts than brains, kid." Admiral Lodon flashed Peter an unnerving smirk. Peter remained firm. "Alright. Let's see what she's got." The Fenestravision brightened and Meg's face appeared. "You! Alumen! Start talking!"

"Well, uh." Meg glanced at Peter, startled. He gave a frantic nod. "We recovered a two kilogram fragment of the projectile. Analysis is not complete but…" Meg took a deep breath. "I believe the metal is tungsten."

"Tungsten?" General Bell's face paled. "Are you sure?"

"Have we raised the alert level in the islands?" Patricia demanded.

"Enough!" Admiral Lodon sprang to her feet, pommel of her tungsten cutlass clanging against the table.

"Can someone fill me in?" President Millenavis stopped looking at the pictures and forced a sheepish grin. "What's so bad about tungsten?"

"Tungsten has the lowest numen sensitivity of any metal." Marius's eyes hardened. "It can't be created, transformed or manipulated. It's a numen user's worst enemy."

"You numen users are pathetic." Admiral Lodon glared at the Generals. "My soldiers risk their lives every day and you imbeciles are scared of an element on the periodic table." She wheeled to face Meg. "Anything else, bright eyes?"

"Yes." Meg sighed. "The fragment was badly damaged, but the projectile-" Meg closed her eyes. "-was in the shape of a septagon."

"No." General Bell breathed, gripping his cane.

"Impossible." Patricia shook her head. "They're dead."

"Not all of them." Marius snarled. "Not Raven."

"Enough." Admiral Lodon repeated a third time, but her rage had been replaced by a resolute frown. Marius's eyes darkened. A hot surge of numen writhed within him. Peter glanced at the Grand Master, concerned.

"Are you and Sam okay?" Peter returned his attention to Meg.

"We're fine." Meg nodded. "Sam and I are at Aprilis P.D. I got some frostbite from the metal, but I heal fast."

"You're not at Central?" Admiral Lodon frowned. Her fist clenched around the hilt of her sword. "Where is the fragment now?"

"Aprilis P.D. will have their analysis in a few hours." Meg's eyes narrowed. "I'll then send the sample to Central for-."

"No." Admiral Lodon interrupted. "Send it now."

"Admiral, please." General Bell leaned forward. "Aprilis P.D. is fully capable of-"

"No." Admiral Lodon cast the General a sideways glare. "They're not." She turned back to Meg. "Send the fragment to Central now. That's an order." Meg did not respond. She continued to watch the angry Admiral, unflinching.

"Good work, Alumen!" President Millenavis clapped his hands, oblivious to the uneasy silence. "Send the sample to Central as soon as possible, and we'll handle the investigation from here." He deactivated the Fenestravision before Meg could respond and began shoving loose papers into his briefcase.

"Uh…Sir?" Patricia Rocklos cringed as the President tossed confidential files into an unclassified folder. "How exactly are we going to handle the investigation? Our investigators are dead or injured."

"Oh." The President was already three steps towards the door. "Really?"

"I have a suggestion." Peter raised his hand. Everyone turned to look at him. Peter could not believe his luck. The meeting progressed his way without any effort. "An old war buddy of mine, Sinon Donafer, retired from the investigation corps two years ago.

He's a professor at Aprilis University. If it's acceptable, I can ask him to join the investigation."

"Great idea!" President Millenavis nodded. "What does everyone else think?"

"Yes." General Bell said without hesitation.

"Alright." Patricia's eyes narrowed.

Marius remained silent, but gave a slow nod of approval.

"Great!" Millenavis smiled. "What about you, Lodon?" The Admiral did not respond. "Uh…Lodon?"

"No objections." Admiral Lodon frowned. She glared at the center of the table, eyes fixed and puzzled.

"Then it's settled!" Millenavis continued towards the door. "Meg, will send the fragment to Central. Peter will meet Sinon at Aprilis University. Great meeting everyone!" President Millenavis was first to leave. Peter followed close behind him; anything to get out of that place.

"Peter." Someone called his name. Peter turned to see Patricia exiting the war room.

"Yes, General?" Peter smiled.

"I heard you have a new student." Patricia beamed. "Congratulations."

"Yes." Peter's eyes glowed with excitement. "Leah Penthes. She's the greatest student I've ever seen; much stronger than Sinon and me at her age."

"I'm glad to hear it." Patricia laughed. "You two were my best students. This Leah girl must be something else."

"Oh she is." Peter continued rambling. "The best in her class, by far. It took them ten hours to fix the stage after her match with Tom. It reminded me of the time Ike-" Peter choked on the last word. His eyes darkened.

"Do you want to talk about it?" Patricia pressed.

"No." Peter turned away. He could feel the tears welling, but he did not want to cry in front of the General. "Not today. You have enough to worry about."

"Alright." Patricia nodded. "Just let me know."

"Thank you." Peter face brightened again. "But I'll be fine. I'll get to see Sinon today."

"You may want to lower your expectations on that." Patricia sighed. "Sinon's been out of the service two years. He's not the same person you knew."

"You've seen him already?" Peter asked.

"A few months ago." The General leaned against the hall window and stared out at the city. "He loves his new job. He may not want to return to this."

"Well." Peter grinned. "At least I'll finally get to see him."

"Yes." Patricia nodded. "I think it will be good for both of you."

"Thank you, General." Peter smiled and turned to leave. Patricia grabbed his arm.

"Please be careful." Patricia's eyes locked with Peter. "I saw what you did in there; taking control of the meeting." She nodded to the war room. "Rising in rank will not help you create a more peaceful world. Trust me. I know."

"I don't know what you're talking about." Peter wrenched his arm from her. He continued down the hall and took the elevator to the Central Docks.

As the doors opened, Peter was greeted by the sweet brine air. Hundreds of docks spread across the Central Harbor. Boatbots stretched as far as the eye could see. Peter scanned his thumbprint and boarded the nearest Boatbot. The computer whirred to life and calculated a new route, avoiding the Helena Bridge. Peter cancelled the suggestion. He wanted to see the devastation first hand. The Boatbot cast-off and sailed into the frigid waters of the Atropa River.

Peter saw Fenestravision footage of the Helena Bridge, but nothing could have prepared him for this. Seven towers bent over the water, webs of cable stretched between them. The stream brewed a dull grey slush of ice and broken metal, scraping against the Boatbot hull. Helpless Carbots bobbed in the water, sinking beneath the waves. Once again, Peter was surrounded by death and destruction.

Aprilis University gleamed through the fog, calm, peaceful and constant. Blue brick buildings lined the peninsula, blending with the sea and sky. Peter smiled. This place was Sinon's first chance at a normal life. It would be great to see him again. Peter disembarked and climbed the cliff-side stairs towards the shimmering glass panes of Prometheus Hall.

Peter followed signs for the large lecture hall on the ground floor. The doors were already open. Sinon pranced across the stage, voice booming through the room. More than two hundred students listened to his every word, scribbling frantic notes and diagrams. Peter smiled and sat in the back row.

"There are two things certain in this world." Sinon smiled and walked to the center of the stage. "Can anyone tell me what they are?" A young man in the fourth row raised his hand. "Yes, Ben," Sinon called on him.

"Death and taxes?" Ben said. The crowd erupted in laughter.

"That may very well be true." Sinon smirked. "But not from a physics standpoint. There are many things in this universe that don't die and there are many more that do not pay taxes." The crowd laughed again. Ben smiled and sat down. Sinon looked up at Peter and gave a brief nod.

"The real answer is: entropy always increases and there's nothing we can do about it." Sinon pressed a small button and the words appeared on the wall behind him. "This is the Second Law of Thermodynamics. It is one of the most important laws of physics. In fact, one could argue that all of physics can be summarized by this one principle. Everything in the universe; where it is, where it's been, where it's going; everything depends on entropy."

"How many people opened a textbook this morning?" Sinon glanced around the room. Roughly half the class raised their hands. "Fair enough, how many people ate breakfast this morning?" More hands raised. "Many of the same people." Sinon grinned. The audience laughed. "How many people breathed sometime today?" Everyone raised their hands. "Congratulations! Everyone in this room increased the entropy of the universe. Any time an object moves; any time an event happens, any time energy is transferred, entropy increases. In many ways, it the defining law of our universe."

Sinon glanced at the clock in the rear of the auditorium. "That's all the time we have today. I will not be assigning written homework on entropy this week, but I strongly recommend reading the section in your textbooks and doing independent research if need be." Most students gathered their belongings and shuffled towards the exit. A few stayed behind to ask questions. Peter remained seated and shook his head, grinning. Patricia was right. Sinon did look happy. When the last student left, Sinon turned to Peter and beamed.

"Peter!" Sinon waved. "Come on down! How've you been?"

"Could be better," Peter laughed. He ran down the stairs to join Sinon on the stage. "What about you?"

"This is the best I've felt in a long time." Sinon withdrew an Accretion Bar from his desk and tossed it to Peter. "I love teaching."

"Aren't we a bit old for this?" Peter unwrapped the bar and broke it in half. He tossed the white chocolate half to Sinon.

"No one's too old for chocolate." Sinon eagerly devoured the bar. "Besides, it's little things like this that make friendships great."

"When was the last time we saw each other?" Peter sat on the desk next to Sinon. "Five years?"

"Three, I think. We did that super-virus mission in Ferox."

"I remember." Peter laughed. "You convinced that big guy the password was 1-2-3-4-5."

"Yeah." Sinon howled. "The doors locked and we didn't have to fight him." Peter laughed until his sides hurt. Sinon brushed a tear from his eye. "Anyways, do you want to grab a bite? We have loads of catching up to do."

"Can't you read minds?" Peter joked.

"I'm a bit rusty." Sinon shrugged. "Besides, I'd prefer a two way conversation."

"Me too." Peter stared at the dark chocolate strip in his hand. "But we'll have to save it for another time."

"Oh." Sinon's smile faded. "Is this about the bridge?" Peter took a deep breath before continuing.

"A transmission ship was attacked during the chaos. Our entire investigation corps was on it. We're treating the survivors' injuries but, in the meantime-" Peter turned to Sinon. "We were wondering if you could assist us."

"I see." Sinon sighed. "I might not be much help. My numen isn't what it used to be."

"It's fine." Peter insisted. "You'll just be investigating and I'll be with you at all times." Sinon paced back and forth, head bowed.

"How bad is it?"

"Half-million dead." Peter's face darkened. "Another million wounded and no power for ten kilometers of the city."

"I had no idea." Sinon stared at the floor.

"We've seen worse." Peter eyes hardened. "And we'll always see worse until someone fixes it."

"Peter?" A worried look crossed Sinon's face. "Are you gonna be okay?"

"Yeah." Peter heaved a long sigh. "It's this world I'm worried about." Peter chewed the dark chocolate. A twisted smile crept across his face. "It's like you said. Entropy always increases." Sinon remained silent. He turned away from Peter and began ascending the lecture hall stairs.

"Come on." Sinon signaled to Peter. "I have something to show you." Peter followed him to the nearby stairwell.

"What is it?" Peter asked.

"It's on the roof." Sinon smiled and began running up the stairs. "Race you?"

"You're on!" Peter grinned. It was just like old times. Peter sprinted up the stairs two at a time, catching Sinon before the fourth floor. When Peter reached the top, Sinon was a floor behind him. "Do you need me to carry you?" Peter teased.

"Yeah. Yeah. Laugh it up!" Sinon panted as he climbed the last few stairs. "Let's see how you do after teaching two classes."

"Fair enough." Peter laughed. "Now what did you want to show me?" Sinon opened the door to the room. Peter's eyes rested on a small wooden box slanted at a 45 degree angle. In the center of the box a square surface reflected the sun. Peter looked at Sinon, perplexed.

"How much do you know about light?" Sinon asked.

"Probably not enough to know how this works." Peter smirked.

"Fair enough." Sinon bent down to adjust the device. "This is a photonic cooler. Some of my students made it. The surface reflects sunlight like an ordinary mirror. But, what really makes this box special is what's beneath the surface." Sinon lifted the box and turned it over, revealing several layers of white and grey substances contained within a transparent glass case. "These are non-linear crystals. Without going into too much detail, these crystals absorb light at one frequency and emit light at a different frequency. In this case, the crystals absorb light from the thermal infrared and emit light in the far infrared." Sinon turned the box over again.

"Okay?" Peter raised his eyebrows. "So, how is that useful?"

"Well." Sinon grinned. "Remember how I said 'entropy always increases and there is nothing we can do about it.'"

"Let me guess," Peter said. "This does something about it."

"Sort of." Sinon nodded. "This device absorbs thermal radiation from the building and emits far infrared radiation; which can easily pass through the atmosphere. Essentially, we are removing heat from the building and sending that energy directly into space. We are decreasing the entropy of the Earth and using space as our own personal heat sink."

"So in other words-"

"Entropy always increases," Sinon answered before Peter could finish. "But we can choose when and where."

"Is it me?" Peter smiled. "Or are you about to accept my offer?"

"I'm your friend, Peter. Was there ever any doubt?"

Chapter 6 – Order Meets Chaos

Sam Pere

"All stars." Meg pointed a diagonal line across the game board.

"One more game." Sam scrutinized the pieces. There had to be some sort of pattern.

"Maybe later." Meg smirked. "We need to get back to the station."

"Fine." Sam repacked the pieces. "But I'm taking it with us." Meg rolled her eyes.

"You're leaving already?" Merc buzzed around Sam's head. "But you just got here."

"Not really." Sam shrugged. "We spent the night; and shouldn't you be in power saving mode?"

"I am in power saving mode." Merc zipped around Sam's apartment. "Can't you see how calm I am?"

"More importantly." Meg dodged the excited robot and proceeded to the door. "Do you have the research I asked for?"

"Right here." Sam grabbed a folder from the kitchen table and handed it to Meg. "The life and times of Detective James Lakon; I marked anything I thought was strange."

"This is great." Meg flipped through the folder as they took the elevator to the garage level. "What does the red mean?"

"Those are inconsistencies in Lakon's past." The doors slid open and Sam walked to the nearest armored truck. "He's supposedly seventeen years old, but the Central Archives only has sixteen years of records on him."

"So he wasn't born in a hospital." Meg sat on the driver's side. "That's not exactly strange. We were at war. You have quite a few inconsistent records yourself, Mr. Pere." She smirked.

"At least I know my real parents died in the war." Sam countered, programming the coordinates of Aprilis PD. The decagonal wheels began to turn. "I can't even find his. The name 'Lakon' appeared out of nowhere."

"That's odd." Meg frowned at the documents.

"And that's not all." Sam pressed. "His records are flawless. Dates can be verified. Places check out. For the last sixteen years, there is not a single moment when James Lakon's whereabouts can't be verified by numerous sources."

"So you're saying his records are too good?" Meg raised her eyebrows. "That's not exactly a crime. Anything else?"

"He's average." Sam grinned.

"That's all you're gonna give me?"

"No, seriously. Look!" Sam nodded to the file. "IQ test: average; police exam: average; detective exam: average; pistol qualification: average. Whenever there's a test, he scores the exact median."

"Well, what are these awards right here?" Meg pointed to some yellow lines along the bottom of the page.

"That's when Lakon joined the force. He was ten years old, the youngest in Aprilis history. IQ test; police exam; detective exam and pistol qualification all in the same day; He broke the records on all four. But, the scores were thrown out for some reason."

"I see." Meg furrowed her brow. "So you think it was a cover up?"

"It has to be." Sam insisted. "Look at his recent weapons test. Lakon is the only person on the force who doesn't use a laser pistol. The fact that he can score average with a projectile weapon is-"

"Extraordinary." Meg nodded.

"I was gonna say weird." Sam cast Meg a suspicious look. "But you get the picture."

"These are good finds." Meg flipped through the pages. "However, they don't prove anything."

"True." Sam sighed.

"But, having only known him for a short time." Meg gazed out the window as they approached the Aprils PD building. "Lakon is not average."

"What should we do about him?"

"I'm not sure." Meg frowned as they pulled into the underground charging station. "Keep an eye on him today."

"You're not coming?" Sam's face paled.

"No." Meg sighed. "President Millenavis insisted on holding the sword ceremony today. You'll be Central's point of contact for the next few hours."

"Me?" Sam's heart raced. "Who's there now?"

"Professor Plummet, I presume."

"Oh, God! Please, no."

"Don't worry." Meg laughed. "You'll only have to put up with him for a few minutes. Then, it will be you and Lakon the rest of the day."

"That's not very reassuring." Sam grumbled as he exited the vehicle.

"You'll be fine." Meg grinned and shifted the truck into gear. "I'll be back before you know it." Sam sighed. This day was not going well.

Sam followed a group of officers to the nearest elevator. Incessant stares and nervous whispers lingered. Sam shivered. The officers towered over him, but Sam could not tell who was more uncomfortable. He bolted from the elevator as soon as they reached the eighth floor.

Aprilis PD was a nightmare of chaos. Detectives, officers and robots raced through the disorganized frenzy. Sam ducked beneath an overburdened evidence bot which promptly collided with a nearby cabinet. Loose paper showered throughout the room, adding to the confusion and panic.

One constant remained. A tarnished bronze shield hung above the entryway, bearing the white stallion of Caerule on the right, the blue rose of Aprilis on the left. Sam walked beneath the shield, past the reception desk and all the way to Sergeant Miles's office.

"Come in! Come in!" Sergeant Miles motioned Sam to enter. "You must be Sam. My son told me you saved his life yesterday. Thank you."

"Uh." Sam hesitated before sitting in the chair opposite Miles. "Yes. Well. I think he saved ours a few times too."

"I'm glad to hear it." Miles beamed. "Protect and serve: that's what we do."

"Right." Sam avoided eye contact. The Sergeant was almost too friendly. "Anyways, can you tell me where he is?"

"Lakon's not working that case!" Miles answered, harsh and abrupt. His smile vanished only to return seconds later. "I'll introduce you to, Al. He's the new detective."

"No thanks." Sam's raised his eyebrows. "Could you just tell me where Lakon is?"

"Sure." Mile's eyes narrowed. "His office is down the hall."

"Thanks." Sam bolted from the office. The Sergeant's reaction left him nervous and confused. Sam hurried past rows of cubicles to a small windowless office on the far wall. "Lakon?" Sam knocked on the half-open door. No answer. Sam stepped inside.

Sam had never seen anyone so disorganized. Mounds of loose paper littered Lakon's desk and a small table in the corner. "Lakon?" Sam asked again, unable to see over the heap of files. He walked around the desk. Lakon's chair was empty.

Sam sighed and cleared a section of the table. He placed the piles in two neat stacks on the floor. Dates and cases were mixed, but Sam wasn't going to waste time deciphering them. He unpacked the Septagon Game and arranged the pieces in the same order as his last match.

Lakon burst through the door, carrying two large boxes of files and holding a half-eaten bagel in his teeth. He turned towards Sam with a stupid wide-eyed stare.

"OR-IYE-TER." Lakon attempted to speak through a mouthful of bagel.

"What?"

"OHM." Lakon lowered his head and spat the half-eaten bagel onto a stack of loose paper. Disgusting! "Oh. Hi there." Lakon repeated, smiling. "Were you waiting for me?"

"Not really?" Sam eyed the bagel still oozing saliva. Was this really the man who saved their lives yesterday? "I guess I'm Central's representative today, at least until Meg gets back."

"Thank God." Lakon collapsed in his chair, reshuffling the mounds of paper so he could see Sam. "Because, not for nothing, the last guy was kind of-"

"Lakon?" An over-excited voice called outside the office. Sam hid beneath the table. Lakon tried to duck behind his desk, too late. "James Lakon, that is you!"

"P-Professor Plummet." Lakon slid backwards. It was a rookie mistake. "How are you today?"

"Great!" Plummet brimmed with energy. "Far better thanks to you." He walked around the desk, pressing further into Lakon's personal space. "Your report was most useful and I admire your attention to detail. The way you guesstimated the superalloy composition; you were only off by two percentage points. Was that a Von Karman integral on the nose cone? How did you account for the change in temperature?"

"Uh." Lakon slid away from the professor until his chair hit the wall. "I dunno. I just kind of-"

"And deriving the parabolic trajectory from those pictures." Plummet continued to ramble. "You accounted for turbulence and everything. I'm amazed how much you did in so little time."

"Right." Lakon forced a weak laugh. "I guess you'll have good stuff to bring back to Central."

"Absolutely!" Plummet agreed. "But I cannot leave until my replacement arrives."

"He's here." Lakon blurted. Sam's heart skipped a beat. "Sam is…" Lakon cast a frantic glance towards Sam. "…in the transmission studio."

"Really?" Professor Plummet stood upright. Lakon lost balance and toppled from his chair. Plummet did not seem to notice. "In that case, I'll be going. Thanks, again, Detective Lakon." With an unnecessary flourish, Plummet waltzed out of the office.

"Thank y…" Sam began.

"Shh!" Lakon signaled Sam to remain quiet. Lakon walked to the door and peered down the hall. "Okay, he's gone." Lakon heaved a sigh of relief.

"Thank you so much." Sam emerged from behind the table.

"Do you have to deal with that a lot?"

"That and worse." Sam laughed. "He's my…chemistry teacher." Sam cringed at the awkward lie, but Lakon did not seem to notice.

"I'm so sorry." Lakon grinned, and nodded to Sam's game board. "What's that you've got there?"

"Oh! This?" Sam glanced at the table, startled. "It's called the Septagon Game. Do you know how to play?"

"No." Lakon shoved the papers off the second chair. "Does it come with instructions?"

"Yeah." Sam handed Lakon the sheet. "It's fairly simple once you get the hang of it; but, no matter what I do, I can't beat Meg."

"I see." Lakon cast a cursory glance at the instructions. "So you're practicing in your spare time. Do you want a real opponent?"

"Sure." Sam cleared the board. "But don't you have work to do?"

"Not anymore." Lakon sighed. "Miles took me off the case." Lakon handed Sam a red half-sphere. Sam placed the piece in the corner of the board.

"That's too bad." Sam handed Lakon a piece. Lakon placed it in a random location and handed Sam another red half-sphere. "You seemed to be making progress." Sam placed the red half-sphere in the opposite corner and handed Lakon a black box.

"Lakon!" a gruff voice called outside the office.

"Yeah, Al!" Lakon shouted.

"Miles asked me to talk to you." Detective Albert Libby strode into the office, carrying an enormous binder. He was at least ten years older than Lakon and did not seem pleased by the situation.

"About what?" Lakon growled without taking his eyes off the board game.

"The Helena Bridge case." Al flipped through the binder, almost dropping it. "Could it have been something other than orbital bombardment?"

"Why are you asking me? You're the lead detective."

"I never asked for this!" Al snapped.

"And yet you got it anyways." Lakon placed the black box in a random corner. "Funny how that always happens."

"Are you going to help me or not?" Al glared at the game board.

"There's a diagram on page 153." Lakon sighed. "Even you should be able to understand it. Anything on that trajectory could've caused the impact."

"Thank you." Al bookmarked the page and stormed out of the room. Sam watched Al walked down the hall.

"He's gone." Sam frowned.

"Now you see what I have to deal with." Lakon grumbled.

"He looked like he wanted to punch you in the face." Sam eyed Lakon's reaction.

"He probably did." Lakon nodded. "People don't seem to like me very much."

"I can't imagine why." Sam shook his head. Lakon was obnoxious at best and arrogant at worst. He flaunted his knowledge one moment and hid behind it the next. Still, there was something about Lakon. No matter what life threw at him, he was always in control. He acted and reacted in the moment, without concern for future or past. Sam almost envied him. Lakon handed Sam yet another red half-sphere.

"You know these are universal pieces, right?" Sam placed the piece in the last remaining corner.

"Yes."

"You shouldn't give your opponent these pieces too early." Sam placed the piece in the last remaining corner. "It gives them too much control."

"Then why aren't you using it?" Lakon asked handing Sam a fourth red half-sphere. Sam looked at the board, confused. None of his previous games looked like this. Most pieces were located near the corners and edges, not threatening anything. This game would not help him prepare for a match against Meg. Was Lakon toying with him?

"Well where would you place it then?" Sam placed the piece next to the two black boxes and handed Lakon a red half-sphere.

"Here." Lakon placed the piece in the center of the board. Now, Sam understood. Lakon was creating the most aggressive board possible. Lakon thrived on chaos. That's why his office was a mess. That's why he remained calm during the bridge collapse. That's why he was always first to react when things went wrong.

The game lasted eight more turns. Lakon won by septagons passing through the center. They played three more games. Whenever Sam blocked a path, Lakon opened two more. Whenever Sam changed his strategy, Lakon did something unexpected. Sam stared at the board, flabbergasted.

"I don't get it." Sam cleared the board in disgust. "This is your first time playing and you're already better than Meg."

"You're a lot better at this than you know." Lakon scratched his chin. "You notice the patterns and you always know when I'm laying a trap; but you never use that to your advantage."

"Well." Sam glared at Lakon. "What am I supposed to do about it?"

"I'm not sure." Lakon frowned. "I think you need to find a playstyle that works for you."

"Of course." Sam's voice dripped with sarcasm. "Why didn't I think of that?"

"Why is this game so important to you?" Lakon leaned back in his chair.

"Because I want to be an agent."

"Why?"

"Because…" Sam's eyes widened. Why did he want to be an agent? The question was obnoxious, but it needed an answer. Sam looked down at the board. "Well…I guess because my parents were. They gave their lives for this country, I guess it must be special."

"That's stupid."

"What?"

"Just because your parents did something you want to too?" Lakon shook his head. "That's the dumbest thing I've ever heard."

"Well, what's your dream then?" Sam spat.

"Me?" Lakon grinned. "I'm going to be President." Sam fell out of his chair laughing. "What's so funny?"

"You just said people don't like you." Sam righted his chair. "And now you're going to be President. Please tell me you're joking."

"I never joke about a person's dreams." Lakon's voice remained firm. "Least of all my own. Now, go on. What's the real reason you want to be an agent?"

"I don't know." Sam furrowed his brow. Add hypocrisy to the growing list of Lakon's flaws. Still, it was such a simple question. What was the answer? Sam thought of Meg; all the places she'd gone; all the people she'd met. His face brightened. "Did you know South Alamus has the largest library in the world?"

"Yeah." Lakon's smiled. "I heard it's twice the size of Central."

"Above ground." Sam's eyes radiated with intensity. "Below, it's even larger than Aprilis. There are five thousand years of books in there; and shelf space for another ten."

"Amazing." Lakon nodded.

"And in Nemo." Sam continued. "They have a skyscraper over five kilometers high. The pyramid is made of silica glass and doubles as an optical computer."

"It must be something." Lakon grinned. "To see all that up close."

"Yeah." Sam trembled with excitement. "There are so many wonders in this world. Even Meg hasn't seen them all."

"And now you'll see them together." Lakon nodded.

"Yeah." Sam sighed and clenched his fist. "I guess we will."

"Is Meg alright?" Lakon eyed Sam's reaction.

"Yeah." Sam straightened to look at Lakon. "She's probably still at the sword ceremony."

"They're still holding that today?" Lakon's face darkened.

"Yes. why?"

"No reason." Lakon climbed onto the table and removed the ceiling tile. He withdrew a small brown package and jammed it into his pocket.

"What was that?"

"Nothing." Lakon replaced the tile and jumped off the table. He strode out of the office and walked down the hall.

"Where are you going?" Sam hurried after him. Lakon did not respond. He proceeded to the large Fenestravison on the back wall where several officers gathered to watch the speech. Sergeant Miles emerged from his office, face pale.

"What is it?" Miles stood at Lakon's side.

"Nothing." Lakon yanked the remote from Al's hands.

"What the hell, Lakon!" Al yelled.

"Sorry, Al." Lakon ignored Al's reddening face. "I'm commandeering this Fenestravision." Lakon spoke directly to the screen. "Give me sixteen extra panels. On the four left, give me views of the stage from every angle. On the four right, give me views of the crowd. On the bottom, give me views of the surrounding buildings. And, on top, give me the highest altitude views possible. Record everything." The image of the podium shrank, but remained centered. The sixteen additional panels appeared around the center screen exactly as Lakon described. He scanned the images, pacing back and forth.

Sam stared at the center panel, heart pounding. Meg and General Bell stood beside the podium where President Millenavis had just taken the stage. Caerule's national anthem sang strong and bold through the screen.

The ocean waves are rough.
Our enemies are tough.
We continue sailing to;
Our Caerule;
Of the just and true.

And we'll sail on the rising tides;
Till the light of the horizon dies;
Our Caerule Blue will guide us through.
Trust in me.

I will trust in you.

Do not cry, oh my beloved;
We are blessed by God above;
Our flag flew though darkness grew.
Our Caerule;
My crew sails for you.

And we'll sail on the rising tides;
Till the light of the horizon dies;
Our Caerule Blue will guide us through.
Trust in me.
I will trust in you.

Fallen free by land or sea;
Your memory lives in me.
We stay true to all we knew;
Our Caerule;
Honors all of you.

And we'll sail on the rising tides;
Till the light of the horizon dies;
Our Caerule Blue will guide us through.
Trust in me.
I will trust in you.

"What's wrong?" Miles put his hand on Lakon's shoulder.

"I'm not sure." Lakon stopped pacing and turned to face him. "I have a bad feeling about this." No sooner had Lakon said it; a bright object dashed across the screens. Sam's eyes widened in terror as the stage exploded in a violent flash of light.

Chapter 7 – Sound and Fury

Meg Alumen

"The President is down," Meg yelled into her Wrist-Pro. "I repeat: the President is down." Meg squinted through the smoke with infrared vision. The panicked crowd stampeded in a disorganized frenzy. Frightened bystanders trampled and collided in a futile attempt to escape the chaos. A high pitched screech rang through the crowd. Meg covered her ears. A second explosion erupted from the northwest exit of the forum. Meg continued to scan the crowd.

"I'll get him out of here." General Bell winced as he slung President Millenavis's unconscious body onto his shoulder. The wooden stage creaked beneath them as flames continued to spread.

"Where's the sword?"

"Get your priorities straight!" Bell grabbed his cane and hobbled down the smoldering stairs. "We'll be lucky to get out of here alive." Meg returned her attention to the crowd, scanning deep into the infrared. Sure enough, an enormous hooded figure strode towards the stage slow and confident. Meg switched to regular vision. The man wore a black cloak with a gold septagon emblazoned on the front. A chill ran down Meg's spine. Was this Raven?

"Aprilis is the cruelest city." The man thrust his arms wide in a theatrical gesture. His voice reverberated throughout the forum. "Meg Alumen, would you be a dear and bring the President to us?"

"He's dead." Meg jumped down, placing herself between the hooded figure and the broken stage.

"You're a terrible liar." The man snarled.

"So are you." Meg encircled herself in a shroud of numen. "You're not The Pale Raven."

"How'd you know?" The man's voice cracked. Meg raised her eyebrows. This guy was a moron. "Oh, well." He ripped off his cloak. Meg's eyes widened. The man was a Feroxan anthrobeast; the head, claws and enormous size of a lion, genetically spliced with the body of a man.

"The name's Abraham Panzer." The lion-man pointed to the immense black septagon tattooed on his chest. Numen surged through his bristling fur. "Not that you'll live to tell anyone." Abraham's face gleamed in the noontime sun, visible to any of the thousand-plus security cameras guarding the forum.

Meg's heart sank. Abraham's sheer stupidity meant two things. First, he was working for someone. Second, he was strong enough to be chosen despite his lacking intelligence. Meg channeled her numen. This would not be easy.

They sprinted towards each other. Meg turned invisible and dodged left. Abraham's claws struck the limestone tiles. BOOM! Rubble blasted across the forum. Meg screamed as jagged shards embedded in her arm. The lion-man charged towards the noise. Meg continued running.

"You can't hide forever, Alumen." Abraham's eyes darted left and right. A trail of Meg's blood ran across the cobblestones. He grinned. Head bowed, Abraham followed the drops. His pace quickened. His teeth barred. His numen raged. "What the-?" He bent down and retrieved a bloodied limestone shard. It lay atop the corpse of a fallen Aprilis citizen. Blood ran everywhere. The trail was cold.

CRACK! Meg smashed a limestone tile against the back of the Abraham's head. The stone exploded and spiraled out of her hand. The lion-man grabbed Meg's neck with one hand and began to lift.

"Reactive armor." Abraham's eyes glowed with malice, saliva dripping from his jaws. "Physical attacks won't work on me." Meg kicked and flailed against the lion-man, but he was too big and too strong. His claws tightened. Meg felt the life being choked from her. It was now or never. She released her numen.

"Argh!" Abraham released his grip as radiation seared across his hand. Meg scrambled to her feet, gasping for air. The lion-man lunged. Meg fired a second laser into his eyes. Abraham fell to the ground.

"Pathetic." Meg withdrew a pair of tungsten handcuffs from her belt. "You wouldn't last ten seconds against Peter."

An ear-splitting screech thundered across the forum. Meg was thrown backwards. The handcuffs spiraled from her grip. Meg's vision swam as she searched for the source of the noise. A dark spot loomed in the distance, growing larger. Meg knew who it was.

"Really?" Sylvania Birnam kicked Abraham across the face as she passed. "You couldn't beat her?" Sylvania spat the last word. She held the Sword of Caerule. Worse, she was holding it wrong. She dragged the scabbard against the ground with no regard for the historic value. "Hello, Alumen. Long time no see."

"Birnam." Meg growled and staggered to her feet. "Don't tell me you did all this for the sword."

"What, this?" Sylvania tossed the sword between her hands, further damaging the artifact. "No. My time is far too valuable."

"If money's what you want." Meg snarled. "Caerule has plenty."

"A tempting offer." Sylvania grinned. "But I'm afraid I must decline." She drew the sword. The blade radiated an intense glow of ancient numen, infused through centuries of Caerule's history. "You see, I've already been hired." She advanced towards Meg, sword raised. "And my word is far more valuable than money."

"Meg!" A familiar voice rang across the forum. Meg's heart sank. He shouldn't have come. "Are you alright?" Sam rushed to her side. His numen twisted and crackled in a raging storm. Meg stared in shock. In terms of sheer power, Sam's numen eclipsed even Peter's, but the inconsistency showed a severe lack of control. Sam's fighting style was not fit to handle such turbulent numen. Peter was right. Sam was not ready.

"I told you to wait at the station." Meg snapped.

"Sorry." Sam glared at Sylvania. "I thought these were special circumstances." Meg returned her attention to the battle. Even two-on-one, their chances were slim. Nevertheless, Sylvania hesitated. She eyed Sam with anger and intrigue. "What can you tell me about these two?" Sam asked.

"Sylvania Birnam manipulates sound." Meg answered. "She's strong and ruthless. Don't fight her unless you have to."

"What about him?" Sam nodded to the fallen Abraham.

"Don't know." Meg shook her head. "His power involves explosions. I'm guessing transformation or manipulation." Meg felt her Wrist-Pro vibrate. She watched in horror as Sam glanced at his own Wrist-Pro to read the alert from Central. "Pay attention!" Meg leapt in front of him.

"What?" Sam looked at her, confused.

"Never take your eyes off the enemy." Meg scolded. She expected Sylvania to attack while Sam was distracted, but the treacherous mercenary remained unfazed.

"Sorry." Sam acknowledged his mistake. "You were right, by the way." He repeated the information from his Wrist-Pro. "Abraham Panzer transforms nitrogen and oxygen into nitroglycerine. If he and Sylvania work together-"

"Get up!" Sylvania kicked Abraham in the ribs. "We're leaving."

"You're not going to kill them?" Abraham writhed in pain.

"You Septagons are so touchy." Sylvania sheathed the Sword of Caerule and turned to leave. "Do what you want, but it's not in my contract. Besides, the harder your job, the more I get paid to do it." Abraham stumbled to his feet. He glared at Meg, then turned to follow Sylvania.

"We need to…We need to." Meg swayed and collapsed onto the tiles. Her body weighed with exhaustion, blood seeping from her wounds. Sam rushed to Meg's side and helped lay her flat against the ground.

"Help!" He called. "Somebody!"

"There you are." Lakon holstered his gun and sprinted across the forum. "Give her this! He tossed a bottle of water to Sam and knelt beside Meg. Lakon withdrew a small First-Aid kit from his jacket pocket and began treating Meg's wounds.

"I'm fine." Meg winced.

"No you're not." Sam raised the bottle to her lips. Meg closed her eyes as the cool water ran down her throat. Lakon rinsed Meg's wounds with saline solution and hydrogen peroxide before wrapping them in gauze.

"I'm telling you, I'm fine." Meg smiled. "Go investigate the scene." Sam and Lakon looked at each other.

"I'll do it." Lakon sighed and rose to his feet. "Make sure she drinks that entire bottle."

"Wait…" Sam began, but Lakon was already gone. Sam continued to watch Lakon with an intense stare.

"What's wrong?" Meg could feel the uncertainty in Sam's voice.

"I don't know." He glared towards the stage. "I'm not sure we can trust Lakon."

"What happened?"

"I'm not sure." Sam shook his head. "At the station, before the explosion, Lakon panicked. I think he knew this attack was going to happen."

"How?"

"I don't know." Sam continued watching Lakon. "But, he's hiding something."

"We have a problem." Lakon returned from the stage, an angry scowl on his face. "Someone tampered with the crime scene."

"And how do you know that?" Sam eyed Lakon.

"Well." Lakon tore off his insulating gloves and threw them on the ground. "The projectile is gone and the impact hole is damaged. It looks like someone smashed it with a wrecking ball;

only there's no sign of the wrecking ball. Do you know who could have done this?"

"There was a woman-" Meg began.

"What makes you think we'd know?" Sam interrupted.

"No reason." Lakon's eyes narrowed.

"Did you find anything useful?" Sam's voice was harsh and accusatory.

"Sam." Meg warned. Lakon remained silent a long time before answering:

"No."

"We'll find more at Central." Meg rose to her feet. She placed herself between Sam and Lakon; anything to break the hostility. "The cameras were on and…" Meg's head felt light. Her legs trembled and her body swayed. Meg fell forward. Sam rushed to catch her, but Lakon beat him to it.

"Here." Lakon offered his shoulder. "You can lean on me." Meg nodded and wrapped her arm around Lakon. His back was strong and steady. Meg heaved a sigh of relief. Everything was going to be alright. Meg hobbled across the forum, leaning on Lakon for support. Sam glared at him but remained silent. Lakon opened the door to the armored truck. "Do you want me to drive?"

"I can manage." Meg smiled. She could already feel her injuries healing as her numen recovered. Lakon returned a cheerful nod and helped her into the driver's seat. Emergency personnel began to arrive. Naval officers established a perimeter. Medics rushed to help the wounded. Lakon turned to Sam.

"Are you going to tell me what's wrong?" Lakon grinned at the boy. "Or are you just going to keep glaring at me like that?"

"How did you know?" Sam's voice shook with anger.

"Know what?"

"Sam." Meg warned again.

"About this." Sam gestured to the devastated forum. "How did you know?"

"Sam." Meg warned a third time.

"So that's what this is about." Lakon laughed and jammed his hand into his pocket. Sam pinned him against the side of the vehicle. Lakon stared down at the boy, unfazed.

"Don't move!" Sam growled. Lakon ignored him and withdrew a small brown package from his pocket. "I told you not to move." Lakon tossed the package to Meg.

"That's the nose cone of the projectile we recovered yesterday." Lakon addressed Meg.

"So you kept a piece after all." Meg frowned. "You realize it's a crime to lie to Central?"

"Meh. Sue me." Lakon shrugged. "As for today's attack; my report should explain how and why I suspected it."

"Why didn't you warn Central?" Sam grit his teeth.

"I did." Lakon glared at the boy. "Do you think you're the only one with trust issues? Did you do any research into the Helena Bridge or did you spend the entire night investigating me?" Sam broke eye contact with Lakon, but did not release his hold.

"I see." Lakon shook his head. "Well, if you had bothered to research the case, you might have realized that the projectile struck a faulty pressure valve less than one centimeter wide. The only people who knew about it were the bridge engineers and Central; and I have not met many bridge engineers who can launch tungsten superalloys from orbit." Sam released his hold and turned away from Lakon.

"So." Meg's fist clenched around the package. "You think we're lying."

"It wouldn't be the first time Central lied to start a war." Lakon brushed the blood and limestone from his clothes.

"A treasonous statement." Meg muttered.

"But true, nonetheless." Lakon remained firm. "Someone from Central was threatened by our findings yesterday. Whoever it was, knew about the projectile fragment." Lakon nodded to the package in Meg's hand. "That piece may be our only hope of solving this case."

"I see." Meg closed her eyes. "Detective Lakon, thank you for your service. Central will take it from here."

"So, that's it." Lakon stared at the ground. "This is good-bye?"

"It is." Meg answered, harsh and firm. "Sam is right. We can't trust you."

"I guess I have that effect on people." Lakon walked alone through the broken forum, glaring at the smoldering wooden stage.

Chapter 8 – Darkness Revealed

James Lakon

"The nurse said you'd be here." Lakon joined Neil Whitney in the front pew of the hospital chapel. Waning candlelight cast shadows across the oaken pillars and stained glass windows. "Neat place. I thought they got rid of these."

"They did, for the most part." Neil sighed. He gazed towards a tarnished brass star on the central altar. "This might be the last one in Aprilis."

"You're not one of 'those people', are you?" Lakon grinned.

"No." Neil shook his head. "Dr. Septem was just a man like any of us. Probably caused more harm than good if you ask me. Still…" Neil glanced around the frescoed walls. "I'm glad they kept it. Sometimes, we need to believe in miracles; here of all places." Lakon took a deep breath.

"How's Paul?"

"I don't know." Neil choked back tears. "The doctors can't explain it. His vitals are fine, but he hasn't woken up yet."

"Cold can do that sometimes." Lakon sighed. "Hypothermia unconsciousness can last-"

"I don't need a damn medical report!"

"Right." Lakon stared at the frayed carpet floor. "Sorry. Bad habit."

"No." Neil dried his eyes. "Don't apologize. You're the reason he's alive right now. I can't thank you enough." Lakon opened his mouth to protest, but was interrupted by the door opening behind them.

"Mr. Whitney?" A nurse walked down the central aisle.

"What is it?" Neil sprang from his seat. His voice cracked, desperate and frantic. "Is it good news? Is it bad news?"

"No...um." The startled nurse stepped backwards. "It's just...you can see him if you want." Neil's face paled.

"Go on." Lakon patted him on the back. "I'll come with you." Neil gulped and nodded.

The nurse led them down a long hallway through a pair of swinging double-doors. The ward was warmer than the rest of the hospital, illuminated by a powerful orange glow. The scent of isopropyl alcohol lingered in the still air. The nurse reached the end of the hall and motioned them to a small room on the left side. Lakon glanced at the nameplates before entering.

Paul Whitney lay in the nearest bed, eyes closed and breaths calm. Neil ran to his side. Lakon stared in shock. The boy didn't have a scratch on him. The crash, the cold, the rescue; none of it had left a mark.

Lakon peered around the curtain. Sure enough, the other boy was in terrible condition. Noah Moby trembled in his sleep. The right side of his face was blistered and blackened with frostbite. His arms remained trapped beneath multiple layers of thick blankets. A cold sweat ran across his forehead. Lakon's heart sank. If he hadn't given Neil such a hard time on the bridge, maybe...

"How is he?" Neil asked.

"Uh…Fine!" Lakon lied, sliding the curtain further to obstruct Neil's view. "Better than expected."

"That's a relief." Neil heaved a long sigh. "I'll get another chair."

"No." Lakon shook his head. "Seriously, Mr. Whitney, it's not necessary."

"No." Neil insisted. "You've had a long day. I'll get it." He rushed out of the room before Lakon could stop him. Lakon sighed. Neil looked exhausted. His day had been worse; no question. Lakon shook his head. There was no sense fighting it now. He sat in the chair and watched Paul Whitney's chest rise and fall with perfect rhythm.

A dull pain throbbed in Lakon's temple. Lakon shook his head. The pain returned, harder and sharper than before. Something was wrong. Lakon grit his teeth. Why wasn't it stopping?

Paul began to cough. His choking grew more and more violent and shook Paul's entire body. Lakon leapt to his feet. "Nurse!" He yelled. "Nurse!" Lakon pushed a small emergency button on the bedside table. No one was coming. Lakon pushed the button again and again. "Nurse!" Paul grabbed Lakon's forearm and breathed a loud gasp. The headache stopped. The coughing stopped. Paul's eyes snapped open. He and Lakon stared at each other.

"Who are you?" Paul asked.

"Uh… James Lakon."

"Paul Whitney." Paul released his grip and collapsed onto the bed. "P-Paul Whitney." Neil returned, dragging an antimicrobial plastic chair. "Dad!" Paul leapt from the bed and embraced his father.

"Paul!" Neil dropped the chair. Lakon stared at Paul. It made no sense. Ten seconds ago, he had been bedridden. Lakon forced a confused smile.

"I'll let you two…" Lakon trailed off. No one was paying attention to him. "Bye." Lakon slipped out the door without another word. He ran out of the hospital and sat against the ledge of the entryway fountain to catch his breath. Lakon rubbed his forehead. It made no sense. He never got headaches.

Lakon stared across the water. In the center of the fountain, a white marble stallion sprinkled water onto a wreath of blue roses. Each drop sent ripples across the pond, a perfect blend of chaos and predictability. Lakon sighed. It was time to go home.

Lakon turned to leave, but stopped before taking the first step. A faint shadow crouched behind the corner of entrance, watching his every move. Lakon's breaths slowed. He pretended to brush himself off, but drew his revolver with a single flick of his wrist.

"Freeze!" Lakon's voice fell calm and cold as he aimed into the darkness. "Place your hands on your head and take three steps forward, slowly." The figure complied, emerging from the darkness, hands raised. "Oh! It's you." Lakon lowered the revolver. "You should be resting."

"I heal fast." Meg smiled. She was still wearing a plastic hospital gown and her bandages looked fresh. "I'm impressed. Most people don't notice me."

"I'm not most people." Lakon turned back to the fountain.

"I know." Meg joined him, staring across the water. "That's why I…" She trailed off.

"What?" Lakon pressed.

"…think you're the only one who can solve this case." Meg looked away. Lakon's eyes narrowed. The answer made sense, but Lakon felt she wanted to say something more.

"I thought you couldn't trust me." Lakon watched her every move. Meg was harder to read than Miles, but she had a weakness. Her thirst for knowledge was as insatiable as his own.

"I can't, but I do." Meg sighed. Lakon smiled and shook his head.

"How long were you following me?"

"Long enough." Meg leaned across the water and plucked a fallen rose that had floated away from the rest. "That man; is he a friend of yours?"

"Who? Neil?" Lakon grinned. "No. I met him on the bridge yesterday, that's all."

"Oh." Meg's face fell. "I see." Lakon sensed the disappointment in her voice. "Do you mind if I…?" She nodded to the revolver still clutched in Lakon's hand. Lakon hesitated. He stared into the water, the reflection of the gun barrel pointing back at him.

"No." Lakon heaved a long sigh and handed her the revolver. As soon as she touched it, Meg's eyes darkened.

"Tungsten bullets." She examined the gun. A solemn frown crept across her face. "I'm sorry I brought you into this." Meg returned the gun to Lakon, and stared at the rose still clutched in her hand.

"You didn't." Lakon sighed, holstering the revolver. "It was my choice from the beginning."

"Just promise me, if something goes wrong-"

"I won't let that happen."

"But if something does." Meg placed her hand on Lakon's shoulder. He flinched slightly at the touch. "Please. Run." Lakon stared into Meg's eyes, glistening soft light of uncried tears.

"You know I can't do that." He removed her hand from his shoulder and clutched it tightly in his own. Meg stared at the ground, crestfallen. "Don't worry about me." Lakon flashed a reassuring smile. "You said it yourself: I'm tougher than I look."

"I know." Meg wrenched her hand from Lakon and turned away. "But you won't be the only one who's hurting." She trudged back to the hospital, blue rose dropping from her grasp. Lakon waited for the door close behind her before beginning the dreaded walk home.

No matter the direction, Miles's apartment was on the wrong side of town. Corroded warehouses lined the winding streets and the air reeked of Carbot refrigerants. The hulking shells of abandoned factories blocked the last light of the setting sun.

The apartment building was as safe as could be expected. Most robberies were confined to the first three floors and the murder rate had declined in recent years. Still, the untargeted apartment on the seventh floor was a rarity seldom found in the Rust District. Maybe they knew better than to mess with a police Sergeant. Maybe they knew better than to mess with Lakon.

When he arrived, the door was already propped open by a box of files. Lakon sighed. Putting away the key, he knocked twice on the open door and entered the apartment.

"Welcome home." Miles greeted in a dull tone. Lakon sensed the frustration in his voice. "I already made dinner." Lakon looked. A small bowl of beef stew remained on the kitchen table. There was no steam. It must have been there for a while.

Chapter 8 – Darkness Revealed

"Thank you." Lakon avoided Miles's gaze and sat in front of the bowl. He grabbed a spoon and began to eat. Sure enough, the stew was room temperature. The meat was rough and the carrots turned to mush. Lakon did not complain. He continued scooping the broth, waiting.

"We missed you back at headquarters." Miles crossed his arms.

"You know where I went." Lakon did not meet Miles's gaze.

"And afterwards?" Miles's eyes narrowed. "Where did you go afterwards?"

"Actually." Lakon locked eyes with Miles. "I went to see Neil." Miles heaved a sigh of relief.

"Did you apologize for yesterday?"

"I tried to."

"How's Paul?"

"Fine." Lakon dropped the spoon and pushed away the bowl. It was time for the real conversation. Miles gave a solemn nod. He reached beneath his chair and withdrew a small yellow toolbox. Lakon's heart sank. Miles placed the toolbox on the table.

"What is this?" Miles rested his hand on the box.

"A toolbox." Lakon sighed.

"What's it for?"

"Holding tools."

"What sort of tools?"

"You tell me." Lakon locked eyes with Miles. Miles remained firm.

"Very well." Miles tore open the latches and dumped the contents on the kitchen table. Ratchets, wrenches and screwdrivers scattered across the plastic countertop. Nuts and bolts tumbled into the discarded bowl of beef stew. Miles studied Lakon's face. Lakon remained unfazed. "How, exactly, did you plan on using this?" Miles grabbed a Phillips-Head screwdriver from the pile.

"Any number of criminal activities." Lakon's voice dripped with sarcasm. "Tightening screws, loosening screws, fixing that doorknob you've been complaining about."

"This doorknob?" Miles pointed to the bedroom door. Lakon sighed and nodded. Miles rose from his chair and began loosening the screws. He twisted the screwdriver with such ferocity that wood and brass shavings littered the floor.

"You're stripping the threads." Lakon complained. Miles ignored him. He threw the disassembled knob on the floor and inspected the crevices of the doorjamb. Dissatisfied, Miles tossed the screwdriver onto the kitchen table and resumed his inspection of the toolbox. He shook the box, banged it against the table and held it up to the overhead light.

"It's too small to have a false bottom." Lakon shook his head.

"You would know that wouldn't you." Miles spat, tossing the box away.

"I don't know how to answer that."

"Because there is no answer." Miles snapped. The room grew silent. At last, Lakon rose from his chair, retrieved the box and began collecting the tools. Miles watched Lakon dump the tools unceremoniously into the box. When he reached for the screwdriver, Miles grabbed Lakon's wrist.

"Go on Miles." Lakon wrenched the screwdriver from Miles's grip. "What's this really about?"

"You shouldn't have gone to that crime scene." Miles's nostrils flared.

"Somebody had to."

"It wasn't your case."

"And whose fault is that?"

"Detective Libby is perfectly capable-"

"Of getting himself lost in a city he's policed for fifteen years!" Lakon threw the screwdriver into the box and clamped the lid shut. "Al isn't able to solve this case and you know it."

"That's not the point." Miles shook his head.

"Then what is the point?" Lakon's eyes burned with rage.

"The point is…" Miles shouted. He stopped and took a deep breath to calm himself. "The point is: I don't want you working with Central." Lakon stared at Miles, stunned.

"What?" Lakon took the chair across from Miles and slid closer to the table. "Why? We're on the same side." Miles hesitated. "Right?"

"For now." Miles turned away. He walked to the kitchen window and stared into the fading sunset. "But, Central is dangerous and you of all people need to be careful."

"Why?" Lakon held firm.

"Because Central has powers far greater than-"

"No!" Lakon interrupted again. "Why me of all people?" Miles froze. Lakon's eyes narrowed. "You devoted your life to this city. And you always taught me to find the truth. Why don't you want me working with Central?"

"Because I don't want to lose you too." Miles's eyes began to water. "I've lost too many friends already. I can't ..." Miles rested against the wall. Tears streamed down his face. "I can't lose you too." Lakon leaned back in his chair. He watched Miles for a long time, analyzing the contours of the Sergeant's face.

"You're a good liar." Lakon frowned after a long pause. "I'll give you that."

"What-" Miles choked through tired sobs.

"What really happened to my parents?"

"I told you. They died in the war."

"On which side?" Lakon pressed. Miles's eyes widened. "I see." Lakon finished before Miles could answer. Miles remained silent a long time.

"Your parents were good people." Miles slumped in his chair. "I don't want you repeating their mistakes." Lakon felt a pang of guilt.

"I'm sorry."

"It's not your fault." Miles shook his head. "Detectives strive to find the truth. I can't keep hiding this from you."

"I guess not." Lakon sighed, rising from his chair.

"Where are you going?" Miles asked.

"Out." Lakon kicked aside the box of files and opened the door.

"James." Miles pleaded. "Stay away from Central. You don't know what they are; what they've done. If you get involved with Central, no good will ever come of it." Lakon hesitated. He closed his eyes, feeling the weight of Miles's words. Then, he turned away, closing the door behind him.

Lakon trudged to the nearest stairwell, climbed the rusted ladder and forced the broken bulkhead open with his shoulder. Cold winds blew from the Atropa River, muffling the sounds of the city. Lakon scanned the gravel and tarpaper until, at last, he found a dry patch away from the leaky water tower. He lay on the flattened rocks, placed his hands behind his head and watched the Carbots stream across the starry sky.

"It's beautiful isn't it?" A cold voice spoke behind him. Lakon wheeled to see a masked man dressed entirely in black. "The way they keep going, ignorant of it all. We spend so much time fighting for ideals; it's easy to forget that most people don't care in the slightest. They repeat the same routines; breakfast, work, dinner; and are perfectly happy living their whole lives that way. You and I are not such people; are we, Lakon?"

"You're him." Lakon breathed. "You're the one behind this."

"Impressive." The figure nodded. "Almost as impressive as that report you gave Central today. Peter and Sinon must have their hands full."

"Who?"

"Really?" The figure laughed. "You don't even know your fellow investigators? All the resources at their disposal, and Central doesn't trust the one person making sense?"

"Stay back!" Lakon drew his revolver.

"Such a shame." The figure stopped. "You're a fighter, Lakon, but do you even know what you're fighting for?" A foghorn blared across the city. The masked man turned towards the noise. Lakon followed his gaze.

The transmission ship drifted along the Atropa River, spreading shadows across the city. Remnants of the Helena Bridge scraped against the battered hull only to be thrust aside by the enormous wake. The ship seemed tired, broken and defeated, but Lakon knew better. Even now, the ship's monstrous communication array continued spinning, always poised to strike.

"Information is the most powerful force in the universe." The masked man continued watching the eerie vessel. "If that ship ever went to war, how many people could it kill?"

"All of them." Lakon bowed his head.

"Correct." The figure nodded, returning his attention to Lakon. "Knowledge and empathy. Perhaps you'd make a good President after all." Lakon's face paled.

"That's right." The masked man advanced. "I could make it happen. Think of all the good you could do for Caerule, for justice, for peace."

"I said: stay back!" Lakon held the gun firm. The figure stopped.

"You know that won't work." An ominous presence radiated from the man. Lakon's eyes widened. Shivers ran through his spine. His fingers trembled and the revolver slipped from his grasp. "Interesting." The figure pressed forward. "So you can sense it after all." Lakon fell to his knees and scrambled backwards to the edge of the roof. There was nowhere left to run. "Perhaps you'll be more useful than I thought-"

Lakon punched the figure in the face, breaking his nose with a satisfying CRACK! The man stumbled backwards. Lakon dove for the revolver. An intense heat seared through the air and the revolver spiraled out of reach. The figure panted, holding his hand in the shape of a gun.

"Alright!" Lakon turned to face the man. "Cut the crap. What's this really about?"

"What?" The figure's voice cracked.

"I've played enough mind games to know how they work." Lakon rose to his feet. "If you were gonna kill me you'd have done it by now." Lakon advanced towards the figure. "I'm not close to solving this case, am I? In fact, I'm so wrong, I'm worth more to you alive than dead; which means you have some other reason for being here." Lakon glared into the black mesh shielding the figure's eyes. Behind him, Lakon heard the faint whirr of Fenestravison drones.

"You're too smart for your own good." The man snarled. He sprinted in the opposite direction, dodged the spotlight of the approaching drones and leapt from rooftop. Lakon ran to the edge, scanning the streets below. The man was gone, vanished into the cold, dark night.

Chapter 9 – Memories of Blood

Peter Turnus

"You of all people should understand." Sylvania's soft voice echoed from the flames. *"I was only following orders."*

"NO!"

Peter roared awake. Blood red blades of numen erupted from his arms shredding the couch cushions. Felt and foam flew in every direction. Peter's head jerked left and right, searching for the enemy. No one was there but Sinon.

"Another nightmare?" Sinon handed Peter a glass of water.

"Worse." Peter panted. "A memory." The HVAC system roared to life, filling Peter's office with obnoxious whirring sounds. Corroded copper wires rattled inside their conduits. Peter extinguished the blades. His fingers trembled as he tried to drink the water. Sinon watched with a concern. "How much did you see?"

"Not much." Sinon placed his hand on Peter's shoulder. "But I felt everything." Peter shivered. Cold sweat drenched what remained of the sofa. The room remained dark, but a faint red glow from the HVAC system washed across Sinon's face.

"I'm sorry." Peter began to cry.

"It's not your fault." Sinon sighed.

"What's wrong with me?" Peter choked back the tears.

"The same thing that's wrong with all of us." Sinon shook his head. "We lose the people we love in defense of a world we hate. Why do you think I left?"

"I'm sorry." Peter dried his eyes. "I'll go back to sleep."

"Not like that you won't." Sinon switched on the lights. "Get up! I brought breakfast." Sure enough, the smell of scrambled eggs and bacon wafted from a pair of take-out boxes on Peter's desk.

"Thank you." Peter pulled up a chair. Sinon handed him a box.

"You'd do the same for me." Sinon sat across from Peter. "Have you told Meg? About the dreams?"

"Not yet."

"And General Rocklos?"

"No." Peter sighed. "I didn't want them to worry."

"Peter." Sinon's voice harshened. "You almost stabbed yourself with that numen blade. If you don't tell them, I will."

"Okay." Peter nodded. "Just give me till tomorrow."

"Today!"

"Fine. Today." Peter stared at his plate. His stomach burned with hunger, but he could not bring himself to eat. Sinon put down the fork. "What's wrong?"

"Everything." Peter buried his face in his hands. "This case. This city. Everything's falling apart. I don't know what to do."

"You could start by trusting me." Sinon began eating again. Peter sighed. Sinon knew him too well.

"It's Meg." Peter's eyes darkened. "Seeing her in that hospital bed...Failing to protect her..."

"...reminded you of Ike." Sinon finished. Peter clenched the blackened dog tag hanging from his neck.

"I will not lose another comrade." Peter's voice shook.

"You may not have a choice." Sinon continued chewing his bacon.

"What?" Peter stared in disbelief.

"Meg almost died yesterday and you had no power to stop it."

"Whose side are you on?" Peter shouted, toppling his chair.

"Yours, you impossible jackass!" Sinon matched Peter's rage. "I'm your friend, Peter. I'm going to tell you what you need to hear, especially when you don't want to hear it."

"We should go." Peter grabbed his coat from the rack and walked towards the door.

"No." Sinon shook his head. "Meg needs her rest."

"Damn it!" Peter threw the coat, toppling the rack. The HVAC system sputtered and groaned with irregular frequency.

"Eat your breakfast, Peter." Sinon shook his head once the noise subsided. "You can't always be there to protect her. But, when the time comes, you'll need your strength." Peter sighed. Sinon was right.

Peter righted his chair and sat across the desk from Sinon. He devoured the eggs, shoveling forkful after forkful into his mouth. Sinon watched in amusement. When Peter finished, Sinon gave him his half-eaten box.

"We'll go to the blood drive, then." Peter spoke through a mouthful of hash browns. "Anything's better than sitting here."

"Agreed." Sinon nodded. "Besides, a trip to the hospital could provide some much needed leads." When Peter finished eating, they left the office and walked to Aprilis General Hospital. As they passed the Central Forum, Sinon struggled to readjust the tungsten bracers digging into his skin.

"I know security's tight and all." He winced as the bracers slid further up his forearm. "But are these really necessary?"

"Sorry." Peter sighed. "Admiral Lodon insisted."

"Figures." Sinon shrugged. "You know, I wouldn't mind if they weren't so damn heavy."

"Think of it as exercise." Peter grinned. "You could stand to lose a few."

"You've put on a few yourself." Sinon laughed.

"It's called muscle."

"It's called denial."

Peter and Sinon bantered across the forum, past the fountain and into the hospital lobby. It was packed. The line for the blood drive snaked around the walls, doubling back four times. Peter and Sinon stood at the end of the line and began to wait.

"White chocolate isn't even chocolate." Peter smirked, continuing their ludicrous conversation. "It's just milk-paste and sugar."

"Sinon?" Professor Plummet emerged from a nearby conference room. His voice was stifled and his nose was stuffed with gauze. "Great to see you, again. How have you been?"

"Never better." Sinon grinned. "I'm a professor, myself, now; believe it or not."

"I heard." Plummet smiled. "I always knew you'd make a great teacher. Thank you both for coming. We've got a special room for agents right this way." He led Peter and Sinon into the conference room. They were in luck. Two donor chairs remained empty and they were next to each other. A nurse tended to Sinon, while the professor assisted Peter.

"What happened to you?" Peter nodded to the professor's nose which had started to bleed again.

"Oh, that." The professor laughed. "I ran into General Bell earlier, quite literally I'm afraid. I probably shouldn't be here, but you saw the line outside."

"It is a great turnout." Peter agreed.

"You're telling me." The professor beamed. "We're running out of space to store it all." No sooner had he said it, a doctor delivered a cart of blood bags from the other room. Professor Plummet thanked the woman and began storing the blood in a small refrigerator alongside packs of water bottles and sports drinks. Peter smiled. It was a good problem to have.

"Peter." Patricia Rocklos strode to his chair, face pale and uneasy. "I need to talk to you. Now!" She clutched an enormous binder beneath her right arm. Her left was taped with gauze from the blood drive.

"It's okay." Sinon nodded as a nurse inserted a needle into his arm. "Go."

Peter rose from the chair and followed the General to a small closet in the rear of the conference room. The General looked left and right before locking the door behind them.

"What's wrong?" Peter's breaths shortened

"Everything." The General pressed a frantic hand against her pocket. The imprint of a large key pressed through her military uniform. "Admiral Lodon's on the warpath and she won't listen to anyone."

"Then that key…" Peter nodded to the General's pocket.

"You saw that." Patricia sighed. "I'm afraid so. With the President incapacitated, Admiral Lodon ordered everyone general-rank and above to carry a key. Two keys together and … well you know the rest." She removed the red key from her pocket and hung it around her neck. Patricia's head bowed and her eyes dimmed with sorrow.

"You don't think she'd actually-"

"I do." The General met Peter's gaze. "But there's nothing you can do about that." Patricia hoisted the binder onto a nearby shelf. "Instead, I need your help with this."

"What is it?" Peter opened the file, bewildered. The pages were covered with complex charts and mathematical formulas. Throughout the report, a recurring diagram showed the Helena Bridge with curved cones protruding from the point of impact.

"This report was written by James Lakon of the Aprilis PD," Patricia explained. "It traces the trajectory of the Helena Bridge projectile and predicted yesterday's attack with stunning accuracy. It's currently our leading theory."

"What is?" Peter turned the page to a wireframe drawing of a satellite.

"Orbital bombardment." The General's eyes darkened. Peter stared at the binder, stunned.

"You're telling me Aprilis PD put this together in one day?"

"I'm telling you one man put this together in six hours." The General closed the binder and lifted it from the shelf. "But that's not the real problem." She pressed a button on her Wrist-Pro and a hologram of a rundown apartment building brightened into focus.

"What is it?" Peter squinted at the blurred rooftop. Someone or something was moving.

"This is Fenestravision footage of James Lakon's apartment building last night." Patricia enhanced the image as the drone zoomed closer. Two figures stood on the roof, facing each other. "The man on the left is James Lakon. The other one..." The masked figure turned towards the camera and a familiar chill ran down Peter's spine.

"No." Peter breathed. His face paled.

"Someone infiltrated Central." Patricia deactivated the hologram. "I don't know who. I don't know why. But, if the Pale Raven is involved, the threat to Caerule could be existential. You need to find Lakon and bring him in, by any means necessary."

"Understood." Peter turned to leave. "Sinon and I will leave immediately."

"Peter." Patricia grabbed his hand. "Trust Meg; with everything."

"I will." Peter nodded, opening the door. He strode from the closet, almost colliding with Professor Plummet who was retrieving another cart of blood bags. Peter hurried past the rows of donor chairs to the entrance where Sinon was already waiting.

"Any leads?" Sinon handed Peter a cold bottle of water, keeping a dark red energy drink for himself.

"Yes." Peter puzzled. "Fenestravision footage. It's the Septagon, no question."

"You don't seem convinced." Sinon held the door.

"I don't know." Peter drank the water. "As much as I hate to admit it, Raven always had a strange honor about him. He never targeted civilians, not like this."

"Honor doesn't always last." Sinon sighed. "Eight years is a long time. People change."

"I guess." Peter glanced over his shoulder and caught a final glimpse of Patricia Rocklos. She handed Professor Plummet the binder, head bowed and eyes solemn. Peter reached for the handle, but was too late. The door closed and locked behind them.

"What's wrong?" Sinon glanced at Peter.

"Nothing." Peter shook his head, uneasy doubt filling his mind. "Let's go. I want to see Meg first." He walked straight to the elevator, scanning the crowd as he passed. Sinon followed close behind. Peter waited for a barrage of questions, but Sinon didn't press any further. Peter pushed the button for Meg's floor and watched the numbers increase, silent and unmoving.

As soon as the doors opened, Peter strode from the elevator, looking left, right, up, down, always moving forward. He made it to Meg's room in ten seconds, certain they had not been followed. Unfortunately, danger lurked in the one place Peter least expected.

"Look out!" Sinon shouted, but it was too late. Admiral Lodon burst from Meg's room, colliding with Peter's chest. Peter gasped as the wind was knocked from his lungs. He fell to the floor. His vision swam and blurred. A sliver streak flashed from the Admiral's metal scabbard and Peter felt the sharp chill of tungsten pressed against his throat.

"Peter!" Sinon's blurred silhouette bumped into the Admiral as he rushed to help his friend. Peter clamped his eyes, bracing for the impact. Lodon's blade remained firm.

"Watch where you're going!" The Admiral sheathed her sword, a vicious scowl on her face. She glared at Sinon, eyeing the tungsten bracers on his arms. Sinon's face paled. "Talk some sense into your student, Peter." Admiral Lodon snarled before marching down the hall. Doctors and nurses pressed themselves against the wall to make way for the angry Admiral.

"Are you alright?" Sinon helped Peter to his feet.

"Yeah." Peter rubbed the back of his head. "What was that about?"

"I don't know." Sinon stared after the Admiral. "But I think we're about to find out." Peter returned his attention to the door. A panicked look crossed his face. Peter burst into the room to find Meg fastening the final straps of her combat boots.

"Are you alright?" Peter rushed to Meg's side.

"Yeah." Meg's expression was livid. "Why?"

"We just ran into Admiral Lodon." Peter watched Meg with concern.

"Literally." Sinon glanced back at the door.

"Did you read her mind?" Meg turned to face Sinon.

"W-What?" Sinon's eyes widened.

"Did you read her mind?" Meg repeated.

"Meg." Peter stared at her in shock. "That would be a breach of-"

"I know the rules!" Meg snapped at Peter before returning her attention to Sinon. "Did you do it?"

"I'm sorry." Sinon shook his head. He raised his arms, showing Meg the tungsten bracers. "Even if I wanted to, I can't; not with these on."

"Figures." Meg rose from the bed and retrieved her blood-stained combat jacket from the closet.

"Come on, Meg." Peter forced a nervous laugh. "You don't think Admiral Lodon's involved?" Meg zipped her jacket and paused. "Do you?" Peter pressed.

"Sinon, could you give us the room?" Meg kept her back turned. "Sam and Leah are training at the Academy. You can wait for us there."

"Uh." Sinon cast an awkward glance between Meg and Peter. "Yeah. Sure." He shuffled out of the room.

"You heal fast." Peter sighed, eyeing Meg's discarded bandages. "Sinon must have taught you that."

"Among other things." Meg's back remained turned.

"He was a much better mentor to you than I ever was." Peter bowed his head.

"Shouldn't I be the judge of that?"

"What's this about, Meg?" Peter pressed. "Whatever it is, Sinon and I will handle it. You're not in any condition-"

"You're going after Lakon, aren't you?" Meg turned to face him.

"How did you-" Peter's eyes narrowed.

"Admiral Lodon delivered a letter." Meg threw a torn envelope onto the bed. Peter recognized Lakon's name in the return address. "Apparently, she's reading our mail now."

"But, what does he want with you?"

"He wants to meet." Meg zipped her jacket and strode to the door. "And that's where I'm going right now."

"I can't let you do that." Peter raised his hand. A transparent blue barrier formed in Meg's path. She wheeled to face him, eyes burning with fury.

"If we're going to solve this case." Meg glared at Peter. "We need to start being honest with each other."

"I don't know what you're-"

"How do you know Sylvania Birnam?" Meg interrupted.

"Oh." Peter's eyes darkened. "That." He heaved a heavy sigh and sat in a small chair facing Meg's bed. "I suppose it's time I told you." He stared at the floor, silent and unmoving.

"Fine." Meg walked past him, drawing her bed curtains with an aggressive flick. Peter bowed his head.

"You know Sylvania Birnam as a mercenary. But, five years ago, she was a student of Lysander Moloch."

"I'm sorry." Meg sighed from behind the curtain. "I didn't know."

"I was about your age, then." Peter clenched his fist. "I felt invincible. I survived the Great War. Nothing could be worse than that, right?" Peter shook his head. "And so, I took a student of my own. Patricia said I wasn't ready. She begged me: 'wait, one more year'. But, I ignored her. 'Ike is ready' I told her. 'I'm ready'."

"Our first few missions were uneventful." Peter closed his eyes. "Ike breezed through on skill alone. 'More' he kept asking me 'more'; and I was eager as he was. We took harder missions, more frequently, further and further from Caerule's shores. We met every challenge, conquered every obstacle, completed every objective without fail, until…"

Peter's face fell. "We were finishing another a mission; nothing dangerous, just escorting some doctors to an allied village. We were walking to the extraction point when Ike saw the smoke. I could have put a barrier in his way, I could have stopped him."

"The entire village had been burned to ash." Peter shuddered. "I couldn't tell the bodies from the bricks. I called to Ike, but the sound died in my throat." Peter's eyes burned with misplaced aggression. "That's when I saw Birnam. She couldn't have been more than fifteen years old. I went easy on her. I showed her mercy, unaware that beyond that hill Moloch was burning Ike alive. Her powers drowned the sounds. I never heard him scream."

"Remember when I told you to never hold back in a fight?" Peter trembled as he spat the words. "I held back once. I hesitated. And now, Ike is dead; because of him; because of her; because of me." Peter's withdrew the blackened dog tag beneath his shirt. All this time and he still couldn't protect anyone. A cold breeze tore through the room, stinging Peter's tear drenched eyes. He glanced at the curtain. Meg's shadow was gone.

"Meg?" Peter leapt to his feet, heart beating rapidly. No answer. "Meg!" He tore open the curtain. Meg was gone. Nothing remained but a large hole cut through the bedside window.

Chapter 10 – Potential Energy

Sam Pere

"What's the matter, boys?" Leah teased. "Getting tired?" She and Artemis exchanged high-fives.

"What's wrong with you?" Sam helped Tom to his feet. "You said you could hold off Leah, no problem."

"For three minutes." Tom snapped. "It's been four. Besides, I don't feel like fighting now."

"Okay, new plan," Sam said. "You take Artemis, I'll take Leah."

"That's not going to work." Tom sighed, but assumed the position opposite Artemis. Sam glanced across the stage at Leah. She had not even broken a sweat.

"Ready ... Go!" Leah initiated the charge. Sam forced numen into his right arm to block the punch. He was not strong enough. Leah's blow connected with Sam's forearm and threw him backwards. Sam fell to the floor. Leah grabbed him by the ankles.

"What are you doing?" Sam asked.

"You'll see." Leah grinned. "Artemis, incoming." Artemis nodded and loosed a numen-charged arrow. Tom absorbed the attack and redirected it into the stage. The arrow exploded in a flash of white light. Tom winced and Artemis increased her distance.

"Now!" Artemis yelled. Leah tightened her grip and hurled Sam across the ring. He collided with Tom and both boys collapsed in a tangled heap.

"Ready for another round?" Leah goaded. She and Artemis exchanged high-fives, again.

"Come on." Tom pushed Sam off of him. "You couldn't last five seconds?"

"Shut up." Sam scowled. "I didn't have time to plan." Tom opened his mouth, but was interrupted by General Bell.

"Tom." The General rose from the ringside bench where he and Sinon had been sitting. "We're leaving." General Bell gripped his cane tighter as he limped past the ring. "Now!" Tom's face fell. He glanced back at Sam for a moment before turning away.

"Sorry." Tom left without another word. Sam stared after him.

"Now what?" Leah asked. "Artemis, do you and Sam-"

"No way." Artemis hopped off the stage. "Even two-on-one we wouldn't stand a chance against you." Leah nodded in acceptance, but seemed saddened by the complement. Sam rose to his feet and joined Leah in the center of the ring.

"I'll continue sparring if you want," Sam offered.

"Thanks." Leah sighed. "But you don't have to do that. You should save your strength in case we need to go back into the field today." Sam gave a disheartened nod and followed Artemis. He sat on the bench next to Sinon.

"Nice fight." Sinon smiled.

"Not really." Sam avoided eye contact.

"Trust me." Sinon stood and leaned against the side of the ring. "You're all much stronger than Peter and I were at your age."

"So I've heard." Sam did not raise his head. Sinon's eyes narrowed.

"You know." Sinon's voice harshened. "We've all been there. Peter, Meg, myself: we're here to help. You just have to ask."

"Well what do you suggest then?" Sam glared at Sinon. "People tell me I'm strong; that I have potential; but I haven't made any real progress in four years. Meg had to beg Peter to make me her student and even then he said no. And yesterday ..." Sam sighed and bowed his head. "I wasn't able to protect her." Sinon stared at Sam a long time, deep in thought.

"What classification is your numen?" Sinon asked after a long pause.

"Creation." Sam gave Sinon a quizzical look. "Why?"

"Numen reflects a user's personality." Sinon paced back and forth. "Creators tend to be spontaneous and optimistic. You're neither of those things."

"Hey!" Sam complained, but Sinon interrupted him.

"Test your numen again." Sinon walked away. "You may learn more about your abilities and yourself." Sam stared after him. Puzzled, he rose from the bench and began the long walk to Professor Plummet's office.

When Sam arrived, the professor's door was already open. The sounds of shuffling paper and frantic scribbling echoed from within. Sam knocked once on the doorjamb and gave the professor a quick wave.

"Sam!" The professor's face paled. He slammed shut the large binder sitting on his desk and stuffed it into a nearby file cabinet.

"I can come back." Sam turned to leave.

"No. No. No." The professor insisted, wiping the sweat from his brow. "Don't worry about it. What can I do for you?"

"Well," Sam hesitated before taking a seat. "I was wondering if you could test my numen."

"Again?" Professor Plummet smiled and shook his head. He reached into his desk drawer and withdrew a small tungsten sphere. "You really shouldn't obsess about numen count. It's just a number, and there are far better ways for you to improve."

"Actually, professor." Sam leaned forward. "I was wondering if you could test classification, not strength." The professor looked at Sam confused.

"Okay…" The professor frowned, returning the sphere to the drawer. "Any particular reason?" Plummet rummaged deeper and withdrew a seven-pointed-star. The center of the star was a tungsten septagon. The points were coated with various other metals.

"I was talking with Sinon earlier." Sam watched as the professor calibrated the device. "He told me that creation did not fit my personality."

"I see." Plummet laughed as he connected the numen tester to his computer. "Sinon was a great numen user, but I think he's wrong on this one. You scored in the ninety-sixth percentile of creators as a fourteen-year-old. That is your strongest category."

"Can I take the test anyways?" Sam asked.

"Sure." The professor handed Sam the star. "You remember how this works? Hold the star between your thumb and forefinger. Then, focus your numen." Sam followed the professor's instructions. A soft, white glow of numen flowed across the star.

Professor Plummet pressed a few keys on his computer and turned the screen towards Sam. A seven-pointed-star appeared. The top-most point turned green. "Still creation." The professor smiled. Sam handed him the star. "But your numen density increased from last time. It may even be stronger than Leah's."

"Thanks, professor." Sam rose to leave. "Sorry for the intrusion." Sam tried to hide his disappointment.

"Not at all." Professor Plummet placed the star in his desk drawer. "It's important to check these things. You don't want to be training in the wrong category." Sam walked to the door, but stopped before exiting.

"Professor," Sam asked. "Can I take the test again?"

"Sam." Professor Plummet sighed. "If the test didn't change in ten years, it's not going to change in eight seconds."

"One more time, professor, please"

"Alright." Professor Plummet withdrew the star from his desk again. "But this is the last time, okay. I have lots of work to do."

Sam held the star in his right hand and channeled his numen. He closed his eyes. Memories flooded back to Sam like a torrent in a raging sea. He remembered Sylvania Birnam, throwing Meg across the forum, advancing towards her, sword drawn. He remembered fighting Leah, hurting through space, a victim of accident and chance. He remembered his parents, Alex and Ester Alumen. He could see them as they were that day at the victory parade, seconds before the shots rang out. "Take care of Sam." They held Meg one last time. "We'll be right back. I promise." Sam's grip tightened as the memories charged with anger, despair and confusion. They all had one thing in common: what Sam wanted; what he needed: control.

"Stop!" Professor Plummet yelled. Sam's eyes snapped open to see the tungsten star glowing red-hot in his hands. He dropped the star and the professor's desk burst into flames. Sam slammed his hands on the table, trying to smother the fire. Professor Plummet dumped a pitcher of water on the desk. Steam erupted from the wood. The fire died.

"Professor." Sam panted. "I'm sorry…your desk."

"Forget the desk." Professor Plummet rushed to check on Sam. "How are your hands?"

"My hands?" Sam asked.

"Yes." The professor grabbed his hands. Sam stared at his palms. There were no burns or cuts anywhere. "You were holding melted tungsten." The professor's voice shook in disbelief.

"I'm fine." Sam wrenched his hand away from the professor. Sam's heart raced. He stared at the desk where the smoldering remains of the tungsten star were now embedded. The outer points had melted leaving only a blackened septagon.

"That's a relief." The professor walked around the desk and collapsed into his chair.

"Professor?" Sam asked. "I thought numen can't destroy tungsten."

"It can't." Professor Plummet stared at the hunk of charred metal. "I don't know. I have no idea how…" Sam looked at the computer screen. The top right corner of the star glowed blue and a warning message flashed across the graph.

"Does that mean I am a manipulator?" Sam asked. The professor stared at the graph.

"I guess it does." Professor Plummet spoke through heavy breaths. "I mean ... I guess it does."

"Sorry about the office," Sam said. "Should I ..."

"No." Professor Plummet shook his head. "Get out of here! Don't tell anyone. You're fine. It's fine." He stared at the computer screen, eyes wide and frightened. He tore a magnet off the file cabinet and began swiping back and forth across the computer's hard drive, arms shaking.

Sam backed out of the office, unnerved by the professor's reaction. Sam turned to run, but a harsh voice stopped him in his tracks.

"Sam!"

"Wha-?" Sam wheeled and clutched his chest.

"Come with me. Now!" Meg walked down the hall, eyes hard and cold.

"Why?" Sam pleaded. "What did I do?"

"What are you talking about?" Meg cast him a quizzical glance. "We're going to Aprilis PD. Now!"

"But?" Sam looked between Meg and the professor's door. He took a deep breath and nodded. "Okay." Sam hurried after her.

Meg did not ask any further questions. She scanned the corridors with an intense scrutiny that made Sam uneasy. She strode past the elevators at a near-sprint, stopping only to look around corners. She flung open the door to the nearest stairwell, glaring up and down the steel steps. Once Sam was inside, she ripped the handle off the door and slammed it shut.

"What-?" Sam began.

"Later." Meg ran down the stairs. Sam struggled to keep up with her. When they reached the bottom, Meg cut the lock with her numen and Sam was greeted by the sweet salt air of the Central docks. Meg tore open the door and ran to the nearest Boatbot. She reached for the biometric scanner, but paused, fingers hovering above the panel.

"On second thought." Meg withdrew her hand. "You should do it."

"What?" Sam's face paled.

"The sensor." Meg nodded to the Boatbot. "Use your thumbprint."

"Why?" Sam protested. "What's going on?"

"His won't work either." A voice called behind them. Meg and Sam wheeled. It was Leah.

"I see." Meg's eyes narrowed. "I guess we'll have to use someone else's"

"Is that a threat?" Leah raised her eyebrows.

"That depends." Meg remained firm.

"Meg?" Sam's face paled. "Please. What's going on?" Leah advanced, eyes locked with Meg. She extended her hand and unlocked the Boatbot.

"I'm coming with you." Leah maintained eye-contact with Meg. "That's my price."

"Deal." Meg nodded. She and Leah boarded the Boatbot. Sam remained on the dock, panicked and confused.

"Get on!" Leah demanded.

"Right, err…Well." Sam's heart pounded.

"It's okay." Meg nodded. "We'll explain on the way."

"You better." Sam shook his head and boarded the ship. The dome closed and their Boatbot sped into the Atropa River. "I just want to go on record saying: whatever this is, it is a terrible idea."

"Noted." Leah grinned.

"We're going to see Lakon." Meg began.

"Of course we are!" Sam threw up his arms in incredulity. "Like I said: terrible idea."

"I know you two got off on the wrong foot-" Meg continued.

"That's an understatement." Sam muttered.

"But." Meg cast him a stern look. "We're not going to solve this case without his help."

"Fine." Sam closed his eyes and crossed his arms. "Just give me time to plan."

"You never change." Leah quipped.

"I heard that!" Sam snapped.

"What were you doing with Professor Plummet anyways?" Meg asked.

"Nuh-uh! No way!" Sam glared across the boat at her. "You don't tell me your secrets; I don't tell you mine. Trust is not a one-way street."

"Fine." Meg smirked. "Sorry."

"You should be." Sam closed his eyes again. "Now be quiet, I'm trying to concentrate." Leah slid to Meg's side and they began whispering about Peter. Sam resisted the urge to start another argument. Peter was the least of their worries. Sam tried to focus on the task at hand, but his thoughts kept shifting back to Sinon's words: *"You may learn more about your ability and yourself."* Sam gazed out the Boatbot window. What had he learned? What was next?

"Is everything alright?" Meg asked.

"Yeah. Fine." Sam gave a startled jolt. "Everything's fine. I'm fine." Meg seemed unsatisfied by the answer, but did not press further.

When they arrived, Sam and Leah followed Meg inside Aprilis PD. The department was calmer than before, but, for once, Sam might have preferred chaos. He glanced towards Miles's office. The Sergeant was gone. Sam took a deep breath. Something was wrong.

Meg strode to Lakon's office, ignoring the other officers' whispers and stares. She held the door for Sam and Leah and looked both ways before locking it behind them.

"It's good to see you again." Lakon finished typing on his computer, hiding behind his cool, nonchalant composure. Sam knew better. Lakon had cleaned his office sometime that morning. The mounds of loose paper were gone and the faint scent of ammonia lingered in the air. Lakon had even gotten a haircut. Who was he trying to fool? He had clearly prepared for their arrival.

"Great to see you too." Meg nodded. "Sorry, again, for yesterday."

"Don't worry about it." Lakon smiled. "I got a bit heated myself." Sam's eyes narrowed. He was missing something, but what?

"Anyways." Meg continued. "I don't have much time. We should get down to business."

"Right." Lakon agreed. "What did you want to talk about?"

"What do you mean?" Meg gave Lakon a quizzical look.

"Your letter." Lakon nodded. "You said it was urgent."

"My letter?"

"You asked to meet."

"Look." Meg replied, annoyed. "If this is another one of your mind games-"

"Mind games?" Lakon interrupted. "You came here, remember." Meg and Lakon began arguing, each exchange more pointless than the last. Sam's eyes widened with fear. He knew what was wrong. Why hadn't he realized it sooner? Every move they made since leaving Central that morning succeeded without resistance. It was so perfect, it almost felt like … a plan.

"STOP!" Sam shouted. Meg and Lakon turned to look at him. "If neither of you sent letters. Who did?" Meg's eyes widened. Lakon's face paled.

"We have to get out of here." Lakon leapt from his chair and flung open the door. He sprinted across the room, vaulting over several desks and pulled the fire alarm on the opposite wall. Loud sirens and flashing lights blared through the police department

"What the hell, Lakon!" Detective Al Libby stormed towards him.

"Do you know a better way to evacuate the building?" Lakon snapped. Al's breaths shortened. He gave Lakon a frantic nod and turned to address the department.

"This is not a drill." Al shouted over the noise. "Get to the nearest exits now!"

"Where's Miles?" Lakon asked. Sam, Meg and Leah rushed to join him.

"Out." Al sighed and gave a solemn nod. He cast a nervous glance at Meg before continuing. "I didn't want to be the one to tell you this, but-."

"Shhh!" Lakon cut him off mid-sentence. He knelt on one knee and pressed his palm against the floor.

"What's wrong?" Meg placed her hand on Lakon's shoulder.

"I'm not sure," Lakon shook his head. "It's just ..." His eyes widened. Sam's heart raced. It was the same look Lakon had seconds before the last attack.

"We have to go. Now!" Sam shouted. He could feel it too; a vengeful presence radiating beneath their feet.

"What is it?" Leah asked.

"The elevator!" Lakon drew his revolver and ran towards the entryway. He pressed himself against the wall, hiding behind the nearest corner. The other officers turned to look at him. Several drew their weapons. Sam turned to face the elevators. The feeling was stronger; faster; closer.

"What's wrong?" Meg flashed Sam a concerned look. Sam opened his mouth to speak, but was interrupted by an eerie song echoing throughout the room. The officers looked around for the source of the noise. Meg's face paled.

The day is here.
We stand as one.
The chains of fear,
Are now undone.

To all mankind;
To every part;
The free of mind;
The free of heart:

Our nations' shame,
Is not our own.
Our only claim,
Is life alone.

The only war,
Is fought within.
The soul is your
One place to win.

We stand with you,
Extend your hand
To others who
Your heart demand.

Together now,
We heed the call,
We will not bow,
We will not fall,
Again.

Chapter 10 – Potential Energy

The elevator doors opened and Abraham Panzer strode into the police department, his lion tail swishing back and forth. He continued humming the eerie tune as the doors closed behind him. Abraham glared around the room. The remaining officers drew their weapons. Abraham grinned. "I'm looking for a man called…" He looked down at his palm and tried to read the name. "James Lak … James Lak … James Lakum. Anyone here by that name?" Lakon emerged from the corner and placed his gun to the back of Abraham's head.

"You're under arrest." Lakon spoke calm and cold. "Place your hands on your head and drop to your knees slowly."

"Tungsten Bullets." Abraham heaved a bone-chilling laugh. "I'm afraid it'll take more than that to stop me." A violent explosion erupted from Abraham and Lakon slammed head-first into the wall. The officers opened fire. Laser bolts deflected off Abraham's ferocious numen. Sam charged, channeling electricity into his fist. Abraham wheeled and struck a vicious slash with his forearm. BOOM!

The blast lifted Sam from his feet. Metal shards and concrete fragments smashed through his numen. Desks and columns splintered. The floor and ceiling burned. Officers and agents were thrown backwards. Sam was not so lucky. He hurtled through the air and plummeted through a broken window in a barrage of fire and shattered glass.

Chapter 11 – Battle of Aprilis PD

Meg Alumen

"Sam!" Meg ran to the ledge. Nothing. Sam was gone, obscured by the stream of fleeing Carbots.

"You should've kept your guard up." Abraham charged towards Meg, channeling numen through his claws. Meg was trapped. Her thoughts for Sam compromised everything. Meg braced for the attack.

"He's mine!" Leah slammed her fist into the Abraham's abdomen. CRACK! The blow threw Abraham careening into a fractured column. "How's Sam?"

"I don't know." Meg's eyes darted across the traffic. She scanned every depth, focus and angle. She shifted between ultraviolet, visible and infrared. Sam was nowhere to be found.

"Don't worry." Leah returned her attention to Abraham. "Sam can take a punch from me. That fall won't kill him."

"I hope you're right." Meg winced as the pain from yesterday returned more vicious than before. "Because I don't think either of us can take this guy alone." Several officers regained their weapons and resumed firing. A crossfire of laser bolts ricocheted off Abraham's ferocious numen. He smirked. Meg felt the intensity of his numen rising. "Get down!" She pulled Leah to the floor. Abraham crossed his arms. A shockwave roared through the air. The floor trembled. The ceiling tore. The columns buckled.

The tower swayed and stopped. Meg raised her head, hoping the worst had passed. It hadn't. The steel screeched. The beams twisted. Meg pressed her face against floor. The structure heaved a final groan before the upper stories separated and plunged to the streets below. Dust spewed through the charred air, mixing with the ash and smoke. Abraham grinned at the devastation.

"Heh." He laughed. "You Aprilisuns … Aprilesans … Aprilisins."

"Aprilisians!" Meg clenched her fist. Abraham did not deserve to live.

"Thank you." Abraham turned to face her. "You Aprilisians need stronger buildings. That didn't even warm me up."

"Bastard." Meg fumed. She felt the sun's rays beating through the thickened dust. The light merged with her furious numen, growing denser, hotter and more violent. Meg embraced the heat. She thrust her fist forwards, firing a frenzied surge of light and numen at Abrahams's heart. He blocked the numen with his arm, but roared as the radiation burned his skin. Abraham dove behind a pile of rubble to avoid the laser.

"You'll pay for that," Abraham shouted behind his feeble cover. Meg redoubled her assault. Flare after flare, she drove Abraham back. Nowhere was safe. He hid behind columns, walls, shattered stone; Meg burned them all. Each strike seared more vicious than the last. Meg's fury knew no limits, but the battlefield did. The dust grew thicker. The light grew dimmer.

Meg forced Abraham towards the ledge. He dove behind a steel desk, the last obstacle between Meg and vengeful victory. A fury of blasts raged across the metal surface. The steel glowed red-hot through the darkened air. Meg unleashed a final volley against the stubborn desk. The light dimmed. The glow faded. Meg's eyes widened in terror.

Abraham blasted the desk aside. His numen writhed with renewed furor, stronger and more savage than before. Meg's heart sank. Yesterday's fight hadn't weakened Abraham at all and, this time, the terrain was on his side.

Abraham lunged. The cramped battlefield left Meg no choice. She had to draw him away from Leah. Meg ran along the ledge. Abraham followed. Each step pressed faster than the last, thrust by the small explosions Abraham projected beneath his feet. He closed the distance in four strides. Meg was out of time and options.

"You're mine," Abraham snarled. His muscles tensed. His numen raged. His fist smashed through Meg's numen, unleashing a barrage of unchecked explosions. Meg couldn't block. The force lifted Meg from her feet and flung her into the last remaining window.

The glass fractured. The frame splintered. Meg looked down. A thin sheet of silica stood between her and a fatal plunge to the streets below. Wiping the blood from her forehead, Meg turned towards Abraham. He charged forward, eager to strike the final blow.

CRACK! A steel beam struck Abraham in the face. The attack sent Abraham reeling. He stumbled to the corner of the building, teetering on the edge. He swayed for a moment and regained his balance; too late. Leah retrieved the beam and struck Abraham a second time. Screaming, Abraham fell from the building and plummeted towards the streets below.

"Thank you." Meg limped towards Leah, heaving a sigh of relief; too soon. An immense explosion erupted from Abraham's claws, propelling him back into the building through a lower story window. The floor shook as support columns continued to fracture. A gaping hole formed in the center. Meg's heart pounded. The repeated thuds of Abraham's steps moved closer and closer. He was almost here.

Sure enough, Abraham emerged from the center hole, brushing the dust and debris from his mane. Leah stooped to retrieve another beam.

"Wait!" Meg yelled, but it was too late. Leah threw the beam at Abraham's head. A blinding flash seared through the dust, hurtling rubble in every direction. The beam ricocheted off Abraham and spiraled towards Leah at frightening speed. Leah dove to the floor as the spinning metal shrieked over her head and embedded itself in the last remaining concrete column.

"Reactive Armor." Abraham grinned. "You won't be able to hit me again." Meg fired another laser at Abraham's heart. Abraham channeled a tremendous surge of numen across his chest, deflecting the blow. "Now that I don't have to worry about her." He jabbed towards Leah. "I can focus on you and your pathetic lightshow." A ferocious wind rushed towards Abraham as he charged his fist with numen. Meg's hair quivered in the strange vortex. She held her breath. This next attack would be bad. "It's over." Abraham advanced towards Meg. "In this form I am invincible." Numen raged across his fur. "I'll start by killing everyone here and, when that bastard Peter shows up, I'll kill him too-" Leah grabbed Abraham's leg and slammed him to the floor.

"You talk too much." She swung Abraham and smashed him into the floor again. Abraham's reactive armor absorbed the damage, but Leah had him by the ankles. She bashed him into floors, walls, columns and desks, never releasing the hold. He thrust his fist at Leah, but a quick flick of her wrist caused Abraham to hit himself with his own attack. "You'll run out of numen eventually." Leah smashed him into a steel beam. Abraham winced as his reactive armor failed to regenerate.

"Here." Meg tossed Leah a pair of tungsten handcuffs. "Put these on him when you're done."

"Will do." Leah caught the handcuffs with one hand and struck Abraham across the face with them. A stream of blood gushed from Abraham's broken nose. "I guess even your reactive armor can't block tungsten." She was about to fasten the handcuffs to Abraham's wrist when an ear-splitting shriek reverberated throughout the building. A shockwave blasted across the debris, striking Leah in the back. The force lifted Leah from her feet, sending her flying into a twisted heap of steel.

"Really?" Meg heard a familiar voice echoing from the crumbling stairwell. "You couldn't last five minutes?" Sylvania Birnam emerged from the stairwell.

"Are you okay?" Meg rushed to Leah's side.

"Yeah." Leah gasped. Her numen absorbed the physical damage, but the attack knocked the wind out of her. Meg glared at Sylvania, but the treacherous mercenary did not seem to be paying attention.

"Where the hell were you?" Abraham staggered to his feet.

"Doing your job." Sylvania tossed something to him. Meg squinted into the sun, but could not see the object against the intense glare. Abraham caught the item and jammed it into his pocket.

"I never asked for your help!" Abraham yelled.

"No." Sylvania agreed. "Your boss asked me for you."

"Fine." Abraham returned his attention to Meg and Leah. "Just stay out of my way."

"You have one minute." Sylvania pressed a button on her Wrist-Pro. "After that, you'd better stay out of my way." Abraham charged towards Meg. But, Meg had prepared for the assault. While Abraham was distracted by Sylvania, Meg absorbed a tremendous surge of radiation in her left hand. She fired the blast into Abraham's eyes, blinding him. Abraham flailed, sending explosions in every direction. Meg grabbed Leah and pulled her behind a pile of rubble. Meg was exhausted and so was Leah by the looks of it. The explosions stopped.

"Did I get them?" Abraham shouted.

"No," Sylvania replied in a dull bored tone.

"Where are they?"

"Behind that." Sylvania spat. Meg heard Abraham's footsteps getting closer and closer. The crunching of rubble grew louder and louder. Meg's heart began to race. The footsteps stopped. Meg looked up. Abraham stared down at them, grinning.

"Found you," he gloated, raising his right fist. Meg channeled numen to her forearms and braced for the attack. CRACK!

A flash of blue light tore through the air and Abraham was blasted backwards. CRACK! CRACK! Two more flashes ripped across the sky, each more powerful than the last. Abraham screamed in agony. CRACK! CRACK! CRACK! The sounds and flashes increased in frequency and intesity until they became continuous. Meg scrambled over the rubble to get a better view. Abraham crouched in the center of the building, driven to his knees by a continuous surge of electricity. The source circled the building, accelerating across the voltage planes with each pass. The speed and power increased until the arc became a raging blue vortex. It was Sam.

"Stay away from my sister!" Sam yelled. The numen and electricity grew more and more violent. Abraham fired random explosions into the air, but Sam was too fast. The last of Abraham's numen was about to fade when a sonic boom knocked Sam out of the sky.

"Time's up!" Sylvania lowered her hand and walked towards Abraham. Sam recovered from his fall and landed on the opposite corner of the building. Leah joined Meg on top of the rubble pile. Sylvania was surrounded, but she did not seem to care. "Did you honestly think you could join the Septagon?" Sylvania kicked Abraham in the abdomen. He keeled and began to gasp. "Please, my cat is stronger than you." Sylvania turned to face Meg. "Alright, which one of you wants to go first? Or do all three of you want to take me all at once? That's fine too."

"I'll hold her off," Meg shouted to Sam. "You and Leah get out of here."

"No way!" Sam's numen crackled.

"Not happening!" Leah assumed a fighting stance.

"Ah! Loyalty." Sylvania smirked. "The source of all bad decisions in the world. Everyone wants to protect someone by destroying someone else. When will you people learn? In the world of 'us' and 'them', it's best to play all sides." Numen erupted from Sylvania's body. She raised her hands and a bloodcurdling shriek reverberated from every direction. The remaining windows shattered. Meg, Sam and Leah covered their ears. The sound raged, endless. Meg's head throbbed. The vibration echoed through her body, ringing in her brain. Sylvania lowered her hands. The sound stopped.

Meg looked up. Transparent blue barriers enclosed the building and a ceiling was beginning to form. Sylvania frowned and readjusted her numen. Meg's heart leapt. Peter was here.

Chapter 12 – Thirst for Vengeance

James Lakon

"Nice to meet you. I'm Detective Al Libby. What's your name?"

"James Lakon." The excited ten-year-old answered.

"Hey, you're the kid who scored perfect on the detective exam."

"I guess so. Miles helped me study."

"He's a great guy isn't he?"

"Yeah. He's my father. Well, close enough, anyways."

"There are all kinds of family, kiddo; some by blood; some by friendship; hell, some even by working in the same office together."

"You mean?"

"Sure thing, little buddy. Welcome to Aprilis PD. We're family now."

BOOM!

The ground shook and Lakon jolted back to the present. He opened his eyes. Nothing. No sight, no sound, only mind. Lakon remained, surrounded by darkness with nothing but his own thoughts.

BOOM!

Gold light seared through the darkness. Hope. Lakon's mind raced. His body writhed. His hands clawed towards the sun, desperate to get warm. Warmth came. Warmth came from blood. Warmth oozed everywhere, seeping through the wreckage.

BOOM!

Rubble shifted and darkness fell again. Lakon stopped moving. His eyes closed. His body wearied. His breaths slowed, soft and shallow. Sleep. Quiet sleep.

NO!

Lakon quivered as his mind fought his body. NO! His thoughts raged, searing images of Meg, Miles and Al into his brain. NO! Lakon's hand tore through the darkness, grabbing someone's arm on the outside.

"Ahhh!" the arm recoiled, but Lakon held firm. The debris shifted, bringing him face to face with a man Lakon had never seen before. The man stared at Lakon with a look of shock and awe.

"Sinon! Come on!" A voice called from above. The man did not answer. He continued to stare at Lakon, perplexed. "Sinon! We need you up here!"

"Coming!" Sinon wrenched his arm away from Lakon and ran up the stairs. Lakon shifted the rocks and tumbled into the stairwell. Limping, he ascended the stairs, shielding his eyes from the blinding sun.

At the top, only horror awaited him. Half of Lakon's fellow officers were dead. The other half were dying. Abraham stood alongside the woman from the forum. They were surrounded by Meg, Sam, Leah, Sinon, and a Colonel that Lakon assumed was from Central. They stood atop a mountain of death and terror. The sight was wretched, crushing and total. Lakon reached for his revolver. It wasn't there.

"Lakon," a weak voice groaned. Lakon scanned the ground and saw Al, trapped beneath the tarnished bronze shield of the Aprilis PD. "Get out of here, Lakon." Lakon rushed to Al's side.

"Come on." Lakon pressed his shoulder against the shield. His muscles strained and failed. It was too heavy. "I'll get you out of here."

"No." Al gasped barely more than a whisper.

"I'll find a lever." Lakon eyes darted across the wreckage. "I'm not leaving you."

"No." Tears streamed down Al's face. "Run." The building trembled. Collapse was imminent. Lakon looked back to Al.

"It's all my fault." Lakon started to cry.

"No." Al breathed.

"I shouldn't have gotten involved."

"No."

"I've been such a jerk to you." Lakon began to cry. "How could you ever forgive me?"

"Come on," Al forced a weak smile. "We're family." The building shook. Lakon watched in horror as the shield pressed tighter on Al's chest. There was nothing he could do. There was nothing anyone could do.

"Sylvania Birnam," the Colonel addressed the woman standing in the middle of the building. "For the destruction of the Helena Bridge and the attempted assassination of President Reginald Millenavis, you and Abraham Panzer are under arrest."

"Peter." Sylvania grinned at the Colonel. "Long time no see. How's Ike doing?" A blast of red light erupted from Meg's fist. Sylvania dodged the laser with ease. Lakon stared in shock. "A touchy subject." Sylvania laughed. "When will you people learn? The more you protect, the weaker you are."

"Ike was not weak." Meg clenched her fist.

"He's dead now isn't he?" Sylvania goaded. Meg stepped forward.

"Meg!" Peter yelled. Meg stopped to look at him. "Stay back!"

"Yes, Meg!" Sylvania taunted. "Listen to your master. We wouldn't want Peter losing another student now, would we?" A devious grin crept across Sylvania's face. Her fist clenched. The air began to tremble.

"As I move in," Peter's voice boomed across the rubble. "Everyone attack at once." What? Lakon remained hidden behind the twisted steel beam. Something was wrong. Something did not make sense.

"Yes Sir!" The other agents took offensive stances. Peter looked at them, confused. Sylvania smirked. Lakon realized what was wrong.

"Peter never said that!" Lakon emerged from behind the shield. "Read his lips!" The agents stared at Lakon, dumbfounded. Sylvania snarled. Behind her, Abraham Panzer groggily rose to his feet. He blinked several times, looking around the entire building as if lost. At last, his eyes met Lakon's.

"Hey! That's that Lakem fellow." Abraham stared at Lakon with a vacant expression. "I thought I killed him."

Chapter 12 – Thirst for Vengeance

"You had two jobs!" Sylvania turned on Abraham, shouting at the top of her lungs. "I did one and you failed the other!"

"Yeah; yeah; I guess I'll kill him now." Abraham raised his arms.

"No!" Sylvania screamed, but it was too late. A massive gust surged towards Abraham. Lakon's lungs burned. His knees buckled. His vision swam. Lakon scanned the shattered remnants of the Aprilis PD. Only Peter and Sylvania remained, holding their breath. The others collapsed, coughing through the dust. Lakon didn't care. Only one thing caught his eye: the pale face of Al Libby, gasping for air, trapped beneath the tarnished bronze seal of the Aprilis PD.

"Stop it!" Lakon screamed. He could not explain it, but, somehow, it felt necessary to address Peter directly. Lakon's lungs seared as he inhaled again. "Stop it!" Lakon shouted again, louder and more forceful than before. Peter turned to look at him. "Before it's too late." Lakon whispered and collapsed to the floor. His vision blurred until Peter was nothing more than a gray spot between the scorched ground and blue sky. The spot writhed between the darkness and light, panicked and uncertain. At last, the spot stopped moving. Lakon felt a rush of cold wind pass over his face. Lakon breathed.

Lakon looked up just in time to see Abraham's fist strike the ground. An ear-splitting crack split the air. The building swayed. Columns crumbled. The floor gave way. Lakon plunged into darkness.

BONG! A solemn clang rang through the shouts and screaming. Lakon's heart sank. He knew what the sound meant. Lakon opened his eyes. How was he alive?

Lakon forced himself to stand. Sure enough, at the base of the rubble, the bronze seal of the Aprilis PD lay broken; the blue rose of Aprilis on one side, the white stallion of Caerule on the other. Lakon did not move the shield. He knew what was underneath. Lakon's eyes darkened.

As he turned away, a light glinted from the rubble. Wedged between pieces of smoldering sheetrock, the reflective muzzle of his revolver lay thirsting for revenge. Lakon kicked the charred panels and grabbed the gun. They would all pay. He would make them pay.

"Leah?" Peter called. "Meg?" The voice shook with desperation. "Sam?" Lakon turned towards the noise, but something held him back. He hid behind a broken concrete wall, waiting.

"We're here." Lakon heard Meg shout. He peered around the concrete barrier. Meg, Sam and Leah scrambled towards Peter. Meg held her hand in the shape of a gun, scanning the rubble with intense scrutiny. "Is Sinon with you?"

"No." Peter's eyes darted across the wreckage.

"Here!" Sinon answered. Lakon's heart raced. The voice was less than an arm's length away on the other side of the wall. "Where are Abraham and Birnam?"

"They must've escaped after the blast." Peter shouted. "God damn it!" Lakon heard Peter's steel-toed book strike against a fallen beam. Something was wrong. Lakon's breaths shortened. The danger was not gone. It was mounting.

"Peter!" A voice echoed across the wreckage.

"A-Admiral Lodon." Peter stammered. A familiar pain shot through Lakon's head. It throbbed, stronger and faster than before. Lakon's hand rushed to his forehead. It was worse than the time at the hospital; much worse.

"What's your status?" Admiral Lodon demanded. Peter's eyes fell.

"I'm sorry, Admiral. The enemy escaped. I take full responsibility."

"Full responsibility?" Admiral Lodon snarled. "Let me remind you exactly what that means."

"What are you talking about?" Peter asked.

"I didn't want to be the one to tell you this." Admiral Lodon looked Peter dead in the eye. "But you're going to find out anyways, so you might as well hear it from me. Central was attacked. General Rocklos is dead."

"No." Peter's eyes widened. The color drained from his face.

"Peter…" Meg began. Peter turned away from her. He climbed a mound of broken rebar and stared across the Atropa River.

"They stole the projectile fragment and her access key." Admiral Lodon explained. "We need to return to Central immediately."

"Yes, Admiral." Peter turned to follow her. Meg remained still.

"Meg-?" Sinon began.

"There's another fragment." Meg interrupted. Lakon cursed under his breath.

"What?" Peter wheeled to face her. Admiral Lodon cast Meg a sideways glance.

"The projectile," Meg continued. "There's another fragment. We agreed to keep it hidden in case-"

"Who's 'we'?" Peter demanded.

"James Lakon." Meg's eyes fell.

"Let me get this straight." Peter clenched his fist and shook his head in frustration. "You're telling me, the man who was at every crime scene, the man who predicted yesterday's attack, the man who lured you, Sam and Leah into this trap asked you to lie to Central and you did?"

"I trust him." Meg met Peter's gaze.

"More than us?" Peter frowned. "Well, let me tell you something, Major Alumen." He spat the words. "General Rocklos and I met earlier today to discuss this James Lakon. Did you know he met the Pale Raven last night?"

"He wouldn't." Meg shook her head.

"There's Fenestravision footage of it!" Peter glared at her. "You disobeyed orders. You put Sam, Leah and yourself in mortal danger. You forced Sinon and me to come to your rescue and now the General…" Peter bowed his head and leaned against a broken wall.

"Peter, I-" Meg began.

"I'm disappointed." Peter turned away from her. Meg stared after him, eyes solemn and sad.

"Do you have the fragment with you?" Admiral Lodon watched Meg with a narrow, piercing gaze.

"No." Meg sighed.

"I see." The Admiral's brow furrowed. "Secure the fragment and return to Central immediately. That's an order."

"Yes, Admiral." Meg paused for a moment, casting Peter a concerned look. Peter did not move. Meg turned away, signaling Sam to follow her. Peter waited for Meg to leave.

"Let's go." Peter nodded to Sinon and turned towards the river. "We'll find more at Central than we will here." Admiral Lodon grabbed Peter's arm.

"I'm not going to tell you what to do." The Admiral slackened her grip. "But, if I were you, I'd focus on the friends I have, not the ones I've lost. General Rocklos would have wanted it that way."

"I know what I'm doing." Peter wrenched his arm away from her. "Come on, Leah." He, Sinon and Leah walked towards the river, leaving Admiral Lodon alone. A tattered blue Caerule flag blew across the clearing, twisting and turning through the turbulent air. The Admiral caught the flag mid-flight. She carried it through the wreckage and tied it to a long rebar rod. The flag waved in the breeze, flying high above the death and destruction.

Lakon had seen enough. He holstered the revolver and ran towards Miles's apartment building. The streets were already teeming with Fenestravision drones. Lakon crept along alleys, hid behind dumpsters, snuck through abandoned buildings, anything to avoid being seen.

As he approached, progress slowed to a crawl. The drones circled lower, more frequently and in greater numbers. What a waste. Lakon scaled the fire escape of a neighboring building and perched on the shadowed ledge of the roof.

Below, drones soared past each other, swarming at any sign of movement. Bystanders, Carbots, stray dogs, everything triggered their sensors. Lakon sighed. It was too easy. He removed a single bullet from his revolver and threw it at a parked Carbot. The street erupted in a violent clash of sirens and flashing lights. Lakon leapt across the gap to his apartment building, forced open the bulkhead and climbed down the down the ladder.

He sprinted to the apartment, propped a chair against the door and rushed to his bedroom to retrieve the yellow toolbox. He ran back to the kitchen, slammed open the lid and grabbed the Phillips-Head screwdriver. Lakon leapt onto the kitchen table and dismantled the ceiling oxygen sensor. He threw the components into the toolbox and jumped off the table. Lakon then turned towards the refrigerator; the argon refrigerator. Taking a running start, Lakon slammed his shoulder into the appliance. The refrigerator crashed to the floor, spilling food and chemicals everywhere. Lakon ripped an argon tank from the rear mounting bracket and slung it over his shoulder.

Last, Lakon looked at the screwdriver in his hand. His eyes darkened. Lakon took a deep breath and slowly unscrewed the bottom cover of the screwdriver handle. A small vial of white powder rolled into Lakon's palm. He jammed the vial into his pocket and turned to leave.

THUMP! A loud thud slammed against the apartment door. Lakon's heart pounded. He drew his revolver and hid behind the doorjamb, waiting. THUMP! The chair fell and the door creaked open. A shadow spread across the floor. The figure stepped across the threshold and the door slammed shut.

"Hello Miles." Lakon sighed and lowered the revolver.

"Lakon." Miles embraced him. "Thank God you're alright. Where were you?"

"Where was I?" Lakon's voice shook with anger. "Where was I? Where were you?" Miles face fell.

"Lakon, you have to understand…"

"Understand what?" Lakon glared into Miles's eyes, livid and unflinching. "You told me to stay out of this. You told me to stop working with Central. You told me to drop the case. And now, everyone is dead."

"Lakon, please-"

"Where were you?" Lakon shouted. Miles turned away. He walked to the kitchen window and stared into the fading twilight.

"Arresting Neil Whitney for the destruction of the Helena Bridge." Miles's voice fell.

"What?" Lakon's face paled. "But he's innocent."

"Do you think that matters now?" Miles spat. "Caerule suffered two, now three, devastating losses and Central has no leads. Did you really think they'd go another day without a scapegoat?"

"But why Neil?"

"Why do you think?" Miles's voice harshened. "As your report so eloquently stated, there were only two groups who knew about that pressure valve: Central and the bridge engineers. Who do you think Central's more likely to blame?"

"No." Lakon dropped the argon canister and collapsed into a nearby chair.

"Neil's wife was a revolution sympathizer." Miles turned back to the window. "He's lucky to have lasted this long. Once Central sets their eyes on you..." Miles trailed off.

"Why did you help them?" Lakon asked.

"What?"

"You always taught me to find the truth." Lakon stared at the floor. "Why did you arrest a man you knew to be innocent?"

"Because." Miles sighed. The last lights faded over the horizon, casting the room into shadow. "I didn't want them to take you too."

"I see." Lakon rose from his chair. He slung the argon tank over his shoulder and grabbed the yellow toolbox.

"Where are you going?" Miles eyed the box.

"To get justice." Lakon turned to leave. "Someone has to."

Chapter 13 – Murderer among Them

Peter Turnus

Entropy always increases. Peter's body produced 700 watts as he sprinted towards the laboratory door. Patricia's lifeless heart produced zero. Peace and war; love and hate; truth and lies; only power mattered in the end. Each step Peter pounded against the tiles, each breath Peter heaved through the cold air, each tear Peter fought to withhold released energy irreversibly into the dark, cruel world. Fate cannot be changed without power, and Peter was losing his.

"Peter." Sinon called. Peter ignored him. He slammed open the steel double-doors, almost striking Sinon in the face. Professor Plummet, General Bell and Grand Master Marius huddled together, whispering in hushed tones. Peter didn't care. He strode to the center of the room and stared down at the pale face of his former mentor.

Fire returned. Memories flooded in a torrent of unchecked sorrow and rage. Peter's fist tightened until blood seeped from his inner palm. Protecting comrades; defending Caerule, his vows were nothing but platitudes, compromised and corrupted by the foul face of failure.

"You!" Peter pointed to Plummet. "Tell me what happened. Now!"

"I'm sorry." The professor stepped forward. Tears streamed down his face. "General Rocklos asked me to run additional tests-."

"What tests?" Peter snarled.

"Heat treatment." Plummet began to ramble. "The properties of tungsten superalloys vary with thermal stress and recrystallization rates. Precipitation hardening can create yield strength anomalies in extreme thermal conditions. Intermetallic nucleation during the reinforcing phase-"

"English!" Peter spat, arms shaking with rage.

"She wanted to know if it passed through the atmosphere." Sinon translated, bowing his head.

"Thank you." Peter's voice shook as he returned his attention to Plummet. "And the results?"

"I'm sorry." Plummet shook his head. "I left to get the equipment, but when I came back..." He mouthed the syllables, but the words would not form.

"Patricia was dead." General Bell finished. He glared at Patricia's corpse, grip tightening on the pommel of his cane. Peter knew that look. It was the face of a man who wanted one thing above all else: vengeance.

"I see." Peter's eyes darkened as he turned towards Patricia's lifeless body.

"Peter." Sinon placed his hand on Peter's shoulder. "Let's go." How long? How long, Peter wondered, before he lost Sinon too?

"No!" Peter tore himself away. "I need to do this." Sinon's eyes fell. He watched Peter for a long time before forcing a solemn nod.

"Okay." Sinon sighed. "I'll help."

"Good." Peter scanned the blood trail. He had to leave emotions out of this; focus on the task at hand. "Stand right there."

Peter pointed to a spot on the floor. Sinon walked around Patricia's body and stood at the place Peter indicated. A lone tear rolled down Sinon's cheek. Peter pretended not to notice. "Good." Peter walked back to the steel double doors. "The killer must've entered here." Peter knelt to inspect the cleanroom floor. "Patricia would've heard the doors even if her back was turned." He walked along the aisle of test stations and ventilation booths. "Here." Peter reached the center of the aisle. A gap in the workstations allowed Peter a direct view of Sinon and the General's body. "This is the first place they'd have seen each other, and..." Peter looked towards Sinon, confused.

"And what?" General Bell asked.

"And she just stood there." Peter shook his head. "It doesn't make sense unless..."

"Unless what?" General Bell asked again. Peter stared across the room at Sinon. Their eyes met and Peter realized what had happened.

"Unless, it was someone she knew." Peter breathed. "Someone she knew very well. That's why she stopped. That's why she hesitated." The room fell silent. Everyone stared at the floor. At last, Sinon sighed and turned to Peter.

"So what happened next?"

"They fought." Peter walked towards the body. "Right here in the center. There are cuts all over the cleanroom floor." Peter stopped to examine a large gash. "Plummet, get over here!"

"Yes, sir." The professor scrambled to Peter's side and squatted to inspect the tile.

"How exactly did Patricia die?"

"She died fighting." Plummet shuddered. "I don't know which wound came first, but." The professor pointed towards the

General's blood-stained chest. "The final one went straight through her heart." Peter knelt over the General's body and examined the wound. It was far deeper and more vicious than the rest. Peter's eyes watered with uncried tears. He had failed her. "The other wounds are too shallow to identify, but that one." Plummet took a deep breath before finishing. "Was caused by a naval cutlass."

Behind him, Peter heard the steel doors slam open; heard the heavy stomp of combat boots; heard the stark, cold voice of Admiral Lodon. Peter's fists clenched and numen flowed through his arms.

"Bell! Peter! Marius!" Admiral Lodon snapped. "Get to the war room now!" Blood-red numen blades erupted from Peter's hands.

"Peter!" Sinon reached to stop him, but it was too late. Peter charged towards the Admiral, forcing all his numen into a single strike.

CLASH! A vicious clang ripped through the room as the Admiral blocked Peter's attack with a flick of her sword. His eyes widened. When had she even drawn it? Peter had no time to react. A blunt pain shot through his body as Admiral Lodon's combat boot smashed into his abdomen. Peter hurtled across the room, crashing head-first into the composite wall on the opposite side of the laboratory.

"Of all the blasted numen users." Admiral Lodon snarled as she advanced towards Peter. "I thought you were different. You fought for Caerule your entire life and now you betray your country?" Peter's head throbbed. Sounds rang and blurred together. Lights danced and brightened until, at last, Peter's vision swam into focus.

"No." Peter gasped and caught his breath. "I saved it." Sure enough, a crimson streak of blood ran down the Admiral's cutlass. Admiral Lodon's nostrils flared as she examined the blade.

"It's over, Lodon." Marius stepped forward. The others cowered at the sight of the angry Admiral. Lodon glared around the room. At last, her eyes locked with Marius. Her gaze was vicious, cold and terrifying. She raised the sword, pointed it towards Marius, then dropped it at the Grand Master's feet.

"Plummet." Marius called, not taking his eyes off Lodon. "Run the test."

"Yes, sir." Plummet scrambled to retrieve the sword. He carried the blade to a nearby work station and began scanning a blood sample. Peter clutched his ribs and tried to stand. Pain burned through his chest, far worse than before. He fell forwards, collapsing on the blood stained floor.

"Are you alright?" Sinon rushed to Peter's side.

"Yeah." Peter groaned.

"I'll take you to the hospital." Sinon placed his hand on Peter's shoulder.

"No!" Peter continued to eye Admiral Lodon. "I need to see this." Professor Plummet stopped scanning the sword and retrieved a piece of paper from a nearby printer. He handed the paper to Marius, face pale.

"You ran it multiple times?" Marius glanced over the paper.

"Yes, sir." Plummet cast a fleeting glance at Admiral Lodon. "The blood matches General Rocklos, no question." The Admiral remained unfazed.

"I see." Marius sighed. "Admiral Lodon, you are under arrest for the murder of General Rocklos. You have the right-"

"I know my rights." Admiral Lodon interrupted. "Get on with it." Marius gave a nod to General Bell. Bell withdrew a pair of tungsten handcuffs and clamped them around Lodon's wrists. The Admiral did not resist. As soon as the cuffs were on, she strode towards the interrogation rooms. Bell and Plummet raced to follow her.

"Good work." Marius returned his attention to Peter, before turning to follow the others. "General Turnus."

Peter stared at Patricia's blood-stained corpse, now alone, helpless, in the center of the room. His promotion was meaningless. Peter felt sick and defeated.

"Peter." Sinon blocked his view. "Please. Let's go." Peter nodded and Sinon helped him to his feet. Together, they hobbled from the laboratory.

"Not the hospital." Peter wheezed as they approached the elevators.

"Where then?" Sinon glanced at Peter concerned.

"You pick." Peter winced. "The forum, the docks, anywhere but there."

"The docks then." Sinon pressed the button. The elevator descended and opened to sweet salt smell of Central Harbor. Peter hobbled across the dock, leaning on Sinon for support. They sat on the end of the pier. Peter withdrew a key from his pocket and unlocked Sinon's tungsten bracers.

"Thanks for that." Sinon winced as he rubbed the irritated skin. Peter threw the bracers into the river. Sinon withdrew an Accretion Bar from his pocket and handed the dark chocolate half to Peter. "I just." Sinon choked back tears. "Can't believe she's gone."

"Not gone." Peter's fist clenched. "Taken."

Chapter 13 – Murderer among Them

"It seems like only yesterday the three of us sat along that hillside." Sinon gazed across the water towards the dark silhouette of Dandelion Hill. "I always hoped we'd go back there some day but-"

"I should never have dropped that barrier." Peter spat.

"What?" Sinon stared in shock.

"At the police station." Peter grit his teeth. "The barrier. I never should have dropped it."

"Meg and Leah would've died."

"And now more will die."

"You made a choice, Peter." Sinon's voice harshened. "For once in your life, you chose comrades over Caerule and I'm proud of you for it."

"Proud?" Peter glared at him. "I failed the General's last order because my feelings got in the way. You think I should be proud of that?"

"Yes." Sinon sighed. "If it had been us, she would've done the same thing."

"That doesn't make it right."

"Peter-" Sinon began. Peter hurled his half of the Accretion Bar into the river.

"Sorry." Peter glared across the water at the shattered remains of the Helena Bridge. "I'm not hungry." Sinon remained silent as he watched the bar drift and sink beneath the waves

"We should leave." Sinon spoke after a long pause. "You, me, Meg, Sam and Leah; we should get out of here before it's too late."

"What?" Peter's eyes widened.

"We could go anywhere, do anything; leave this all behind and go wherever the future leads us. The mountains of Ardor, the skies of Borea, the jungles of Ferox: we could visit them all, or none, whatever we want."

"Our mentor was just murdered." Peter stared in disbelief. "Don't you want revenge?"

"No." Sinon's eyes darkened. "I've seen what vengeance does to people. Avengers hurt no one but themselves." He turned towards Peter. "And their friends."

"All the same." Peter shook his head. "I can't leave Caerule. Not now."

"I understand." Sinon heaved a long sigh. "I guess I should've known. I want to be there with you but…"

"But what?" Peter pressed.

"I can't do this anymore." Sinon's eyes ran red with tears. "I can't sit by and watch this world destroy itself again. You're strong, Peter; stronger than I could ever hope to be. You've seen the worst this country has to offer and still you keep fighting for it. Why?" Sinon cried. "Why do you keep fighting when there's nothing left worth fighting for?"

"I never had nothing; I always had you." Peter remained firm. "You, Meg, Leah, Ike; I always had someone worth protecting even when I didn't have something."

"I see." Sinon brushed the tears from his eyes. "You're a good friend Peter; the best I've ever had."

"Then you'll stay?"

Chapter 13 – Murderer among Them

"I'm sorry." Sinon rose to his feet. "I'm leaving whether you're with me or not."

"You'll come back." Peter smiled. "You always do."

"I hope you're right, Peter. I hope you're right." Sinon walked away, leaving Peter alone. Moonlight clashed with the darkness, spreading across the water an uneasy mix of fire and shadow.

Peter stared towards Dandelion Hill, now blocked by the grim silhouette of the moored transmission ship. Memories returned; of Sinon, of Patricia, of warm summers long since faded. Peter began to cry. Why was the past always brighter?

Peter turned away, vicious hatred burning in his heart. Admiral Lodon was not working alone. There was one more that escaped justice. Peter's blood-stained fist clenched as he spat the name: "James Lakon." A violent flash split the night, plunging the city once more into fire and chaos. Peter's eye widened. The explosion echoed across the water and flames billowed from the upper floors of Sam's apartment building.

Chapter 14 – Protocol Zero

Sam Pere

Chaos reigned in Aprilis. Carbots collided. People fled. Smoke poured into the night sky. Sam stood frozen at the base of the tower, trying to think of a plan. Nothing. Sam's mind raced faster. His eyes grew wider. Useless; hopeless; helpless; Sam's thoughts left nothing but panic and desperation.

"Let's go!" Meg sprinted ahead of him.

"What?" Sam's face paled. His voice drowned in the deafening hysteria. Sam ran after her, elbowing his way through the frenzied crowd. A random knee slammed into Sam's chest, almost knocking him to the ground. He pressed himself flat against a wall to catch his breath. The mob was deadlier than the fire. They stampeded in random directions, followed oblivious leaders, and trampled each other without mercy. Sam was alone, fighting against a hostile horde that wanted to go the other way. It didn't matter. He couldn't lose Meg. Not now. Not ever. Sam channeled his numen and forced himself through the crowd.

At last, he fought his way to the riverside entrance of the high-rise. People spilled from the emergency stairwell. Sam scanned the crowd, his frantic heart pounding. Meg was nowhere to be found.

Sam's eyes turned upwards towards the flames. Why had she run ahead? Sam pushed through the entrance and began climbing the narrow stairs. The crowd thinned and their echoes faded. Sam quickened his pace.

Chapter 14 – Protocol Zero

At last, he reached the landing. The air blackened with smoke and dust. Sam shielded his eyes and stumbled through the hall, guided only by memory. Flames raged through the smog. Sam coughed and gagged as the heat intensified. The light reached towards him and... Sam felt a hand on his shoulder.

"Here." Meg guided Sam to a metal box on the far wall. Her numen glowed red and gold, strengthened by the flames. "Give it power."

"What?" Sam choked.

"The box." Meg pointed to a severed wire at the top of the breaker panel. "Give it power." Sam channeled his numen and completed the circuit. The overhead sprinklers sprang to life, dousing the hall in a gross shower of filthy water. The fires sputtered and died. Sam released his numen. The water stopped.

"I thought these things had emergency power." Sam brushed the disgusting water from his eyes.

"They did." Meg frowned at the panel. "The emergency power was cut." She turned away and walked towards the smoldering ruins of Sam's apartment.

Sam's face fell. The floors were charred and blackened. The walls were torn and twisted. Ash blew through the cold night air, covering the death and destruction beneath. The only light shone from the rising moon. It peered through the dying smoke, casting dark shadows across the floor. Even light left nothing but darkness.

Meg's eyes glowed with numen as she scanned the devastation. Sam scrambled to help. Kneeling in the soot, he plunged his blackened arms into the ashes. The dust was lifeless but warm. Sam sifted through the wreckage until his fingers rested on something sharp and cold.

"Found him." Sam choked, trying to hold back tears. He brushed off the shattered remains of Merc. There was not much left of the robot. His frame had fractured in multiple places and his eyes lay broken on the floor.

"How is he?" Meg knelt at Sam's side.

"Beyond repair," Sam ran his hand across Merc's shattered display screen. It was not right to cry over a robot, not now, not with so many people dying.

"And the fragment?" Meg began to place the tarnished components one-by-one into a large evidence bag.

"Gone." Sam traced his fingers over the small pouch where they hid the projectile in Merc's chest cavity. He was so cheerful then. Even now, Sam remembered the way Merc zipped around the room, happy to help in any way he could.

"Too bad." Meg rose to her feet and brushed herself off. "Then we have no leads.

"I wouldn't say that," Sam muttered.

"What was that?" Meg flashed Sam a warning look.

"You heard me!" Sam raised his voice. "There's only one person who knew we had that fragment. Now it's gone and he's nowhere to be found."

"There are many ways to get information." Meg frowned. "Never trust a fact unless you trust its source."

"Even if that source is Peter." Sam spat. His voice was bitter and his words were charged. Meg turned away. She walked towards the crumbling Fenestravision wall and stared over the city.

"There are different kinds of trust." Meg spoke after a long pause. Her face remained shrouded in shadow. "I trust Peter with my life, but I trust Lakon with this case." Sam shook his head. He should've known. Why Lakon of all people?

"You love him." Sam's eyes darkened. "Don't you?"

"Is it that obvious?" Meg sighed. A cold wind shrieked through the room. Sam's grip tightened around the shattered remains of Merc's display screen.

"Why?"

"I don't know." Meg turned back to the city and stared across the Atropa River towards Central. "I guess because he lives in the moment. He always looks forward and never looks back. History is forged by people like that; for better or worse."

Sam opened his mouth to protest, but was interrupted by a beeping noise from Meg's Wrist-Pro. Meg pressed a button and answered the call.

"Hello Peter."

"Meg." Peter's voice crackled through the transceiver. "Thank God! Are you and Sam alright?"

"We're fine." Meg answered. "But the fragment is gone. How are things at Central?"

"Bad." Peter sighed. "Lodon won't talk and-"

"Lodon?" Meg interrupted.

"Sorry. I forgot you weren't there." Peter continued. "Admiral Lodon murdered General Rocklos. She's being interrogated as we speak."

"That...Can't be." Meg shook her head.

"We caught her red handed." Peter choked the words. "Patricia's blood was all over the Admiral's sword. I...I failed her."

"We're on our way, sir." Meg tried to reassure him.

"Please, hurry." Peter sighed. "Things are much worse than I thought. Protocol Zero. Over and out." Meg's Wrist-Pro gave a soft click and the call ended.

"No." Meg breathed.

"What's wrong?"

Meg did not respond.

"What does 'Protocol Zero' mean?" Sam pressed again. Meg bowed her head.

"War."

Sam's face paled. Meg turned away. She leaned against a crumbling wall and stared into the dark reflection of Central fading into the Atropa River. Sam sat in the pile of ash, grip tightening around the remnants of Merc's display screen. What could he say? What could he do? At last, Meg broke the silence.

"Sam." She continued to look across the city. "Do you still want to be an agent?"

"What?" Sam puzzled.

"You may be young." Meg's eyes darkened. "But you know what war is. Do you want to go through that again?"

"Don't say that!" Sam sprang to his feet. "There has to be another way."

"I don't know." Meg sighed.

"What are our options?"

"We could leave Caerule."

"No!" Sam shouted

"We could stay and fight the war."

"No!" Sam repeated, louder than before.

"Or…" Meg trailed off.

"Or what?"

"Or we could attack Central ourselves."

"What?" Sam's heart raced.

"I don't know who's behind this." Meg glared at the marble-white buildings looming over the river. "But we know they're inside Central. We need to stop their war plans, and I need to meet with Admiral Lodon undetected."

"But how?"

"Actually." Meg turned to look at Sam. "I was hoping you'd think of something."

"Me?"

"Yes." Meg continued. "Your rigid planning is frustrating at times, but you are good at it. I've always thought so." Meg's eyes radiated a calm certainty Sam wished he could find in himself. This was crazy. How could she be so confident? Sam's mind raced, trying to find an answer. So many questions remained. Sam stared at the twisted remains of Merc still clutched in his hands. His fingers ran across the broken circuitry, now cold and lifeless.

"Central's wires are made of tungsten." Sam closed his eyes. "Aren't they?"

"I assume so." Meg sighed. "You won't be able to-"

"I'll do it." Sam answered before Meg could finish.

"Uh … Great." Meg's eyes narrowed. "You'll do what, exactly?"

"Whatever I need to." Sam turned to leave. "Follow ten minutes behind me. You'll know when it happens." Meg nodded. Sam left without another word. He ran down the tarnished stairwell, dodged through the panicked crowd and sprinted along the coastline.

As he approached the Aprilis docks, Sam's heart leapt. The light of a returning Boatbot shone through the encroaching mist. What luck! Sam's feet pounded on the planks, spreading booms and ripples across the water. He ran towards the pier, so focused he almost missed the startled shadow ducking behind a nearby Boatbot.

"Who's there?" Sam froze. No answer. "Show yourself!" Nothing. Sam's breaths shortened. He channeled his numen, enveloping the dock in a blue-white glow. The darkness receded and the figure came into view. "Tom?"

"Sam?" Tom scrambled to his feet. "What are you doing here?"

"Returning to Central." Sam tried to be as vague as possible. "What are you doing here?"

"Bringing my father a change of clothes." Tom held up a blue paper bag. "Sorry, I thought you were one of them."

"No worries." Sam's eyes narrowed. Tom was always calm and collected. What could have frightened him? A solemn bell toll broke the silence, announcing the arriving Boatbot. A dark figure emerged from the craft. Tom's face paled. Sam squinted through the mist. The figure stepped towards them, boots creaking on the tired planks. The light of the Boatbot died and the shadow vanished. Through the darkness, Sam could only hear the creaking boots, closer with every step. At last, the figure stepped into the glow of Sam's numen. It was Sinon.

"Sinon." Sam smiled, relieved to see a familiar face. "Thank God! We were waiting for a Boatbot and-"

"Didn't want to scan your fingerprint." Sinon frowned. Sam shivered. How much did Sinon know?

"I'll start the Boatbot." Tom raced past them, avoiding eye contact. Sinon cast a quizzical glance at the boy.

"I'll help." Sam turned to follow Tom. Sinon grabbed his arm.

"Whatever you're doing." Sinon's voice was calm, but stern. "Don't. Central is a dangerous place right now, especially for you." He released Sam's arm and strode into the looming darkness.

"Let's go!" Tom called.

"Right." Sam hesitated before following his friend. He boarded the Boatbot as Tom finished programming the coordinates.

The boys did not speak on the way to Central. Sam closed his eyes, analyzing various plans and scenarios. Tom looked out the window, watching the city lights darken one by one. As soon as they reached the Central docks, Sam leapt from his seat and prepared to leave. Tom did not move. He continued staring into the distance, shifting only as the waves beat gently against the hull. At last, he broke the silence.

"You're planning something, aren't you?"

"What gave you that idea?"

"I'm terrified right now." Tom shuddered. "And you're calm as could be."

"Life's random." Sam smiled and shrugged. "Sometimes, you just have to roll with it." He left without another word. Tom sat in the Boatbot alone.

Sam ran to the nearest door, dodging the security cameras with ease. Again, he was in luck. The lock remained severed where Meg had melted it earlier that afternoon. Sam ran up the stairwell to the same floor. Sure enough, the handle remained broken, but only from the inside. Once it closed, there would be no turning back. Sam took a deep breath and walked through the door.

The hall was dark and empty. Footprints littered the floor where military personnel no doubt rushed to more important buildings. Charts and memos had been torn from the walls, perhaps in some futile attempt to review every document mentioning Admiral Lodon. The last remaining light emanated from Professor Plummet's office. Inside, the sounds of the professor's scribbling resonated through the halls. Sam smiled. At least someone was still searching for the truth.

BANG! A door slammed open at the end of the hall. The professor's scribbling stopped. Sam's heart pounded. Eyes frantic and fearful, Sam dove into the nearest office and hid behind the door. An enormous shadow rushed past Sam's hiding place and barged into the professor's office.

"Master Marius." Plummet stuttered. "Great news! I think I found the satellite that-"

"Shut up!" The Grand Master interrupted. "You know why I'm here."

"W-well … I'm not sure exactly-"

"Don't lie to me!" Marius spat. Sam's body stiffened. "Raven remained silent for eight years. Why would he surface now, in Caerule of all places?"

"I don't know wh-"

"The test!" Marius slammed something on the professor's desk with a loud thud. "Did you honestly think you could hide it from me?" Sam peered at the reflection in a nearby office window. Sure enough, Marius held the blackened remains of Plummet's numen tester. "It's not your job to protect students, Plummet." Marius spoke calm and cold. "Your job is to destroy the Septagon. You will help me do that, whether you want to or not."

Marius snatched the tungsten septagon from the professor's desk and stormed out of the office. He took three steps towards the elevator and stopped. He stood for a moment, teeth gritting, nostrils flared. Then, he turned towards Sam.

Sam pressed himself behind the door. He clamped his eyes shut, struggling to suppress his numen. Marius entered the room, brushing against the door as he passed. Sam felt the heated rasp of the Grand Master's breath on the other side of the door. Marius reached for the light switch. Sam forced a sliver of numen to his index finger and severed the circuit just in time. Marius flicked the switch several times. Nothing. Marius glared around the office and left in the direction of the elevators.

When the sound of the descending elevator reached Sam's ears, he heaved a sigh of relief. Shivers ran up and down his body. His hairs stood on end. Sam crept from his hiding place, slipped past the professor's office and weaved through the dark corridors until he reached the bottom floors of the command center.

All the offices, including Peter's, were empty. Sam bit his lip as he scanned the vacant passageways and cryptic cellars. It was worse than he thought. Everyone must be in the war room.

Sam ran to the end of the hall. He forced open the door of Patricia Rocklos's old office which doubled as the generator room. Sam sprinted past the rows of turbines to an enormous electrical box on the far wall. Fingers trembling, he ran his hand over the metal, feeling the ebb and flow of the currents. Sure enough, the wires were tungsten.

Sam pressed against the box, driving the entirety of numen into the circuitry. Useless. "No!" Sam pounded against the box. "No!" He failed a second time. Meg was counting on him. Caerule was counting on him. Sam strained against the box with all his might. Nothing. "No." Sam whimpered. He slid to the floor, held his face in his hands and started to cry.

The HVAC system rumbled to life, bombarding the room with shrill creaks and echoing rumbles. Sam stared at the corroded ducts, eyes watered and blurry. The whirring stopped and a massive wave of heat surged throughout the room. Sam brushed the tears from his eyes. He had a plan.

Chapter 15 – Central Powerless

Meg Alumen

One minute the bold white pillars of Central shone, tall, proud and invincible; the next: darkness. The blackout tore across the island, grinding the gears of war to an abrupt and total halt. Meg breathed a sigh of relief. Sam did it.

Meg switched her Boatbot to manual and veered away from the docks. She channeled numen to her hand, absorbed radiation from the overhead floodlights and melted the filaments with a single slash. The Boatbot neared the treacherous shore and faded into the shadows of Central.

Meg's eyes glowed with numen as she shifted her vision to infrared. She weaved between the sunken rocks and beached the Boatbot at the nearest shoal. Meg removed her boots, tied them together and flung them over her shoulder. She rolled up her pant legs and reengaged the Boatbot's autopilot. The craft squirmed and whined, trying to break free from the sandbar. Meg jumped into the shallow water, waded ashore and pushed the Boatbot's bow into the river. The robot paused for a moment to recalculate its course, and then sped around the rocks in the direction of the Central docks.

Meg refitted her boots as soon as she reached dry ground, carefully watching the waterline. Sure enough; low tide. She didn't need to cover her tracks. Soon, the entire sandbar would be underwater. Meg crept along the shoreline, past the remains of the Helena Bridge and through the crumbling forum.

No sooner had her feet touched the cobblestones, Meg heard the faint whirr of an approaching Boatbot. Heart pounding, she wheeled towards the river. Darkness. Meg's thoughts raced to her own Boatbot. Had she programmed it wrong? The whirring stopped. Meg's eyes widened in realization.

Scrambling across the shattered limestone, Meg dove behind the wreckage of the rotting wooden stage. She channeled her numen, adapting her refractive index until she was completely invisible. Meg's breaths shortened. Who could have followed her?

A dark figure rose from the river, blacker than the night, holding what appeared to be a gun. Lakon? A familiar chill ran down Meg's spine. No. Not Lakon. The figure stopped on the edge of the forum, scanning the crumbling ruins. Its face turned towards the stage and Meg, once again, felt the bloodthirsty stare of unknown eyes. How? The figure strode towards Meg, murderous numen seeping from its body. No escape.

"LODON!" A furious shout echoed through the cold, still air. Meg wheeled. Master Marius stormed across the forum, eyes burning with rage. Meg turned back to the river. Nothing. The figure faded into the darkness, leaving no trace but the sinking fear in Meg's heart. Marius stomped to the courthouse, slamming the glass door behind him, shattering it into countless jagged shards.

Meg raced after him. Marius was dangerous, but in darkness death was certain. That thing wanted blood and somewhere, this night, would find it. Meg shuddered at the thought. She ducked through the shattered door frame, tip-toed across the fragmented glass and followed Marius along the damp, twisting halls towards the detention center. When he arrived, Marius proceeded to the first interrogation room and flung the door open. BANG! Meg barely managed to slip inside before the door slammed shut.

On the other side of the one-way mirror, Peter wheeled towards the noise, almost knocking the gas lantern off the metal table. Admiral Lodon remained unfazed. She sat across from Peter, handcuffed to a steel chair. Marius snatched an extra lantern from a nearby shelf and proceeded through the second door, Meg following close behind. He slammed the lantern on the table and glared at Admiral Lodon.

"What did you do?" Marius snarled.

"Plummet went to check the generators-" Peter began.

"Not you!" Marius interrupted without taking his eyes off Lodon. "Her!"

Admiral Lodon remained silent. Her eyes locked with Marius, burning with a vicious hatred that sent shivers down Meg's spine. Marius returned the glare. Cold, hard and callous, he met the Admiral's gaze, watching her every move.

"I'm sorry, sir." Peter hesitated before breaking the silence. "She hasn't said a word."

"Is that so?" Marius's lip curled. "Then perhaps it's time we tried 'alternative' methods."

"Sir?" Peter's face fell.

"I'll get authorization." Marius directed Peter without looking at him. "Find Plummet and demand an update. I want Central up and running within the hour. Go!"

"Yes, sir!" Peter stammered. He fled the room and sprinted down the hall. Marius grinned as the door clicked shut.

"We found your satellite." He leered across the table. "Did you honestly think this power failure would stop us? You of all people should know: the tides of war cannot be stopped. Your navy will destroy that satellite or I will hang every one of them for treason." Lodon's eyelid twitched. "There it is." Marius laughed. "I always wondered which was stronger: your discipline or that untamed rage. You can't hide anything from me. I will break you, Lodon; and then I will destroy the Septagon once and for all." He turned to leave.

"Marius!" Admiral Lodon's voice cut through the air. Marius wheeled to face her. "If you could choose between saving Caerule or destroying the Septagon, which would you choose?"

"Easy." Marius smirked. "I would destroy the Septagon, no question."

"How sad." Admiral Lodon shook her head. Marius snarled and stormed from the room. His angry stomping faded into the distance.

"What do you want, Alumen?" Admiral Lodon looked towards her. Meg's heart jumped.

"How did you-?" Meg turned visible.

"Don't waste my time!" Admiral Lodon snapped. "What do you want?"

"The truth." Meg met the Admiral's daunting stare.

"And why do you think you'll find it here?" Admiral Lodon's voice was bitter and untrusting.

"Because." Meg sat across from Admiral Lodon. "You're the one person in Central I know to be innocent." Lodon's eyes locked with Meg, cold, hard and unflinching.

"Go on." She spoke after a long pause.

"Everything points to you." Meg started to ramble. With all the luck and preparation to reach this point, she had not dared hope for this moment, let alone plan for it. "The bridge, the forum, Aprilis PD; each attack required inside knowledge and a severe hatred of Central. You had both; opportunity and motive. Patricia's blood on your sword just provided the evidence-"

"Get to the point!" Lodon spat.

"One thing doesn't make sense: Birnam." Meg continued. "You'd never trust anyone that much, least of all a numen user." The Admiral remained silent. She leaned back in her chair, watching Meg with unsettling scrutiny.

"You're smart, Alumen." Admiral Lodon frowned after a long pause. "Far smarter than anyone gives you credit for."

"Still, I don't understand." Meg pressed. "You knew you were being framed and you did not resist. Worse; you remained silent. Why?"

"Isn't it obvious?" Lodon's jaw tightened. "The culprit was in that room. Any protest from me would have given information to the enemy."

"Then you know who it is?" Meg leaned forward.

"No."

"Do you know who it's not?"

"No."

"But you must know!" Meg's face paled. "There was such a short time-window. Who had access to your sword?"

"No one!" Admiral Lodon insisted. "From the time Rocklos died to the time Plummet examined it, that sword never left my side."

The lights switched on and a small overhead camera whirred to life. Lodon lunged forward and struck Meg's face with a vicious head-butt. Meg fell to the floor, blood pouring from her nose. The Admiral towered over her, straining against the handcuffs.

"Serves you right, you pathetic numen user." Admiral Lodon snarled. "I'll never tell you a God-damn thing." Footsteps thundered from the hall. Now Meg understood. Lodon was saving her. Marius burst through the door, followed closely by General Bell.

"You!" Marius grabbed Meg's neck and pinned her against the wall. Blood spewed across his pearl-white robes. "What are you doing here?"

"Interrogating a prisoner." Meg choked as Marius's hand tightened around her throat.

"On whose authority?" Marius snarled.

"Mine." Peter burst into the room. Marius's grip slackened and Meg fell to the floor, coughing. "Are you alright?" Peter knelt at her side.

"Yes." Meg gasped. "I think so."

"You had no right-" Marius began.

"No, you had no right!" Peter spat at Marius and pointed towards Admiral Lodon. "That woman murdered my mentor. Did you honestly think I would leave her unguarded?"

"Did you find anything?" General Bell asked, but retreated into the corner after a hostile glare from Marius.

"Does it look like I found anything?" Meg wiped blood from her nose. Marius glared around the room, the soft glint of the security camera catching eye. He stared at the blinking green light, dumbfounded. Then, he turned towards Meg.

Chapter 15 – Central Powerless

"Where's Sam?" Marius spat, a vicious snarl twisting across his mouth. Meg's face paled. Sam stood in the doorway, eyes wide with terror.

"With me." Peter turned to face Marius. "I couldn't find Plummet, so I asked Sam here for help. As you can see." Peter gestured to the overhead lights. "I think I made the right decision."

"Those wires are made of tungsten are they not?" Marius glared at Sam. Sam's breaths shortened.

"Actually, sir." Peter continued. "The failure started from the HVAC system in my office. I told you countless times we had to get it fixed. If not for Sam here, we might never have gotten the power back."

"Is that right?" Marius continued to watch Sam with vicious scrutiny. "Then I suppose thanks are in order." The Grand Master extended his hand. Sam hesitated before shaking it. "Peter! Bell!" Marius snapped and turned to leave. "Let's go. We have a war to plan."

"Yes, sir." General Bell followed him. Peter remained behind with Meg.

"Don't worry." Meg winced as she rubbed the bruises on her neck. "I'm fine."

"I know you are." Peter snapped. "Get up!"

"Peter, I-" Meg rose to her feet.

"Not here." Peter glared at Lodon. "You. Sam. Hallway. Now!" Peter stormed from the room. Meg and Sam followed him into the hall. Peter severed the nearest security camera with a barrier blade and wheeled to face them, eyes burning with rage. "What the hell were you thinking?"

"I can explain-" Meg began.

"Explain what?" Peter fumed. "How you disobeyed a direct order? How you cut power to our military headquarters? How you met with a traitor who murdered Patricia less than four hours ago? What did Lodon tell you anyways?" Meg opened her mouth to speak, but hesitated. Peter's eyes burned with irrational fury. Would he even listen?

"Nothing." Meg lied.

"Nothing?" Peter shook his head. "How can I trust you if you won't trust me?"

"Sir, I-"

"I don't want to hear it!" Peter spat. "You and Sam committed treason today and I covered for you. Next time..." Peter bit his lip. "Next time, I won't." He turned away and strode down the hall in the direction of the war room. Meg stared at the floor.

"Meg." Sam began. "I'm sorry-"

"Don't apologize." Meg sat against the wall. "You did well; better than I could have hoped."

"And Lodon?" Sam pressed. "Did she really say nothing?"

"Not exactly." Meg bowed her head.

"Then why didn't you tell Peter?"

"I don't know." Meg sighed. "I didn't think he would listen."

"What?" Sam gritted his teeth in frustration. "Everything we did; everything will be wasted if Peter doesn't get that information. Plummet found the satellite. They're going to shoot it down unless-"

"Plummet found it?" Meg's eyes narrowed.

"Well…yeah." Sam cast Meg a quizzical glance. "Who else?"

"Stay here." Meg leapt to her feet and ran after Peter. "Watch Admiral Lodon. Someone may try to kill her."

"What?" Sam's face paled.

"Just watch her!" Meg shouted and continued running. There was no time to argue. Was she already too late?

Meg reached the war room just in time to hear the door click shut. Damn! Meg grit her teeth. Outside, Peter might have listened. In there, nothing was certain. Sam was right. She should have told Peter. Meg pressed forward and barged into the war room.

"We have to act now-" Marius turned away from President Millenavis. "Alumen!"

"Meg!" Peter jumped from his chair.

"Sir." Meg ignored both of them and addressed the President directly. "There's been a mistake, please don't do this."

"Uh…what?" President Millenavis bobbled his folder, spilling confidential files across the table. Meg channeled numen to her eyes and scanned whatever documents she could.

"Get out!" Marius fumed, grabbing her by the arm. Meg wrenched herself free.

"Sir." Meg snatched a loose paper from the table. "That satellite has payloads from all seven Great Nations, including ours. Please, sir, don't shoot it down."

"What?" General Bell flipped through his own file. He stared at the diagram, hand resting on the page.

"Enough!" Marius towered over Meg, blocking her path. "One more word and I'll throw you in that cell with Lodon."

"Why don't we have a vote?" Millenavis beamed an awkward smile entirely inappropriate for the situation.

"What?" Marius's face paled. Meg heaved a sigh of relief. President Millenavis never could resist democracy. It was the only thing he was good at.

"Great idea, sir." Meg stepped forward. "I vote: no."

"You don't get a vote." Marius snarled. "You're not supposed to be here."

"Agreed." President Millenavis nodded before Meg could protest. "Marius, how do you vote?"

"Yes, of course!" Marius stared at him, dumbfounded by the turn of events.

"Great!" Millenavis made a small tally mark with his pen. "General Bell?"

"No." General Bell breathed, still staring at the page.

"Bell!" Marius shouted. General Bell jolted his attention away from the files.

"No!" General Bell repeated, more forceful than before. "I'm with Meg. Don't shoot it down."

"What?" Marius stared at General Bell, eyes wide with shock.

"One for, one against!" President Millenavis checked another tally, excited by the turn of events. "That just leaves Peter."

Peter remained silent. He flipped through his binder, reading every word. The room watched and waited. At last, he reached the final page.

"Please, sir-" Meg pleaded as Peter closed the book.

"Marius." Peter ignored her. "Plummet was certain of these calculations?"

"Yes." Marius nodded, breaths short and shallow.

"Very well." Peter turned to President Millenavis. "I vote: yes. Shoot it down."

"No." Meg's body stiffened.

"Two for, one against!" President Millenavis checked the last tally with an unnecessary flourish and began punching codes into his laptop.

"Peter…" Meg's lip trembled with frustration and pain. "…Why?"

"I'm sorry Meg." Peter sighed and shook his head. "I just can't trust you." The display screen flicked on and an image of the satellite came into focus.

"I'm sorry too." Meg turned to leave.

"Where are you going?"

"To find someone I can trust." Meg flung open the war room door. "Before it's too late." She strode into the dark bowels of Central as the satellite exploded in a violent flash of light.

Chapter 16 – Hunter and Hunted

James Lakon

Abraham Panzer was being hunted. As soon as he entered his apartment, he double bolted the door and pressed his eye against the peephole. Bump-Bump. His feral heart pounded against his chest, panicked and uncertain.

Grunting, Abraham pulled away from the door and switched the Fenestravision to the building's security cameras. His tail flicked back and forth. His eyes scanned the screens, searching for his phantom pursuer. He watched and waited. Bump-Bump.

Eyes fixed on the screens, Abraham withdrew a sandwich and beer from the argon refrigerator. His senses bristled, so focused on the unseen enemy he did not notice the blinking red light on the refrigerator door. The oxygen sensor had been severed. Bump-Bump.

Abraham carried his meal to a small table in the center of the room. He watched the Fenestravision as he ate. His eyes darted between screens with increasing frequency. The enemy was close. But, once again, Abraham had underestimated. Bump-Bump.

A sharp hiss emanated from the bedroom. Abraham leapt from his chair and ran for the exit. He unbolted the door and grabbed the handle, but a cold voice stopped him in his tracks.

"Run if you want." James Lakon emerged from the bedroom, eyes hard and callous. "Either way you're already dead."

"Oh!" Abraham laughed. "It's only you." Grinning, he released the handle, his last and only chance of escape. He wheeled to face Lakon, muscles tensed, claws poised to strike.

"I wouldn't do that if I were you." Lakon withdrew a vial of white powder from his pocket.

"What's that?" Abraham smirked.

"The antidote." Lakon sat at the opposite end of the table. "To the poison you just drank."

"Poison?" Abraham's laugh shook the room. "And to think we considered you a threat. I've trained my whole life to join the Septagon. I'm immune to every poison on the planet."

"Are you willing to take that chance?" Lakon rolled the vial between his hands. Abraham's smile weakened as his eyes followed the bottle back and forth.

"Even if you did poison me." Abraham's breaths shortened. "I could always take the antidote by force."

"Then why haven't you?" Lakon's eyes locked with Abraham. Abraham's face paled.

"What do you want?" Abraham's voice trembled with panic.

"The truth." Lakon glared across the table. "Sit down!" Abraham hesitated, then sat in the chair opposite Lakon. "Who do you work for?"

"I don't know his real name." Abraham stammered, eyes fixed on the vial. "No one does. Not even when he was in the war."

"Who?" Lakon feigned indifference. Curiosity was leverage and Lakon knew better than to show his.

"Raven." Abraham gulped and shuddered.

"Never heard of him." Lakon lied.

"You must have!" Abraham's eyes darted between Lakon and the vial. "He was the right hand man to God, himself. He survived the Field of Fate when God, himself, did not. He is…" Abraham squeaked. "The most dangerous man in the world."

"Then why would he need you?" Lakon faked a bored sigh.

"I don't know." Abraham shook his head. Lakon seized the vial and prepared to throw it against the wall. "I swear! I don't know." Abraham screamed and whimpered. "He calls, I go. He'd kill me if I don't. You have to believe me. Please."

Lakon hesitated, then slid the vial to Abraham. Abraham unscrewed the cap and downed the contents in one gulp. He threw the empty bottle across the room, shattering it. Abraham grinned. He rose from the chair, towering over Lakon, teeth bared to strike. "Just out of curiosity." Abraham curled his claws into fists. "How did you manage to poison me?"

"Simple." Lakon remained unfazed. "I told you it was the antidote." Before Abraham could recover from the shock, Lakon drew his revolver and fired. The tungsten bullet tore through Abraham's chest, narrowly missing his heart. Lakon fired again, but the shot ricocheted off Abraham's skin.

Abraham smashed the table aside. He grabbed Lakon by the neck and pinned him against the wall. Lakon kicked the lion-man's chest, ribs and abdomen, but Abraham did not flinch. His claws tightened, digging deeper into Lakon's throat. "I warned you." Abraham snarled. "It would take more than tungsten bullets to stop me."

Lakon felt the life being choked from him. A strange heat radiated from Abraham, strong and hostile. Lakon's legs fell limp.

Chapter 16 – Hunter and Hunted

His vision swam. The heat surged from Abraham, overwhelming everything except...

Lakon raised his revolver and fired. Abraham howled in pain. Lakon fired again. The claws loosened and Lakon fell to floor, revolver slipping from his grasp. Abraham stumbled backwards, falling to his knees. It was just as Lakon expected; both shots entered through the original bullet hole. Abraham neglected the vulnerability. No. He was no longer able to defend it.

Abraham thrust his forearm in a vicious slash. Feeble smoke puffed from his fist. Abraham repeated the motion. Nothing. Lakon scrambled to his feet. He leaned against the nearest wall, panting.

"Your power requires air. Doesn't it?" Lakon wheezed short, shallow breaths. Abraham's eyes widened. "I thought so." Lakon grinned. "Well, there's not much left, for either of us." Argon gas continued to flood the room, but Lakon could not help but lord over his defeated prey. The color drained from Abraham's face. Lakon outsmarted him and Abraham knew it.

Abraham lunged for the revolver, but Lakon was faster. He kicked Abraham across the face, breaking his nose with a satisfying CRACK! Abraham collapsed, gagging and gasping.

"Please." Abraham coughed and sputtered. "Anything."

"What's the next target?"

"They'll kill me." Abraham pleaded.

"And you think I won't?" Lakon retrieved the revolver. Tears welled in Abraham's eyes. Lakon had broken him. It felt good.

"Alright." Abraham wept into the carpet. "I'll tell you." Lakon held the gun firm, ready, waiting. "The next target is-"

Before Abraham could finish, an ominous presence surged through the room. Lakon dove to the floor just in time. The wall exploded. A vicious heat seared over his head. The blast struck Abraham, tearing through his blood-stained chest. Abraham fell, eyes wide with terror.

Lakon stumbled through the rubble and pressed himself against the splintered remains of the wall. He squinted through the dust. A dark figure stood on the opposite building, holding its hand in the shape of a gun. Lakon raised his revolver. CLICK! The hammer struck the empty chamber, useless and futile. Lakon grabbed another bullet from his belt; too late. The figure was gone, vanished into the cold, dark night.

"Lakem!" A weak voice coughed from the rubble. Lakon waved through the soot and smoke to find Abraham, legs crushed beneath mounds of shattered brick, chest impaled by a rebar rod.

"You're still alive." Lakon's eyes darkened. Thunder boomed in the distance and rain poured through the gaping roof.

"Lakem, please." Abraham begged, his once proud mane stained with blood. "I don't want to die alone." Cold air rushed through the room, purging the remaining argon.

"Okay." Lakon sat on the rubble next to Abraham and began reloading his revolver. "I'll stay with you until the end."

"Thank you." Abraham wept, tears mixing with the rain. "I'm sorry…for everything."

"I'm sorry too." Lakon avoided eye contact.

"I never wanted to be a monster." Abraham sobbed. "People always used me for my strength, but I would have given anything to be smart like you. All I ever wanted was to be part of something greater than myself, to make a difference in this world, to be treated as human."

"It wasn't poison." Lakon bowed his head.

"What?" Abraham wheezed.

"The vial." Lakon bowed his head. "It was a sedative. I wanted to take you alive." Lakon finished reloading the revolver. Thunder boomed a second time.

"I see." Abraham forced a weak smile. "I guess, in the end, you were the only one who ever cared about me."

"You don't know anything, do you?" Lakon sighed. Abraham whimpered, ashamed to answer the question. "It's okay. Save your breath."

Abraham writhed, forcing the rod deeper into his chest. He jammed his broken hand into his pocket and withdrew a blood-stained metal shard. Lakon recognized it immediately. It was the tungsten fragment he had given Meg. Abraham lifted the fragment as high as he could and placed it in Lakon's outstretched hand.

"It's all I have." Abraham cried. "Please let me be useful to someone."

"Meg?" Lakon stared at the metal in disbelief. He trusted Meg. How did Abraham get this fragment? The wheels turned in Lakon's mind. Meg was leading Central's investigation. She was at every attack. She was the only one who knew where the fragment was located.

"I have one last question." Lakon's fist tightened around the tungsten shard. "When Raven uses his power, does he hold his hand in the shape of a gun?"

"Yes." Abraham nodded, eyes red with tears.

"I see." Lakon rose to his feet. "I'm sorry I lied."

"About what?"

"About wanting to take you alive." A final gunshot tore through the night, masked by the booming thunder.

Chapter 17 – Betrayal

Sam Pere

"You might want to wait in the Carbot." Meg sighed as they pulled up to the broken apartment building. She leaned her head against the window and gazed weary-eyed at the superstructure.

"I can handle it." Sam opened the Carbot door and stepped outside. Meg shook her head, but did not press further. When they arrived at the apartment, Peter was waiting for them, arms crossed.

"Hell of a crime scene in there." His eyes locked with Meg's. "Bastard was poisoned twice and crushed beneath a wall before Lakon shot him in the head."

"You seem sure it was Lakon." Meg tried to walk past him, but Peter blocked her path.

"Who else could it be, Alumen?" Peter's face twisted with rage. "We have Fenestravision footage of him leaving the building!" Peter jabbed several buttons on the blood-stained remote in his hand. Nothing. "Goddamn it! Who set this thing to manual?"

"Do you mind if I take a look?" Meg's voice was blunt but tired. Peter stepped aside, inviting Meg with an exaggerated gesture. Sam followed close behind.

As soon as they entered, Sam gagged at the ungodly stench. The crucible of toxins infesting Abraham's corpse accelerated the decomposition process. The room smelled of death. Leah stood in the opposite corner, examining a severed wire from the apartment's oxygen sensor. Sam scrambled over the rubble to join her.

"Anything interesting?" He whispered.

"No." Leah whispered back. "I wanted to get away from that smell."

"Me too." Sam nodded. "We could check the other room if you want."

"The smell's not the only thing I'm avoiding." Leah glanced towards the corpse. Meg examined the body, writing notes on a small pad. Peter loomed over her, bitter scowl on his face.

"How long has Peter been like that?" Sam turned back to Leah.

"Don't know." Leah returned her attention to the wire. "He hasn't said a word to me and rages at everyone else." Peter glared in their direction. Sam averted his gaze.

"Find anything?" Peter frowned at Meg.

"Not yet." Meg remained unfazed.

"Fine." Peter scowled at the rotting corpse. "Tell me when you do. We need to know everything about his and Lakon's relationship?"

"Relationship?" Meg repeated with a dull sigh. "Didn't know they had one."

"He tricked Abraham into drinking poison." Peter snarled. "Only a friend could do that."

"Or an enemy." Meg rose to leave.

"He lied to you, Meg." Peter stood in her way. "Don't let feelings cloud your judgement."

"Look who's talking." Meg muttered.

Chapter 17 – Betrayal

"What was that?" Peter fumed.

"You heard me!" Meg scribbled a final line on her notepad. Sam and Leah held their breath. "I agree with Peter's assessment. James Lakon is our primary suspect in the death of Abraham Panzer."

"Good." Peter nodded. "Plummet will be glad to hear it."

"Plummet?" Meg cast Peter a quizzical glance. "He's here?"

"Found it!" Professor Plummet's overexcited voice rang from the bedroom. He burst through the door carrying the shattered remains of an argon canister. "That Lakon fellow is something else. I bet Abraham never saw this coming. Oh! Hi Meg." Plummet extended his hand.

"Who arrived at the scene first?" Meg hesitated.

"Oh! That would be me." Plummet smiled and shrugged. "I live in the building across the street." He pointed through the shattered wall to the neighboring apartment complex. Meg's face hardened. "Uh…Meg?"

"Sam." Meg strode to the door. "We're leaving."

"Err…What?" Sam looked at her, confused. Peter's eyes narrowed.

"You heard me. Let's go." Meg continued walking.

"Err…Right behind you." Sam called after her before turning back to Leah. "Sorry. I'll…We'll catch up later." He chased after Meg, sprinting down the stairwell. He finally reached her on the ground floor. "Okay." Sam huffed in annoyance. "You have to tell me what's going on." Meg scanned the upper floors for pursuers, then pulled Sam behind the bottommost staircase.

"Did any of that seem strange to you?" Meg demanded.

"Yes." Sam grinned. "But you're my sister, so I'm used to it by now."

"I meant the crime scene!"

"Oh…." Sam puzzled. "Well the rotting lion corpse was a bit unusual."

"Besides that!" Meg fumed. "The bullets and poison could have been Lakon, but that wall was destroyed by a numen user."

"Maybe it was Abraham." Sam offered.

"No" Meg shook her head. "The apartment imploded. That blast came from the outside."

"Okay…" Sam raised his eyebrows. Where was Meg going with this? "And that means what, exactly?"

"Don't you think it's strange that one person handled the all the evidence in this case?"

"Well…yeah!" Sam nodded. "I warned you about Lakon from the start."

"Not Lakon."

"Okay?" Sam watched Meg, concerned. "Well, he is our prime suspect."

"Why didn't I see it sooner?" Meg cursed under her breath. "Al is dead, Sinon left and Lakon's missing. Only one person is left investigating the case and only one person had access to both crime labs."

"Professor Plummet?" Sam's cast Meg a quizzical glance. "Surely you don't think-"

Chapter 17 – Betrayal

"I do." Meg's eyes radiated a cold certainty made Sam uneasy. "I read the witness statements for Patricia's murder. Plummet claimed to be getting thermal test equipment at the time, but that equipment was already in lab. In fact, it's permanently stationed there."

"Maybe it was an oversight." Sam stammered, desperate to change the subject.

"Plummet wouldn't forget something he uses daily." Meg shook her head. "Besides, you're missing the point. Plummet getting equipment isn't unusual. What's suspicious is he didn't return with any."

"Please, Meg." Sam begged. "Don't do this again."

"One thing does not make sense." Meg ignored him, pacing back and forth. "Lodon's sword. No one had access to it after Patricia's death. The tests could have been faked, but that blood was real."

"Because she was lying!" Sam snapped, failing to maintain his composure. "She and Lakon have been lying to you from the start. Lodon murdered General Rocklos. That's why her blood was on the sword." Meg did not react to Sam's outburst. She stared past him, towards the exit where a large poster was taped against the door.

"What's this?" Meg brushed past Sam and tore the poster from the door.

"It's nothing." Sam read the poster over Meg's arm. "Central held a blood drive yesterday. That's one of the announcements."

"Who ran it?" Meg demanded.

"Professor Plummet." Sam answered without thinking. Meg's eyes glowed with newfound intensity. Sam realized his mistake. "No, Meg. Please, don't."

"This is it." Meg brandished the poster. "Plummet had the General's blood before the murder. He planted it on the Admiral's sword before he murdered the General. It all fits."

"No it doesn't." Sam pleaded. "You're ignoring the evidence because you want to believe Lakon's innocence."

"He is innocent." Meg insisted.

"No he's not." Sam countered. "He lied about the projectile fragment. He met Raven on the roof of his apartment. He probably murdered Abraham and is plotting revenge against God knows who. Stick to the plan, Meg." Sam continued, rage building. "If you stuck to the plan this case would be solved already. If you stuck to the plan, General Rocklos would still be alive. If you stuck to the plan, mom and dad wouldn't-" Meg slapped him across the face.

"I'm sorry." Meg's eyes widened in horror. "I didn't mean…"

"No." Sam turned away. "You meant it. And so did I." They stared at the floor. Silence remained an impenetrable wall between them.

"You're right." Meg spoke after a long pause. "My theory is biased, unlikely, and I have no evidence to support it. But, on faith alone, I trust it. Lakon is innocent. Of that much, I am certain."

"And how do you plan to prove it?" Sam's face darkened, afraid to know the answer.

"We have to ask Lakon ourselves." Meg looked towards the door.

"You know where he is?" Sam bowed his head. It was worse than he thought.

"I think so." Meg nodded. "If he's alive, I know where he'll be." Meg strode through the door, determined and resolute.

"I'm sorry, Meg." Sam whispered under his breath. He turned to follow her but, behind his back, Sam activated the homing beacon of his Wrist-Pro.

Chapter 18 – Culprit Realized

Meg Alumen

Light is the harbinger of entropy. Meg strode between the fog-wrapped ruins of the Helena Bridge, beckoned by the soft glow of the Aprilis Lighthouse. Embracing the radiance, she could see the opposite shore; the bold pillars of Central; the white marble fountain wreathed with roses. Sight is strange like that. The future shines so bright the present remains blind.

If Meg had been watching, she might have noticed the yellow toolbox, jutting from the uneven snow. She might have noticed the blood-stained footprints creeping fast behind her. She might have noticed that Sam was no longer following. Meg continued towards the light, inching closer to the edge.

"Meg!" Sam screamed through the fog, a high-pitched screech followed by silence. Meg ran towards the noise. Nothing else mattered; not the case; not Caerule; not even herself. Meg charged through the fog without thinking to use her numen.

"Sam!" Meg found him. Sam shivered in the snow, handcuffed to a steel cable. His eyes widened as Meg approached.

"Meg! No! It's a trap!" Sam clanged the tungsten handcuffs, too late. Meg felt the cold kiss of a gun barrel press against her cheek.

"Don't use it." Lakon spoke calm and cold. "If you use it, I'll know."

"Lakon?" Meg instinctively began channeling numen. A hand seized her neck and pinned her against an overturned Carbot.

"I said don't use it!" Lakon pressed the gun harder. Meg's numen faded.

"It was you." Meg breathed, desperate to hide her fear. "You killed Abraham."

"Are you with them?" Lakon's glare burned with indiscriminate rage.

"I know you're innocent." Meg rambled. "Plummet handled the evidence. He had the General's blood. He's been manipulating us-"

"Shut up!" Lakon released his grip on Meg's neck and withdrew a round tungsten fragment from his pocket. "Are you with them?" Meg's eyes widened in realization.

"It was you!" Sam writhed against the tungsten handcuffs. Even with his numen suppressed, steam spewed from the icy pavement. "It was you all along!" The cables strained and snapped, showering the bridge with sparks.

"Enough!" Lakon cocked the revolver. Meg smelled the awful stench of fresh-burnt gunpowder. Sam's face paled. The ice stopped melting. The cables stopped shaking. Sam's breaths froze in the cold, unmoving air.

"Sam." Meg struggled to suppress her fear. "Don't worry. It'll be alright. I promise." Sam gave a frightened nod, tears welling in his eyes.

"Are you with them?" Lakon repeated, holding the fragment in his palm.

"No." Meg met Lakon's gaze. All the anger; all the sorrow; all the fighting, fear and failure melted. She could see Lakon's soul as sure as he could see hers. Both were lost; both confused; both were trapped, scared and helpless.

"Sorry." Lakon sighed and lowered the revolver. "I had to be sure." He pulled a small key from around his neck and tossed it to Sam.

"Did you solve the case?" Meg pressed, curiosity overpowering her momentary relief. "Do you know who's behind this?"

"No." Lakon shook his head. "But I think you might. That masked man, the man in black, he-"

"You!" A dark figure charged past Meg and tackled Lakon into the fog.

"James!" Meg screamed. She heard Lakon gag and gasp for breath. Meg followed the sounds of struggle. She swatted through the mist focusing the fading light to her palm. She found the figure straddling Lakon's chest. "Don't move." Meg aimed at the figure's head, holding her hand in the shape of a gun. It was Peter.

"Stay out of this, Alumen!" Peter spat. Blood red barriers extended from his hands in sharp blades. Lakon writhed in panic, sensing the danger, but unable to see the source.

"Please, sir. Don't make me do this." Meg's voice was firm, but her numen flickered with uncertainty. Peter tightened his grip. Lakon stopped resisting.

"I'm sorry, Meg." Peter raised his blade. "This is for your own good."

"No!" Light erupted from Meg's hand. The blade swung. Two screams split the air. Two bodies fell to the cold ground. Blood stained the snow.

Meg's eyes welled with tears. Had she gone too far? Had she not gone far enough? Had she lost them both? Meg prayed for some sign of life. Lakon moved first.

Staggering to his feet, Lakon retrieved his revolver from the snow. He clutched his neck, still bleeding where Peter's numen grazed him.

"Don't move." Lakon pointed the gun at Peter, hands trembling.

"Of all people!" Peter glared at Meg, slamming his fist into the ice. "I never thought you for a traitor."

"I said: don't move." Lakon winced, struggling to steady the revolver.

"Freeze!" Leah emerged from the mist, holding a Carbot-sized icicle in her hand. She glared at Lakon, poised to strike.

"Drop it!" Meg aimed at her. Even without the fog, Meg doubted if she could stop Leah. Nevertheless, Leah hesitated. Meg heaved a sigh of relief, too soon. A burning pain surged through Meg's back. She fell to the snow, arms and legs quivering. Meg's vision swam into focus. "Sam?"

"I'm sorry Meg." Sam stood over Meg, electricity arcing between his fingers. Tears welled in his eyes as he fastened the tungsten handcuffs around Meg's wrists, locking them with a soft click. "It's over."

"Good work Agent Pere!" Peter nodded. Lakon backed towards the edge of the bridge, eyes searching for his next move. "What are you going to do?" Peter goaded. "Jump?"

"You'd love that wouldn't you?" Lakon spat. "One more victim for this monument of death." Blood red blades extended from Peter's arms. Lakon raised his revolver.

"STOP!" Meg wrenched away from Sam and flung herself between Peter and Lakon. Both hesitated. Meg turned to Lakon. "James. Before, when you pointed your gun at me, when you thought I was responsible; why did you think that? Was it the fragment or something else?"

"Stand aside Meg." Peter snarled. Meg ignored him.

"James, please." Meg begged. "Trust me."

"It wasn't the only reason." Lakon continued to watch Peter.

"What was it?" Meg pressed. "Tell me."

"The masked man, the man in black." Lakon met Meg's gaze. "He moves just like you, holding his hand in the shape of a gun."

"But I learned that technique from…" Meg's eyes widened in terror. The color drained from Peter's face. A cold wind tore across the bridge as Meg spoke the name: "Sinon."

"It can't be." Peter's numen faded. He stared into the fog, eyes wide and vacant. "It can't be." Peter walked to the edge of the bridge and stared into the blackened river. His feet teetered on the edge as he gazed upon the death and destruction.

"Sir?" Leah's eyes widened. Peter did not respond. Meg watched in horror as he began to lean forward.

"Peter!" Meg yelled. Peter jolted at the sound of Meg's voice. He shivered and stepped back from the edge.

"I don't get it." Lakon sat against an overturned Carbot. "If none of you told him, how did he know?"

"Sinon can read minds." Peter sat next to Lakon, head bowed. "He's been playing us from the start. Why didn't I see it sooner?"

"But what about Admiral Lodon?" Meg asked.

"We went to the blood drive before visiting you." Peter bowed his head. "We ran into Admiral Lodon shortly afterwards. He did it right in front of me." Peter reached into his pocket. Lakon flinched. Peter withdrew an Accretion Bar, broke it, and handed the white chocolate half to Lakon.

"So what now?" Lakon hesitated before accepting the bar. Meg sat on the other side of Lakon. Sam and Leah rushed to join them.

"Now?" Peter ate the chocolate calm and slow. "I suppose, we fight." Meg stared across the water towards Aprilis University. Sinon would be facing the combined might of Central and the Caerulean Navy. Not even Raven, himself, could withstand such an onslaught. Meg shivered in the thickening fog. Why was she still so afraid?

Chapter 19 – Confrontation

Peter Turnus

"Do not underestimate him!" Peter warned the perimeter team. The line was four units deep, surrounding Prometheus Hall in a 500 meter arc. Tanks blocked the roads. Destroyers patrolled the coast. The monotonous beating of helicopter rotors reverberated through the sky.

"We should take him now!" General Bell scanned the host of agents and naval units converging on Aprilis University. "If we wait any longer, we'll lose the element of surprise."

"He already knows." Peter stared at the large glass doors. The sky darkened and lightning flashed in the distance.

"All the more reason to go now!" General Bell glanced towards the nearest railgun battery where Meg, Sam, Leah and Tom were waiting. "The six of us are more than enough to take him."

"Alright." Peter glanced around the perimeter team again. It would have to do. "Let's go!"

"Yes, sir!" Sam and Leah advanced. Meg and Tom hesitated.

"Tom! Go!" The General hobbled towards the building, cane scraping along the ground. Tom stared after Sam and Leah for a moment, then bowed his head and followed his father's lead. Meg remained behind.

"Any word of the sword?" She cast a nervous glance towards Peter.

Chapter 19 – Confrontation

"No." Peter shook his head. "I assume Birnam has it, wherever she is."

"Right." Meg forced an unconvinced nod and hurried after Sam.

"I should go too." Lakon watched Meg leave, eyes grim with worry.

"No!" Peter insisted, turning to face Lakon. "We've been over this. You can't even see numen. You'll only get in the way." Lakon frowned, unsatisfied by the answer. "Besides." Peter placed his hand on Lakon's shoulder. "I need someone out here I can trust."

"Fine." Lakon retreated behind the sandbag wall, but continued to watch Meg, nervous and concerned. "But if you want to take your friend alive, don't let him get to me."

"Whatever." Peter shook his head and ran to regroup with the others.

"Meg?" General Bell asked as they approached the gleaming entryway. "If you don't mind me asking, why do you care about that sword so much?"

"You mean besides the fact it was used to frame Admiral Lodon?" Meg raised her eyebrows.

"Well, yeah."

"I don't know." Meg sighed and glanced towards the approaching ships. "I guess because it's a reminder of what Caerule is. Our country was founded on the principles of truth, loyalty and justice. That sword represents everyone who fought for that dream. Now, I guess, it's our turn."

"Well said, Meg." Peter led the way, throwing open the glass doors. His determination turned to fear as soon as he saw the students' reaction. There wasn't one. The activities inside Prometheus hall remained undisturbed. Some students pointed to the tanks and ships before returning to their books. Others paid no attention and just kept reading. Sinon's sickening sweet voice echoed from the lecture hall, cheerful, captivating and composed.

Meg and Sam positioned themselves by the far entrance. General Bell and Tom took the near entrance. Peter joined Leah in the middle. Peter gave a quick nod and all three teams entered.

"There's not much time." Sinon continued teaching the students. He was wearing the same black outfit during his rooftop meeting with Lakon; this time without the mask. "But, before I go, I want to teach you about a subject near and dear to my heart." Peter walked down the central aisle, one cautious step at a time. "Who here knows what an ideal system is?" Several hands shot up. "Yes, Ben." Sinon pointed to one of the students.

"An ideal system transfers energy without a change in entropy."

"Correct." Sinon smiled at the student. Peter recognized the expression immediately: pride. "An ideal system is the pinnacle of physics. All energy is conserved. No loss. No waste. No entropy. An ideal system is simple, efficient and predictable. It is the ultimate goal of mankind." A chill ran down Peter's spine. The combined forces of Caerule were hunting him and Sinon was more concerned about his lecture.

"How many of you lost family in The Great War?" Sinon's smile faded. Several of the students raised their hands. "I'm sorry." Sinon sighed. "I lost friends too; before the war; during the war; after the war..." A tear rolled down Sinon's cheek. Peter could almost see the boy who saved his life so many years ago; the brave child who remained strong when Peter couldn't; the loyal friend who always stood by Peter's side. "And even now…" Sinon's eyes locked with Peter's. Peter looked away. Sinon always played mind games with his opponents, but this was too genuine. Peter's numen trembled. Meg flashed him a concerned look.

"As you know, an ideal system is impossible." Sinon continued to stare in Peter's direction. "There is always loss. There is always waste. There is always entropy." Peter stopped his advance. "But, I know we can do better." Sinon almost seemed to be pleading with him. "Look around you. The waste of knowledge; the waste of opportunity; the waste of human lives. All to support a system as brutal and corrupt as the nations that control it." Several students shifted uncomfortably in their seats.

"At some point you will come to realize the injustice of this world and you will have a choice." Sinon stopped and the foot of the stairs. "Fight back or perpetuate it." Peter did not meet Sinon's gaze. Sinon shook his head and retreated behind a small podium in the center of the stage. "I made my choice and I do not regret it." Sinon glanced around the room. Some students looked confused. Others were on the verge of tears. Sinon sighed again. "I'm afraid we're out of time. You've been a wonderful class. Thank you for listening." The students gathered their books and shuffled out of the classroom. Sinon leaned over the podium, head bowed. Peter clenched his fists.

"Sinon!" Peter took a step forward. "You are-"

"Save your breath, Peter." Sinon interrupted without looking. "I know why you're here."

"Then it's true?" Peter glared at his former friend.

"You already know the answer." Sinon met Peter's gaze; cold, hard and remorseless.

"I see." Barriers extended from Peter's arms in sharp blades. The light from their numen illuminated Peter's face with a ghastly red glow.

"Wait." Sinon raised his hand. "Let the students leave."

"So." Peter paused, enraged by the hypocrisy of Sinon's words. "You suddenly care about innocents?"

"I never stopped caring, Peter." Sinon remained firm, eyes glistening with uncried tears. "Do you know what it's like to be inside someone's mind as you kill them; to feel their hopes and dreams seconds before crushing them to darkness? I've always cared, Peter. And I always will."

"You murdered half a million people." Peter sprinted down the stairs. "You murdered innocent civilians." Peter advanced towards Sinon until only the podium stood between them. "You murdered our mentor in cold blood and you used me to get to her." Peter's numen writhed and twisted in anguish.

"Heh!" Sinon gave a weak laugh, brushing the tears from his eyes.

"What's so funny?" Peter spat.

"You blame me for everything, don't you?" Sinon grinned and shook his head. A thin veil of numen flowed around his body, calm and controlled. "You forget, Peter. When Patricia died, I was with you the whole time." Peter's eyes widened.

"Meg!" Sam yelled. Peter turned, too late. General Bell drew a dagger from the hilt of his cane. The blade glowed, morphed and grew. Peter recognized it immediately: the Sword of Caerule.

SLASH! A vicious surge of numen erupted from the sword in a jagged arc. The slash screamed across the room, eviscerating desks, chairs and the concrete foundation. Leah shrieked as the attack clipped her shoulder, but she was not the target. The slash charged towards Meg, shocked and defenseless. Sam lunged forward, pushing Meg out of the way, taking the full force himself.

CRACK! Peter could not tell if the noise came from Sam or the concrete. Wires, glass and rusted steel cascaded from the ceiling. Peter ran to help, but a searing blast of numen pierced his back, tearing through his chest. Peter fell to his knees.

"You should've kept your guard up." Sinon held his hand in the shape of a gun aimed at Peter's heart. Sinon fired a second blast. Peter deflected with his numen blades. A third blast caught Peter's arm. Sinon channeled numen for a fourth and final strike, but an avalanche of concrete forced him back. Peter raised his palm, creating a domed barrier above his head. Rubble rained on Peter, burying him in a slurred mix of stone, glass and dust. Peter was surrounded by darkness. Sinon cursed.

"We need to leave now!" General Bell shouted somewhere above Peter.

"He's not dead." Sinon spat.

"We can't wait any longer." The General insisted. "Admiral Lodon is on her way. We have the boy. Let's go." Sinon cursed again.

"Peter!" Sinon yelled through the rubble. "I know you can hear me! When you get out of there, do not follow us. Take Meg and Leah and go somewhere far away. I do not want to kill you, but, if I ever see you again, I will." Sinon sprinted up the stairs, leaving Peter buried and alone.

The light grew dimmer. The weight crushed heavier. The air breathed weaker. Peter closed his eyes. He had been here before. He could almost see it; a wave of debris hurtling towards him. No escape. No hope. There was only the reassurance of a young boy, a friend, saying: *"You can do this. I know you can. Trust me."* Peter heard the scraping of rock against rock. "Sinon?" Peter whispered. Was it real or only a memory? Peter felt warm relief as a great weight was lifted from him and a dazzling white light greeted his eyes.

"Found him!" Meg's hand radiated a bright glow, illuminating Peter's weakening barrier. Leah scrambled to remove the rubble crushing on the dome. The barrier faded. As the cavity collapsed, Meg and Leah reached inside and pulled Peter to safety. He fell to his knees, gasping for breath.

"We can't stay here." Leah pointed upwards. "Look." The roof of Prometheus Hall was gone. A barrage of lights danced across the sky. Gunfire boomed in the distance.

"Stay close to me." Peter rose to his feet. "No matter what happens." Meg and Leah nodded. Peter climbed over the crumbling ruins of Prometheus Hall with Meg and Leah following behind him. When he reached the top, Peter's heart sank. The battle lines had broken.

"Sam!" Meg charged down the hill. Peter looked. Sinon, General Bell and Tom clashed with the remaining regiments. Sam's unconscious body lay on the General's shoulder.

"Meg, Wait!" Peter yelled, but Meg paid no attention. The ground shook. Peter chased after her. "Meg!"

"Get down!" A dark figure darted behind a sandbag bunker and pulled Meg to the ground. A tungsten projectile struck the hillside, showering them with dirt. The man held Meg's wrist and would not let go. It was Lakon.

"They have Sam!" Meg wrenched away from Lakon. Peter rushed to Meg's side and created a barrier above their heads.

"You can't save him if you're dead." Lakon countered. Tungsten slugs rained from the sky, obliterating everything. The earth blackened. The hill trembled. The stench of melting slag filled the air. The bombardment was brutal and total. Peter winced as projectiles ricocheted off the barrier. Meg, Leah and Lakon huddled around him.

The scattered remnants of the perimeter team fell one by one. Gun batteries shattered. Helicopters crashed to earth. The last survivors surrounded Sinon in a small circular clearing, untouched by the projectiles. They fought for comrades. They fought for Caerule. They fought for lives, both theirs and others. Sinon killed them all the same.

"Miles." Lakon's face paled. One man remained. The Sergeant was unarmed and his leg was broken. Miles held his ground, the last one standing between Sinon and Aprilis. Sinon aimed his hand like a gun at Miles's heart. Miles looked at Lakon one last time. A light flashed through the darkness and Miles crumpled to the earth. "No!"

Lakon abandoned the barrier and sprinted towards the clearing. Without looking, he dodged left and right, avoiding the tungsten projectiles. Lakon never slowed down and never looked back. He charged forward, reaching the clearing without a scratch.

Sinon, Tom and General Bell continued along the shoreline, destroying everything in their path. Lakon remained alone, staring over Miles's lifeless body. The clearing closed around him. Rain fell, blurring with the projectiles. Lakon remained, silent and motionless. Then, he was gone. Peter squinted through the darkness: nothing.

The projectiles slowed and stopped. The rain withered and died. Dust settled, blanketing the bodies with soot and ash. Peter released the barrier. "It's all my fault." Peter surveyed the devastation, the waste of knowledge, the waste of opportunity, the waste of human lives. "I underestimated him."

A faint buzzing rang from Meg's Wrist-Pro. She pressed a button and Lakon's vengeful voice crackled across the line: "I found them."

Chapter 20 – War Erupts

James Lakon

Lakon crept along the edges of the dock, hiding in the long shadow of the transmission ship. Corpses of fallen sailors lay strewn across the waterfront. Sinon strode towards the gangplank, not bothering to check his surroundings. It was the General that worried Lakon. Every few steps, Bell turned with a sudden jerk, scanning the abandoned loading crates. Lakon avoided him every time, so far.

"Bell!" Sinon already climbed halfway up the gangplank. "If you're going to waste time, at least do something useful and cut the moorings." General Bell growled, shifting Sam's unconscious body to the opposite shoulder.

Lakon took advantage of the distraction. He sprinted across the dock and dove behind a pallet of explosive shells. Bell turned. His eyes rested on the pallet. Lakon exhaled, watching the General though a small gap in the munitions. Bell drew his sword. With a swift slash, the mooring lines fell. Steel cables snapped and smashed against the dock. Frayed wire rope struck the pallet, tearing a long gash in Lakon's leg. Lakon bit his lip, stifling his urge to scream. The General glared at the pallet again, then followed Sinon up the gangplank and disappeared inside the ship.

Lakon gasped in pain, leaning against the pallet for support. The gangplank was suicide. Even if he reached the top, the General could be waiting on the other side. There had to be another way. Lakon looked around. The repairs had been rushed if they had been completed at all. Spare parts and steel cables were strewn across the dock. Lakon grinned.

Grabbing a cable, Lakon tied several knots around the pallet's centermost munition. He looped the cable through nearby racks of oil drums. Lakon fastened the cable to a severed mooring line. Lakon ran down the dock, repeating the process for every cable the General had cut. After tying a crate of depth charges to the sternmost mooring line, Lakon climbed the cable to reach the main deck.

The ship shuddered and the propellers stirred to life. The communication array started spinning with slow, steady rhythm. Lakon crept to the nearest hatch and descended the main stairwell. Voices echoed through the narrow passageways.

"Give me the keys, Bell." The sound was soft, but Lakon felt the eerie threat in Sinon's words.

"We don't have to do this!" General Bell's shout boomed through the ship harsh and abrupt.

"It's too late. We have no choice." Sinon insisted in a dull, bored tone. Lakon hid behind the galley door and peered through a gap in the hinges. Sinon sat at the central table, eating sardines from a tin. He did not seem to care about General Bell towering over him. Sylvania Birnam sat on a countertop behind them, shaking her head in disapproval.

"I'm leaving." Sylvania slid off the countertop and walked towards the exit. General Bell and Tom stared at her, eyes wide with shock. Sinon remained unfazed.

"Where do you think you're going?" Sinon continued to face forward

"My mission was to clear this ship, not defend it." Sylvania kept walking. "Besides, war's bad for business."

"Not if we win." Sinon finished the can of sardines. Sylvania's hand rested on the doorframe.

"You of all people should know." Sylvania's voice was harsh and unflinching. "It's unwise to underestimate your opponents." She left without another word.

"Couldn't be helped." Sinon shrugged, tossing the empty sardine tin into a recycling bin. "Still, she was useful while it lasted. If she gets out of this city alive, I might consider hiring her again."

"Sinon." General Bell bowed his head. "Please. There has to be another way." Sinon paused, eyeing the General with intense scrutiny.

"You know there's not." Sinon spoke calm and cold. "We have no choice."

"We always have a choice." General Bell insisted. Sinon's eyes narrowed.

"Give me the keys, Bell." Sinon remained firm. "I will not ask again." The ship lurched forward. The room echoed the high pitched screech of grinding metal. Lakon braced himself.

"What is Birnam doing?" The General covered his ears.

"It's not her." Sinon snarled. "Lakon…" Lakon's heart fell. Had Sinon noticed his presence?

"Lakon?" General Bell asked. "What do you mean Lakon?"

"Lakon!" Sinon clamped his eyes shut. "He must have anchored us to the dock." Lakon, once again, felt a dull pain growing inside his head. Lakon grit his teeth. The pressure surged faster this time. Worse, it seemed to be moving. Left and right, up and down, backwards and forwards, the pressure pushed and pulled.

Lakon pressed a hand against his forehead, wanting desperately to scream.

"Uh." Tom hesitated. "What did he use for an anchor?"

BOOM!

An explosion rocked the ship, reverberating along the starboard hull. Fires flashed across the exposed compartments, smashing the frame against the opposite dock. Lights flickered and the ship plunged into darkness. Lakon sighed with relief as the pain eased from his head. Emergency lights flooded the passageway with an eerie dim glow.

"You, check the backup. You, check the deck." Sinon's orders were followed by the shuffling of feet. Lakon peered through the doorjamb. Sinon stood alone, back turned. Lakon drew his revolver. Sinon's hand curled into the shape of a gun. Their breaths resonated soft, slow and shallow.

Sinon turned towards Lakon. He scanned the shadows, wary and methodical. His eyes rested on Lakon's hiding spot. Lakon held his revolver along the doorjamb, aiming at Sinon's heart. Sinon walked forward, raising his hand.

"Backup power is live." General Bell returned through the opposite door. Sinon broke his concentration and wheeled to face the General.

"Lodon's ship is on the horizon." Tom was right behind his father.

"That just leaves-" Sinon began. An intense heat tore through the hull, smashing through the armored walls. A green disc barrier careened towards Sinon, surging with so much numen even Lakon could see it. Tom and the General dove to the floor. Sinon stepped forward and caught the disc with one hand.

"Peter." Sinon snarled. His grip tightened, shattering Peter's barrier in his clenched fist. A monstrous presence flooded the room. Dark, cold and unyielding, Lakon felt his spirit breaking as Sinon's aura clashed with his own.

"Give me the keys!" Sinon snapped. General Bell trembled as he withdrew the keys from his pocket. Sinon snatched them from his hand. "I need fifteen minutes. Go!"

"Yes, sir." The General's voice weakened. "Go on, Tom." The boy stared at Sinon, frozen, paralyzed by fear. "Tom. Please. Go." The terrified boy nodded and shuffled out of the room. General Bell remained.

"Go ahead!" Sinon's lip curled as he spat the words. "Ask!"

"Did you plan it?" The General avoided eye-contact. "Did you plan it, so we'd have no other choice?" Sinon clenched the keys in his fist. He glared at Bell a long time before answering:

"No."

General Bell nodded and left the room. Sinon tossed the keys, catching them with the same hand. A satisfied grin crept across his face. Sinon strode to the nearest stairwell, and descended into the bowels of the ship.

Lakon slid down the wall, revolver slipping from his grasp. This was nothing like Abraham. Beating Sinon was nothing but a foolish thought. There was no hope.

Lakon brushed the tears from his eyes. Miles stood up to Sinon. Alone and fearless, he resisted even in the face of death. There had to be a way.

Blue lights danced across the walls of the galley. Lakon rose to his feet. Unlike Miles, he was not alone. Naval and police boats gathered across the harbor; Aprilis and Central reunited once more.

They raced towards the transmission ship, determined to save what remained of their country.

Lakon holstered his revolver and ran towards the stern of the ship. He could not defeat Sinon without help. He needed a plan.

Chapter 21 – Agent of Caerule

Sam Pere

For the second time today, Sam found himself captured. He pushed and pulled, trying to wrench free from the tungsten handcuffs. The restraints dug deeper into his wrists. All this time, he had been nothing but a liability. Sam stopped struggling. Peter was right. He was not ready.

Sam's chest seared renewed agony as his scar from the Sword of Caerule flared again. Sam hunched forward, burdened by the pain. Outside, the rhythmic booming of artillery fire clashed with the ship's countermeasures. Shockwaves echoed across the hull. Sam winced as the vibrations reaggravated his wounds. A loud crack reverberated across the hull. The ringing stopped. Sam squinted at the bars of his cell. Typical. Not only had they handcuffed him to a steel bench, they locked the door as well.

"Could this get any worse?" Sam leaned against the wall. A new sound greeted his ears: the soft gurgle of flowing water. Sam looked back at the door. Sure enough, a steady stream of brine spilled through the steel bars.

"Sam!" A voice called. "Sam!"

"Here!" Sam clanged the handcuffs against the bench. "I'm in here!" Sam heard frantic splashing. A bright light shone into the cell. It was Lakon.

"There you are." Lakon lowered the flashlight. "I need your help."

"You need my help?" Sam stared at Lakon, flabbergasted. "In case you haven't noticed, I'm not doing so hot myself."

"These bars are steel." Lakon ignored Sam's sarcasm, examining the hinges of the door. "If I got you out of those handcuffs, do you think you could break them."

"Probably." Sam rattled the handcuffs again. "Get me out of them and we'll find out."

"There is a way." Lakon drew his revolver and pointed it at Sam. "Trust me."

"Wait! Wait! Wait!" Sam squirmed at the sight of Lakon's gun. "Give me the battery."

"What?"

"The battery in the flashlight: toss it here." Lakon shrugged and holstered the gun. He unscrewed the bottom of the flashlight, and extracted a thick metal cylinder from the base.

"You ready?" Lakon reached through the bars, holding the battery in his outstretched hand.

"Yeah." Sam readjusted himself on the bench. Lakon tossed the battery into Sam's lap. It began to roll. Sam shifted to the side, widening the gap in his legs. The battery tumbled through, allowing Sam to catch it with his thighs. "Get out of the water!"

"What?"

"Get out of the water. Now!" Sam felt the battery slipping. Lakon retreated from the door. The splashing of feet grew fainter. Sam closed his eyes. The water was almost at his knees. It was now or never.

Sam closed his eyes and focused on the battery. He felt the electrons strain against their metal prison. Sam took a deep breath. This wasn't a battery. It was a bomb. Between his legs, Sam held the electrical equivalent of a kilogram of dynamite. Sam took a deep breath and completed the circuit. The room crackled with blue light.

Electricity surged through Sam's body, mixing with his numen until he could not tell them apart. Sam channeled the current to his wrists. The tungsten glowed, warped and melted. It did not hurt. It was invigorating. Tungsten slag fell into the water, erupting in a cloud of steam. Sam blasted the door with one hand and sprinted through the flooded passageway. Lakon waited for him, sitting cross legged on a wooden bench that ran along the back wall.

"Is it safe?" Lakon sighed. He seemed both bored and annoyed.

"Yeah." Sam grinned, electricity crackling around him. "I'm in complete control."

"Great!" Lakon jumped into the water. "Follow me."

"How are Meg and the others?" Sam jogged to catch up to him.

"Better than us at the moment." Lakon drew his revolver as they approached the center passageway. "I think Sinon's gonna nuke someone."

"WHAT?" Sam squeaked, too loud. The sound carried along the corridor. Lakon pulled Sam behind the entrance and peered around the corner. Sam's heart pounded. How many nukes did Sinon have? What were his targets? Had he already fired them?

"In here." Lakon crept to a side storage bay. Sam forced a weak nod and followed him. Inside, large computer connected to a breaker box with a thick black cable. Three cables ran from the box into the ceiling. Lakon closed the door behind them and tore open the breaker box. "What can you tell me about this?"

"Uh…" Sam's fingers trembled as he placed his hands on the breaker box. He felt the currents flowing through the wires, but something was wrong. "The main power's not working."

"I know." Lakon stood guard at the door, leaning his ear against the metal. "I destroyed it. What about the backups?"

"T-There are two." Sam wiped cold sweat from his brow and returned his attention to the box. "One at the bow and one midship." Lakon cursed under his breath.

"Can you destroy them from here?"

"No." Sam shook his head. "These are tungsten cables."

"You just destroyed tungsten handcuffs."

"That's different." Sam's breaths shortened.

"How so?"

"It just is, alright!" Sam tore himself away from the box and sat against the wall. Lakon knelt beside him.

"Okay, Sam, I'm going to level with you." Lakon glanced at his watch. "We have nine minutes and forty three seconds. After that-"

"I can't!" Sam clamped his eyes shut, panting. "I'm sorry. They're too far away. I can't."

"Fine." Lakon flung open the door in frustration. "I guess I'll have to wing it." The door clanged against the wall as Lakon stormed down the passageway.

"We need a plan." Sam chased after him.

"No time." Lakon pressed forward. "You know what this ship is just as much as I do." Sam's frantic eyes scanned the corridors, just in time to see a dark shadow descending the main stairwell.

"Look out!" Sam pulled Lakon to the ground. A blast of numen shot past them. Sam looked to the source. Tom emerged from the stairwell and blocked their path. Sam moved in front of Lakon, protecting him from a second attack. The attack never came. Tom stood in the passageway, a solemn frown on his face.

"Sorry." Lakon rubbed the back of his head.

"There's nothing we can do about it now." Sam's numen crackled as he glared at Tom. He needed a plan. Worse, he had to communicate it to Lakon without Tom knowing. "You know that game we played?" Sam asked. It was just about the only thing he and Lakon had in common.

"Yeah." Lakon furrowed his brow in confusion.

"I'm going to play to my strengths." Sam's eyes remained fixed on Tom. "I suggest you play to yours." Lakon puzzled for a moment, then nodded in agreement.

"Got it." Lakon turned and sprinted to the sternmost stairwell. He descended deeper into the vessel, splashes receding in the direction of midship. Tom's eyes darted back and forth, unsure who to follow. Sam advanced, calm and controlled.

"Don't move." Tom channeled his numen. Sam pressed forward. "This is close-combat." Tom's eyes widened. "You can't win." Sam channeled his own numen. "I'm serious. Stop!"

"No, Tom." Sam locked eyes with him. "I'm done with tricks. I'm done with plans. And, most of all I'm done running away-" Sam cut the last word and sprinted down a horizontal side passage. Tom tripped at the sudden change of movement. Sam's bluff worked. He reached the end of the passageway and fired a blast of electricity as Tom rounded the corner. Tom absorbed the blast and redirected it with twice the power, too late. Sam was already gone, charging along the portside passageway towards the bow.

Sam didn't need to fight. He just had to reach the bow first. A blast of numen struck Sam's back. His ankle twisted and Sam fell to the floor. Tom was faster than Sam remembered. He might even be faster than Leah. Sam scrambled to his feet, ignoring the pain in his foot. Tom was almost on top of him.

Sam dove into a side compartment, slamming the door behind him. He pressed his shoulder against the door and welded the edges with his numen. WHAM! The door shuddered as Tom slammed against it. WHAM! Sam scanned the room. Along the opposite wall, a door to the central passageway lay open. Sam had an idea.

Extinguishing his numen, Sam abandoned the door and hid behind a large crate. WHAM! Cracks split through the welds, splintering the metal. Tom was almost through. WHAM! The door fell, clanging against the floor. Sam held his breath. Tom stepped through the shattered doorway.

It was just as Sam thought. When Tom saw the open door, his eyes widened. He sprinted across the compartment and ran down the opposite passageway. Sam emerged from his hiding spot, stepped over the fallen door and exited the same way he entered.

Sam limped towards the bow. Across the ship, he heard the desperate slamming of doors as Tom searched for Sam in the wrong place. The slamming stopped and the stomping of Tom's feet faded into the distance. Sam's heart sank. He knew where Tom was going.

At last, Sam reached the generator room. Sure enough, Tom stood guard outside. His arms quivered, eyes darting back and forth. Sam clenched his fist. There was no way to plan around this. It was the only entrance.

"I'm here, Tom." Sam hobbled into the main hallway. Tom's head turned with a jerk. "Stand aside, and no one has to get hurt."

"I can't do that, Sam." Tom's eyes were sad but firm. "I'm sorry."

"I thought you wanted to be an agent. I thought we were going to protect Caerule together." Sam's numen crackled as he spat the words. "You're willing to die for this?"

"No." Tom shook his head. "I'm willing to die for him. You lost your family. You've felt that pain as much as anyone. My father…" Tom's eyes began to water. "He's the only family I have."

"You had us." Sam stepped forward. He felt pity for Tom, but that didn't matter now.

"I suppose I did." Tom smiled.

"Stand aside, Tom." Sam's eyes hardened. "I will not ask again."

"You won't have to." Tom's numen flowed around his body, calm and resolute. "I made my choice."

"And I've made mine." Sam clenched his fist. Lights shattered. Sparks flew. Lightning cracked across the halls. Tom retreated to the door, eyes wide with terror. "I don't know how to control this power." Sam stared at the numen surging through his arm. "But this time." He turned towards Tom. "I'm not the one who has to."

Sam and Tom lunged towards each other, fists colliding in a vicious clash of blue and white light. Steel glowed in the darkness. Tremors echoed through the ship. Sam fell to the floor, metal searing against his skin. He flinched as residual current shot through his arms. Even electricity hurt now. His whole body ached and throbbed. Rogue currents surged through Sam's nerves without numen to protect them. Sam closed his eyes. He had given everything. He hoped it was enough.

A faint rattling jolted Sam's attention. Something moved behind him. A hand pressed on Sam's back. Sam's heart sank. Tom bound Sam's arms and legs with tungsten wire and propped him against the smoldering wall.

"Wha…What happened?" Sam's vision blurred into focus.

"You lost." Tom sighed. The left side of his face was charred and blackened. Sam winced and turned towards the generator room.

"No." Sam heaved a sigh of relief. "I am an agent of Caerule and I completed my mission." The door melted and the entire generator room had been incinerated. Tom forced a solemn nod. He hoisted Sam onto his shoulder and walked towards the main stairwell. Sam was captured a third time.

Chapter 22 – Impossible Choice

Meg Alumen

"Admiral Lodon is on her way." Peter shouted over the whomping helicopter rotors. Meg saw the apprehension reflected in his eyes. "Until then, our primary objective is stopping Sinon, by any means necessary." He jumped and landed on the deck twenty meters below. Meg looked down. The ship was sinking into an ocean of fire. Smoke billowed from the hull and flames spread across the water.

"Don't worry." Leah nodded. "Sam will be fine." She leapt from the helicopter and landed a few meters behind Peter. Meg sighed. She hoped Leah was right. Meg encircled her body with numen and jumped. She felt the air surging hot and turbulent. Her lungs burned and her eyes stung with soot and smoke. Sam was down there, somewhere. Meg feared the worst.

As soon as she landed, Meg scanned the ship in infrared. She could not see a thing. The heat was too strong. "Find anything?" Peter glared at the center gun turret. He seemed troubled by something.

"Bottom of the ship, near the middle." Meg stopped scanning. "It's the only place that isn't burning." Peter nodded but his eyes remained fixed on the turret.

"What's wrong?" Leah rushed to join him.

"Get behind me." Barriers extended from Peter's arms, forming long red blades. A jagged surge of numen sliced through the turret. Peter leapt in front of Meg, deflecting the attack with his blades. His arms quivered, but the barriers held.

"Not bad." General Bell emerged from the smoldering ruins of the gun turret. He advanced towards them, holding the Sword of Caerule. "If you fought together, you might actually be a threat to me."

"You killed General Rocklos." Peter stepped forward. His eyes darkened and his numen flared.

"I did." Bell nodded, tapping the sword against the deck. "She fought for Caerule to the bitter end. I can't stand such people." An artillery shell spiraled towards the General with frightening speed. Bell's smile faded. He sliced the shell in half, but a large fragment struck his leg. Bell winced.

"Peter!" Leah tossed a second shell between her hands. Peter stopped. His breaths fell long and heavy. "We've got this. Focus on the mission." Peter nodded but his eyes remained dark and cold. He retreated towards the center stairwell.

"By all means, go!" General Bell sneered. "Sacrifice two more students for this pathetic country." Peter stopped. His hand rested on the railing.

"Peter." Meg tried to calm the uncertainty in her voice. Peter looked at her. "We'll be fine. Trust me." Peter nodded again and continued down the stairwell. Meg stared after him. It was for the best. No matter how this ended.

"You're a terrible liar." General Bell shook his head. Numen surged into the sword, radiating malice and despair.

"You're right." Meg sighed. A steady stream of numen flowed across her body. "But I will keep that promise." General Bell raised the sword. Leah tensed her throwing arm. Meg channeled radiation to her fist. Their bodies remained still, but their shadows danced in the crackling blaze.

General Bell moved first. Faking a step towards Meg, he turned and slashed towards Leah; too late. Leah hurled the shell with vicious speed and force. The attacks landed simultaneously. The slash clipped Leah's shoulder but was deflected by her numen. The General was not so lucky. The shell impaled his upper chest. Meg unleashed a blast of radiation. The shell glowed red and the General howled in pain. He dropped the sword and stumbled backwards.

BOOM!

A vicious heat seared across the deck as the helicopter exploded above their heads. The wreckage crashed into the ship's communication array, showering the deck with burning scrap metal.

"Look out!" Leah screamed. Meg dove behind an anti-air gun. The burning communication toppled, crushing the General's leg. Bell screamed.

"We have to destroy their defenses." Meg used her numen to melt the barrel of the anti-air gun. "Any reinforcements will-"

"It didn't come from the ship." Leah shouted.

"What?" Meg's face paled.

"That missile didn't come from the ship." Leah repeated. "It was friendly fire." No sooner had she said it, two Caerule fighter jets attacked each other and crashed into the Helena Bridge. In the distance, Admiral Lodon's flagship was firing in all directions, besieged by unknown enemies. Meg's face paled. She knew Sinon was behind this, somehow.

General Bell took advantage of the distraction and channeled his numen. Leah ran for the fallen sword. If she grabbed it, this would all be over. The General thrust out his weak hand. The sword slid across the deck towards him.

"No!" A bright laser surged from Meg's finger slicing the sword in half. The top of the blade spun across the deck. The bottom half glowed red-hot as the hilt leapt into the General's hand. Bell grinned.

SLASH!

The General's attack struck Leah full-force, slamming her against the helicopter wreckage. She crumpled to the deck, motionless.

Meg turned invisible and dove to the floor. A wild series of slashes rang above her head. Cables snapped. Guns shattered. The remnants of the communication array were smashed aside. Meg shuddered. The General's power was overwhelming. He was using half a sword in his weak hand and could still sink the entire ship if he wanted. The slashes stopped.

"Not bad, Meg." General Bell cut the debris trapping his leg. Blood poured from the melted shell embedded in his chest. "You almost had me, but I know your power better than you know mine." Meg surveyed the devastation. Clouds of ash and dust swirled from the wreckage, dimming the raging fires. Meg had no light. She had no hope.

"And now to find you." The General limped towards Leah, sword raised. Meg absorbed whatever radiation she could. Infrared, ultraviolet, microwaves: all parts of the spectrum surged to Meg's fist. It would not be enough. Unless…

Meg leapt to her feet and began absorbing whatever visible light she could find. Her body darkened, turning blacker than the ash strewn deck. Before General Bell could react, Meg fired the blast, striking him in the heart. It was not enough. The attack failed to pierce the General's numen. Bell stumbled backwards, clutching his chest. He grinned.

"You'd sacrifice all of Caerule rather than watch her die." General Bell shook his head. "Perhaps there's hope for you after all."

"You never gave a damn about Caerule." Meg spat.

"I don't, but I did." General Bell's eyes darkened. "I gave my soul for this country. I lost ten thousand men on the Field of Fate. I lost my wife. I lost my first born son. I ordered my family to their deaths because that's what the mission required. And Caerule called it a victory. They called it a victory because we killed a man who did nothing but defend himself." Meg's face paled.

"That's right, Alumen." General Bell examined the broken sword, reflecting the flames that raged around it. "Your parents gave their lives, their sanity, to kill a man I now know to be innocent. Your Caerule is a lie; as false and misguided as the history this sword represents. 'Truth, Loyalty, Justice.'" He read the inscription. "That dream died long ago, if it ever existed at all." General Bell stood over Leah. "I can't take back the things I've done. But, I can set things right." His hand tightened around the sword. Meg prepared to charge.

"Don't move." A nervous voice stopped her mid-stride. Tom emerged from the main stairwell holding Sam's unconscious body. Tom surrounded his hand with numen and held it against Sam's neck.

"Good work, Tom!" The General aimed the broken blade at Leah's heart. "What'll it be, Meg? The mission or Sam's life. Stand down or they both die." Meg glanced at Sam. His face was burned. His arms were limp and lifeless. Meg's heart sank. It was all her fault. Meg fought to hold back tears. There was only one answer.

"No." Meg's eyes darkened.

"Please, Meg." General Bell met her gaze. "Don't make the same mistake I did."

"No." Meg repeated, louder and more forceful. Sam, Leah, Peter: she failed everyone.

"Don't make me do this." General Bell shook his head. "This sword is stained with enough innocent blood."

"No." Meg repeated a third time. The fire raged around her, trapped in an endless cycle of destruction.

"I see." General Bell bowed his head. He turned to Tom with a solemn nod. "Do it."

"What?" Tom's face paled.

"Kill him." The General's words were sad, but firm. "Kill him now." Tom hesitated. His hand shook and his numen began to flicker. "Do it!"

"No." Tom lowered his hand.

"What?" The General spat.

"No." Tom's numen faded. He placed Sam's body on the deck and backed away. The General grabbed Leah by the neck and dragged her towards Tom. Meg fired a desperate blast of numen at the General's head. He deflected with the broken sword and continued walking. The General returned his attention to Tom.

"Do it, Tom!" The General towered over his son. "Think of your brother."

"I am." Tom's eyes welled with tears. "He wouldn't have wanted this. Mom wouldn't have wanted this."

"Fine." The General stood over Sam's body and raised the sword. "I'll do it myself." The blade fell and the ship echoed a resounding clang.

General Bell's eyes widened in terror. Admiral Lodon stood between Sam and the General, blocking his sword with her own. Meg stared in shock. Lodon moved so fast. Where had she even come from?

"I suppose you already know." Admiral Lodon glared at the General, calm and cold. "How I handle traitors on my ships."

Chapter 23 – Fight for Peace

Peter Turnus

The door to the operations room creaked and swayed with the ship, obscuring the digital clock that counted the seconds; eight minutes left. Peter crept towards the room, chills spreading through his body. Sinon was behind that door, waiting in the darkness.

The door swung and Peter rushed inside. Red blades extended from his arms. Scarlet shadows swept across the floor. Peter looked left, right, up, down. Nothing. The only movement came from the ticking clock; seven minutes left.

BOOM! Peter wheeled. The door closed and locked. An ominous presence flooded the room, writhing and twisting until malice seeped from the walls themselves. Peter's breaths shortened. Was this really Sinon?

Peter turned to the computer. Two keys remained in the terminal switched ON. A world map dominated the screen, littered with red dots. Underneath, a small nuclear generator whirred, so close and yet so far; six minutes left.

Peter ran towards the generator cable. One strike would end it. He ran for Meg. He ran for Leah. He ran for Caerule, ignoring the danger that lurked in the shadows.

BANG! A blast of numen hurtled towards Peter. He spun, blocking the attack with his blade. The force lifted Peter from his feet, smashing him against a steel column. There was no time to recover. Sinon fired a second shot, then a third. Each volley surged more vicious than the last, forcing Peter to expend more numen. His defenses were failing. He had to attack.

Peter lunged, unleashing a fury of slashes. Sinon dodged every time. Peter's mind flooded with desperation. Each step drove Sinon closer to the generator, but each swing drained Peter's fast depleting numen.

With the next strike, Peter's fears were realized. Sinon dodged both blades and delivered a devastating punch to Peter's abdomen. Peter winced as the blow smashed through his defenses. Again, there was no time to recover. Sinon's attacks bashed the weakest layers of Peter's numen, forcing Peter further from his goal.

The walls were fast approaching. Sinon was driving Peter into a corner. There was one thing left to do. Peter leapt back and created a large barrier. Sinon stopped attacking. He scanned the edges of the barrier. It was a perfect shield. Peter was surrounded on all sides. He struggled to catch his breath.

"Stay there, Peter." Sinon glared through the transparent wall of numen. "In five minutes this will all be over."

"You'll start a war!" Peter slammed his fist against the barrier.

"No!" Sinon roared. "I'll end one!" Explosions thundered across the hull. Peter stumbled, but preserved the barrier. "I thought you were better than this, Peter. You swore to create a more peaceful world. You fought for it, killed for it, sacrificed students; and how much closer are you?"

"Closer than you." Peter spat, glaring at the world map. "Destroying cities. Massacring innocents."

"You don't know me at all, do you?" Sinon shook his head, eyes pained with disbelief. "You see that map on the wall and you think that's me? It's been here longer than you and I have been alive. That's what you've been fighting for; endless war and a world held hostage."

"By you!" Peter shouted. "Held hostage by you! I know what this ship is. No peace can come of it. You can't win!"

"I already have." Sinon nodded to the upper decks. "You think that's Caerule fighting up there?" Peter's face paled. The booms of cannon fire spread away from the ship, chaotic and frenzied. "Transmission ships." Sinon gestured to the screen. "Are the largest communication networks in the world. In Lodon's hands, they send orders to Caerule's fleet, but in mine…" Sinon examined the numen flowing into his palm. "I control the world."

"No." Peter breathed.

"That's right." Sinon's face was solemn and sad. "The world's militaries are destroying each other in a battle of my design. Every password, every protocol, every paranoid security measure is mine to command. When that clock hits zero, the last recall codes will be erased. Then, not even Admiral Lodon can stop them."

"Impossible." Peter shook his head. "There's always a failsafe."

"There was." Sinon nodded in agreement. "A network of satellites launched by the Great Nations after the war. Unfortunately, trust is such a fleeting resource. The last satellite was destroyed by Caerule less than twelve hours ago."

"No." Peter pounded against the barrier.

"I'm sorry, Peter." Sinon sighed. "You should have trusted Patricia. You should have trusted Meg. I knew you wouldn't. I was counting on it."

"Why are you telling me this?" Peter's eyes welled with tears. "You never reveal your plans. You're too smart for that." Another shell struck the ship. Steel snapped and cracked. Below, Peter heard the hiss of rushing water.

"Why?" Sinon stepped forward. "Because every second I waste saves millions of lives, and somewhere, deep down, you know that to be true."

"You're insane." Peter grit his teeth. "You betrayed Aprils! You betrayed Caerule! And you betrayed me!" They glared at each other, unmoving, like reflections in a mirror.

"You know." Sinon watched his numen flicker like soft candlelight. "When I first discovered my power, I was…disappointed. Everyone, could do something, create something, change something. I was useless, doomed to watch the brightest stars of our generation waste their gifts, slaughtering each other on the orders of lesser men. Why?"

"I joined the war to find that answer." Sinon clenched his numen charged fist. "I read the minds of every soldier, general, and politician. I felt the pain of every, mother, wife and child. I traveled every nation, every battlefield, asking the same question: Why?"

"I never found the answer." Sinon held his hand in the shape of a gun and began to raise it. "Everyone will go to war if given the right reason. Even good men like you. How can peace be possible if people kill each other for believing different lies?" Sinon met Peter's gaze. "I soon realized my 'useless' gift was the strongest weapon of all: the truth. I will end this war. I'm the only one who can."

Numen surged to Sinon's outstretched finger. He was betting everything on one attack. Peter closed his eyes, concentrating his numen into the barrier. It wasn't enough. Sinon held his hand steady, aiming at Peter's heart.

A shot tore through the darkness followed by a resounding scream. Peter's eyes snapped open. A second bullet tore through the weakest layer of numen around Sinon's leg. Sinon screamed again. The bones snapped and Sinon fell to his knees. Lakon fired a third shot; too late. The bullet glanced off Sinon's numen. Sinon raised his hand and fired. The blast struck Lakon's chest. He hurtled through the darkness striking the far wall with a devastating crunch. The revolver spun across the floor, barrel pointing into the shadows.

Peter dropped the barrier and charged. Sinon blocked the blades with his arms. He was no longer able to dodge. Peter slashed with renewed vigor, driving Sinon back. Peter felt his numen weakening, but, for once, Sinon was weakening faster. One way or another, the battle was about to end: two minutes left

Peter slashed his arms for a finishing blow. Sinon caught the blades mid swing. Numen raged around them, growing stronger as they pushed against each other. A ball of light glowed inside the blades as numen surged in both directions. The ball exploded. Peter stumbled backwards. Sinon fell to the ground.

Using the last of his numen, Peter created a single blade and lunged towards Sinon; too late. Sinon raised his hand and fired. The blast struck Peter above the heart, tearing through his previous wound. Peter fell to his knees. His numen faded: one minute left.

"I'm sorry, Peter." Sinon staggered to his feet. "You're not a bad person. You just chose the wrong side."

"You're right." Peter stared at the floor. "I chose to trust a friend. I guess I was wrong." Sinon nodded. A thin veil of numen encircled his body. He raised his hand.

Click!

Sinon turned towards the noise. Lakon leaned against a steel column, panting. He retrieved his revolver and pointed it towards Sinon. Peter stared at Lakon, stunned. How was he alive?

"You!" Sinon snarled. "If vengeance means that much to you, come on! Take it!" He was losing control. Peter had never seen Sinon so flustered.

"I knew it." Lakon grinned. "You can't read my mind." Sinon's eyes widened. Lakon's arm began to turn.

"No!" Sinon screamed. Lakon fired. The bullet struck the generator, shattering the connector in a shower of sparks.

Chapter 24 – Mysterious Stranger

James Lakon

"No." Sinon fell to his knees.

The clock stopped with seven seconds remaining. The screen flickered and the room plunged into darkness. Lakon slid down the column. It was finally over.

Lakon flipped open the cylinder of his revolver. One bullet left. He closed the cylinder, loading the final round into the chamber. Sinon's back was turned: a perfect target. Lakon took a deep breath and raised the revolver.

BANG! Artillery shook the compartment and General Bell's flailing body crashed through the ceiling. Admiral Lodon jumped after him. "Please." The General tried to crawl away. His whole body was shaking. "I surrender! I surrender! I surrender!" The Admiral's sword slashed through the air. "Mercy!"

"You don't deserve it." Admiral Lodon held the sword steady against his neck. General Bell whimpered. She kicked Bell's face into the floor. The General collapsed, weeping. "What about you, Sinon?" Lodon advanced towards him.

"I…" Sinon continued to stare at the black screen in disbelief. His voice was weak and uncertain. "…Surrender." Admiral Lodon's sword rested against the back of Sinon's head.

"Pathetic." Admiral Lodon snarled. A thin trickle of blood ran down the blade. "You sacrifice others, but never yourself." Sinon did not respond. "Take them away!" Lodon sheathed her sword. A team of naval officers handcuffed Sinon and the General. "And get a medic down here!" Admiral Lodon knelt by Peter's side.

"The recall codes." Peter winced.

"Plummet's already sending them." Admiral Lodon nodded. "What's left of them anyways."

"How are Meg and the others?" Peter groaned, clutching his chest.

"Better than you by the looks of it." Lodon helped apply pressure to his wound. "How did you beat Sinon like this anyways?"

"I had help." Peter winced. James Lakon holstered his revolver and limped into the moonlight.

"Who the hell are you?" Admiral Lodon eyed his approach.

"James Lakon, Aprilis PD."

"I'm sorry for your loss." Admiral Lodon sighed.

"I'm sorry for yours." Pain spread through Lakon's ribs, but it was nothing compared to the pain in his heart. Too many good men died today. The Admiral did not respond. She stared at the ground in absolute silence. The medics bandaged Peter's wounds and loaded him onto a stretcher. "I'll follow them out." Lakon began to walk towards the door.

"Lakon." Admiral Lodon rose to her feet. "Thank you." Lakon nodded and proceeded to follow the medical team. Admiral Lodon stayed behind. She retrieved a fallen helmet and brushed it with her sleeve. Light shone through a gaping hole in the crown. Lakon turned away. It was too painful to watch. Sinon killed everyone in his way. Lakon's hand crept towards his chest. The bruise had almost healed. How was he alive?

As soon as they reached the main deck, the medical team loaded Peter onto a helicopter. Meg rushed to Lakon's side.

"How's Peter?" She asked.

"He'll live." Lakon replied. "How's Sam?"

"He's fine." Meg heaved a sigh of relief. "He and Leah will make a full recovery."

"Thank God." Lakon breathed; finally, some good news.

"Are you hurt?" Meg eyed Lakon's chest.

"What? No!" Lakon withdrew his hand from his shirt. Meg did not seem convinced. "Okay, Sinon shot me."

"What!"

"I'm fine." Lakon protested. "It didn't break the skin."

"You should still get it looked at." Meg glared at the spot with intense focus.

"I said: I'm fine." Lakon covered the spot with his hand. Meg shook her head. She walked to the starboard side and gazed across the harbor. The water was dark except for a pale streak of moonlight rising above the Helena Bridge. Lakon looked towards the gangplank. Three steps and he could leave this all behind. He could go to a new city; maybe even a new country. Lakon sighed and joined Meg at the railing.

"What's wrong?"

"Come back to Central with us." Meg gazed into his eyes. "This isn't over. We need you. I..." Lakon waited for her to finish, but the words never came. Meg's face glistened in the moonlight. Lakon turned away.

"I'm sorry." Lakon shook his head. "Not today." He proceeded to the gangplank.

"James." Meg turned to face him. Lakon's hand rested on the railing. "Do you love me?"

"I'm not sure." Lakon sighed. The past few days had been such a whirlwind of emotion. "But I'm willing to find out." Meg forced a solemn nod. Lakon proceeded down the gangplank and wandered into the cold night, alone.

The city was quieter than Lakon remembered. Wailing sirens faded into the distance. The twinkling streetlamps returned one by one. The faint whirring of Carbots streamed overhead. Each one had a destination. Lakon was searching for his.

At last, he arrived at the ruins of Aprils PD. Mountains of steel and concrete littered the streets, twisted and broken. Lakon climbed the rubble and stared across the tired city. Central had stopped burning. Power returned to Aprilis University. The fallen fragments of the Helena Bridge slowly washed away. Overhead, the tattered Caerule flag waved from its rebar rod, torn but triumphant.

Lakon looked down. A dark figure stood in the center of the wreckage, head bowed over the broken bronze shield. Lakon's eyes burned with fury.

"YOU!" Lakon sprinted down the rubble, drawing his revolver. The figure flinched and wheeled. It wasn't Sinon. "Sorry." Lakon stopped and lowered the gun. "I thought you were someone else."

"No worries." The man clutched his chest, panting. "I get that a lot." His hair, shirt and jeans were pitch-black, but his pale skin shone in the moonlight. There was something familiar about him. Lakon couldn't quite place it. The man withdrew an inhaler from his pocket, fumbled it between trembling fingers and dropped it in the dust.

"I'm sorry." Lakon holstered his gun and retrieved the medication. "It's all my fault."

"Thank you." The man wheezed and took a frantic drag from the device. Lakon watched him concerned.

"Do you need to go to the hospital?"

"No." The man shook his head. "I'm fine now."

"James Lakon." Lakon extended his hand. The man hesitated before shaking it.

"Jet Lightbringer." The man forced a weak smile. His eyes were tired, but his grip was strong.

"Were you looking for something?" Lakon asked.

"Someone, actually." Jet nodded. "Sergeant Miles?"

"I'm sorry." Lakon sat against a broken slab of concrete and stared at the ground. "Sergeant Miles was killed a few hours ago."

"I see." Jet's smile faded. He sat on the concrete slab beside Lakon. "Were you two close?"

"Yes." Lakon closed his eyes. "He was like a father to me."

"I'm sorry." Jet sighed. "He was a good man."

"He was." Lakon nodded. A lone tear trickled down his cheek. "I failed him."

"How so?"

"Detectives find the truth. Policemen protect others." Lakon stared across the smoking rubble. "I used to think they were one in the same. But, in these past few days, I chose the former and Miles the latter."

"Sometimes it's hard to know what's right." Jet bowed his head.

"You sound like you're talking from experience." Lakon felt an odd kinship with Jet. They understood each other, perhaps better than anyone else ever could. Their connection fascinated Lakon, but Jet remained reserved.

"You might say that." Jet turned away. "I lost a father too. That pain of being the last survivor never goes away."

"So what'll you do now?" Lakon pressed.

"Now?" Jet rose to his feet. "I guess I'll move on. Other people need my help. But, Miles..." Jet paused. "I hoped Miles could help me for a change."

"I guess I never appreciated all the ways he helped me." Lakon stared at the broken bronze shield. "I never got the chance to thank him. No. I had plenty of chances. I just never..." Lakon cried, no longer able to hold back the tears. His voice choked and his jaw trembled. Jet knelt and retrieved something from the ground.

"Here." Jet placed the tarnished Aprilis PD badge in Lakon's hand. "I think Miles would have wanted you to have it."

"Thank you." Lakon choked through uncontrolled sobs.

"Just be careful, Lakon." Jet turned to leave. "If you spend your life pursuing truth, you might not like what you find."

Chapter 25 – Interrogation

Meg Alumen

"I thought you'd never allow another friend to die."

"You are not my friend."

"Your words lie, but your mind tells the truth."

Meg watched Peter through the one-way mirror. It was an awful sight. Peter limped around the interrogation room, leaning on a cane for support. He insisted on doing the interrogation immediately. Meg's heart sank. She should have stopped him.

"Shut up!" Peter's voice cracked as he slammed his fist on the table. "Where are the weapons?"

"Everywhere." Sinon's arms rested on the table; wounds already healed. "Hidden in plain sight." His tungsten handcuffs glinted in the fluorescent light.

"Stop lying!"

"I've never lied to you, Peter." Sinon spoke calm and cold. "Go ahead! Ask your real question!" Peter stared towards the one-way mirror. Meg could not tell if he looking at her, Sinon or his own reflection.

"Why…" Peter paused. His eyes were tired and full of sorrow. "Why did you do it?"

"Why didn't you?" Sinon's voice was soft and sad. "They say you truly see a man when he is brought to his lowest point. I'm disappointed." Was he talking to Peter or himself? Meg grit her teeth. This interrogation was a battle and Sinon was winning.

Peter stumbled, dropping his cane. Meg threw open the door and caught Peter before he hit the ground. Cold sweat dripped down Peter's arm. His body was heavy and limp.

"That's enough." Meg glared at Sinon as she carried Peter out of the room. She sat Peter in a chair and slammed the door behind them. Sinon stared through the glass as if concerned. The sight made Meg sick.

"I'm sorry." Peter gasped, clutching the wound in his chest. His bandages had begun to redden. "I can't break him."

"It's not your fault." Meg bit her lip.

"What about General Bell?"

"Nothing." Meg shook her head. "He's more afraid of Sinon than us."

"That's bad." Peter tried to push himself out of the chair, but Meg held him down.

"You've done enough."

"What, this?" Peter shrugged his shoulder, loosening the muscles around his wound. "Don't worry. I've had worse."

"It's not your body I'm worried about." Meg looked into Peter's eyes. Sinon was a master of mental torture. She was amazed Peter had lasted this long. Peter closed his eyes and nodded his head in acceptance.

"Uh, Meg?" Professor Plummet entered the room. His face paled as he saw Peter's condition.

"What is it?" Meg asked without taking her eyes off Peter.

"Uh! James Lakon to see you."

"I'll be right there." Meg's face brightened for a moment. "Sir, are you-"

"Go." Peter forced a weak smile. "I'll be fine."

"Watch him for me." Meg rose to her feet and turned to Plummet

"I'm not that kind of doctor." Plummet countered, but knelt to inspect Peter's wounds. Meg glanced at Peter one last time before leaving. He continued to watch Sinon through the mirror and Sinon almost seemed to be staring back. Meg turned away.

As she left the interrogation room, Meg was greeted by the sounds of Lakon's excited voice echoing through the hallways. It was the first cheerful sound Meg had heard all day.

"I just spoke with the President. You'll be out of here within the hour."

"Really? Thank you!" A voice answered, overcome with excitement. "Does Paul know?" Meg rounded the corner to find Lakon talking to Neil Whitney through the bars of his cell. Under one arm, Lakon held a tightly wrapped package.

"I called him five minutes ago." Lakon smiled. "He can't wait to see you."

"Thank you." Neil brushed tears from his eyes. "I was worried I'd never see him again." He and Lakon embraced each other through the bars. Neil released the hug, grinning. "Miles must be thrilled."

"Yes." Lakon's eyes watered. He pretended it was happiness, but Meg could tell the difference. "I'm sure he is."

Chapter 25 – Interrogation

"He told me not to give up on you." Neil continued rambling. "All the way to Central he kept telling me: 'Don't worry. Lakon won't let you down.' Please, the next time you see him, thank him for me."

"I will." Lakon dried his eyes. "It's great to see you, Neil." Lakon turned towards Meg and began walking down the hall. By the time he reached her, Lakon regained his composure.

"I thought you weren't coming back today." Meg grinned.

"It's past midnight." Lakon joked.

"It's good to have you back." Meg nodded.

"Thanks." Lakon quickened his pace. "How's Peter?"

"How'd you know?"

"Lucky guess." Lakon continued to face forward. His eyes emanated an odd sense of concentration and intensity.

"It makes no sense." Meg shook her head. "Sinon shouldn't be able to read minds while wearing tungsten handcuffs. But, he beat every interrogation we've thrown at him. And, I have a bad feeling his plan isn't over."

"Same here." Lakon nodded, shifting the package to his opposite arm. "But, I think I have something to even the odds."

"What's in the box?" Meg nodded to the package.

"You'll see. Please don't look just yet." Lakon walked to the interrogation room and held the door for Meg. He gave a quick nod to Peter and proceeded to the one-way mirror. He stared through the glass, locking eyes with Sinon.

"He can't see you; you know." Professor Plummet said.

"No." Lakon agreed. "But he knows I'm here." Lakon reached for the door.

"Wait!" Meg took a step forward, but Lakon had already walked inside.

"Let him go." Peter leaned forward. The color had returned to his face and his eyes reflected the same intensity as Lakon's. "I want to see this."

Lakon placed the package on the table and sat in the chair opposite Sinon. Sinon's eyes narrowed.

"You're not used to losing are you?" Lakon grinned.

"Neither are you." Sinon glared at him.

"Me?" Lakon shrugged. "Nah! I lose all the time, but I always find a way to get even."

"I see." Sinon leaned back in his chair. "And how do you plan on doing that? I've destroyed everything you care about and, in twelve hours, I will be dead."

"Eleven hours and fifty four minutes." Lakon grinned without looking at his watch. "I can hardly wait. Unfortunately, I'm not your executioner. But, you and I both know some things are more valuable than life."

"Like what?" Sinon spat.

"Information." Lakon's eyes narrowed.

"I suppose you're gonna ask where the weapons are." Sinon smirked, crossing his arms.

"No." Lakon shrugged. "I already told President Millenavis to take down the Fenestravision network." Sinon's smile faded.

Chapter 25 – Interrogation

"Neat trick hiding projectiles in the drones. I'm surprised I didn't figure it out sooner. Something so basic we almost forget it's there."

"You have no idea." Sinon snarled. "You have no idea what these people have done."

"No." Lakon agreed. "But I know what you've done and I know you're not working alone." Sinon remained silent. He stared across the table with a calm, cool composure. "I guess we'll do this the hard way." Lakon sighed and began unwrapping the package.

"What's that?" A panicked look crossed Peter's face.

"I don't know." Meg was startled by Peter's reaction.

"You didn't check?"

"He asked me not to."

"Get him out of there." Peter began to push himself out of the chair. "I don't like where this is going." Meg reached for the door. "Wait!" Peter raised his hand. Meg looked through the glass again. Lakon finished unwrapping. Meg recognized the contents immediately. It was the Septagon Game she had given Sam.

"So, you have played this game." Lakon placed the board in the center of the table

"Once or twice." Sinon tried to remain deadpan, but his eyes glinted with intrigue. He was lying. Meg grit her teeth. Sinon played this game hundreds of times with her alone. Lakon was walking into a trap.

"Good." Lakon grabbed a red-half sphere and held it above the board. "If I win, you answer one of my questions."

"And if I win?" Sinon eyed the piece.

"I answer one of yours."

"What is he talking about?" Peter looked at Meg.

"I have no idea." Meg shook her head. What information could Lakon have to interest Sinon? Sinon stared at Lakon for a long time. Then, without saying a word, he reached across the table and accepted the red-half sphere. Click! Sinon placed the piece in the center of the board. He leaned back in his chair and waited for Lakon's reaction. Lakon grinned.

In eighteen turns, it was over. "All stars." Lakon pointed along the diagonal. Sinon remained silent. "Who do you work for?"

"No one." Sinon's eyes narrowed as he examined the board. "This operation was mine and mine alone. But the Septagon..." Sinon smirked. "The Septagon does have a leader." Sinon nodded towards the mirror. "They know him as the Pale Raven. They call him the most dangerous man in the world, but I know he's the only one who can save it. His vision for the future is more beautiful than any I could have imagined. I will achieve it, no matter what."

Lakon raised his eyebrows. Meg recognized the look immediately. He had no idea what Sinon was talking about. Lakon paused for a moment. Then, he cleared the board and handed a black box to Sinon. Sinon placed it in the center.

In thirty turns, it was over. "All waves." Lakon pointed along the left side. "Now..." He leaned back in his chair, crossing his arms behind his head. "What was your real reason for attacking Caerule?"

"I told you before." Sinon did not look at the board. He continued to watch Lakon with an odd fascination. "Peace-"

"Bullshit!" Lakon interrupted. "If peace was your real goal, you wouldn't have taken Sam."

"You are too smart for your own good." Sinon's lip curled. "Peace is the ultimate objective, but so many steps in between. I guess you could call this attack a catalyst. My victory got the pieces moving and my defeat..." Sinon smirked. "Well, let's just say an old friend has finally come out of hiding."

"What does he mean by that?" Meg cast a nervous glance towards Peter.

"No idea." Peter shook his head. "I don't know why he's telling Lakon any of this."

"This time, you go first." Sinon cleared the board and handed Lakon a piece.

"Fair enough." Lakon placed the piece in the center of the board. He glared across the table, but flinched as Sinon met his gaze. Meg leaned forward. Something was wrong. The energy in the room had changed.

"That man I killed. Sergeant..." Sinon snapped his fingers as if trying to remember the name.

"Miles." Lakon growled.

"That's it!" Sinon laughed. "Sergeant Miles. You didn't trust him much, did you?"

"Shut up." Lakon muttered.

"Don't worry." Sinon's grinned. "He never trusted you either. Do you want to know what he really thought of you?"

"Couldn't care less."

"He only wanted a good son." Sinon shook his head. "Someone who'd protect the innocent and help others in need. But you couldn't give that to him, could you? There is darkness in you and Miles always knew it was there."

"I don't know what you're talking about."

"He was afraid of you, Lakon." Sinon's lip curled. "He lied to you, your entire life. I know more about you than you know about yourself."

"Shut up!" Lakon pinched the top of his nose, brow furrowed. He seemed to be in pain. "You think reading minds lets you know them? What about the lives you ended; families you ruined; cities you destroyed? Tell them how much you understand, how much you know. You waste too much time reading other minds and not enough examining your own."

"All Septagons." Sinon placed the final piece in the space closest to Lakon. Lakon's eyes widened. Sinon leaned forward. "I have seen many minds, Lakon. You're right about that. I have seen the hopes and dreams of countless people all over the world. You're afraid, Lakon. You're afraid because with all that knowledge, with all that understanding, with all that collective wisdom, I made my choice. You say I'm wrong. Maybe I am. Perhaps the truth lies within the one mind I could not reach. So what is it Lakon? How do you plan to save this world?"

Lakon remained silent.

"I see." Sinon shook his head. "You condemn me, but have no answers yourself. Or perhaps you will not share because your darkness is even worse than mine."

Lakon remained silent.

"No answer." Sinon leaned back in his chair. "In that case, I have one last question. What will you do when Caerule betrays you as well?" Sinon's eyes shifted to the door. "Too late."

Chapter 25 – Interrogation

BANG!

The door swung open and slammed against the wall. The one-way mirror shattered. Grand Master Marius stormed into the room. His eyes raged and his voice snarled.

"Alumen. Courtroom. Now!"

Chapter 26 – An Unjust Trial

Sam Pere

"Sit down!" Marius dragged Sam by the arm and flung him onto a cold stone chair in the center of the courtroom. Sam winced as the force re-aggravated the burns on his back. Meg leapt from her chair, fists clenched. Marius glared at her.

"Abuse children on your own time, Marius." Admiral Lodon goaded from the left judicial bench. She continued chewing a large wad of bubblegum and drummed impatient fingers on the wooden stand. "Some of us have work to do."

"That's enough." President Millenavis warned from the center bench. He banged the broken Sword of Caerule like a gavel, obliviously putting his fingerprints on the evidence. "Both of you." Marius snarled and took his seat as the third judge. "This court will come to order."

"Agent Pere!" Marius addressed the courtroom.

"Yes, sir?" Sam trembled.

"You took at numen classification test at 12:34 yesterday afternoon?" Marius continued.

"I…" Sam opened his mouth, but the words drowned in his throat.

"Answer the question!" Marius demanded.

"The witness has rights!" Meg rose from her chair.

"Not on these charges." Marius shouted over her.

"Order!" President Millenavis cast a warning look at Marius. "Both of you." The President turned back to Sam. "Agent Pere, please answer the question."

"Yes, sir." Sam stared at the floor. "I took the test." President Millenavis sighed and turned to Admiral Lodon.

"How do you want to handle this?"

"As quickly as possible." Admiral Lodon picked her teeth with a fingernail.

"Very well." Millenavis nodded. "Marius, call the first witness."

"The state calls Eisenhower Plummet Sr." Marius's eyes narrowed. Sam craned his neck to see a pale-faced Professor Plummet emerge from the rear of the courtroom. He walked past Sam and sat in a stiff wooden chair in front of the judicial bench. Sam could not tell which of them was more frightened. "Professor Plummet. You administered a numen classification test on Agent Pere at 13:24 yesterday afternoon."

"Y-Yes Sir."

"And, during this examination, the numen tester was destroyed."

"Yes, Sir."

"And, what material was this tester made from?" Sam could feel the hatred writhing in Marius's eyes.

"Tungsten, sir." Professor Plummet bit his lip and stared at the floor.

"There you have it." Marius turned to face the President. "Sam's numen melted tungsten. And that can only mean-"

"Thermal runaway!" Plummet interrupted. Marius wheeled. The professor's eyes shone renewed intensity.

"Thermal runaway?" Marius snarled. "The metal ignited on your desk!"

"The tester is made of other things." Plummet rambled, giving a quick nod to Sam. "The internal components are silicon, copper, gol-"

"But it's tungsten." Marius slammed his fist on the bench. "Sam's numen melted tungsten!"

"No!" The professor locked eyes with Marius. "Sam's numen heated the semiconductors and that caused the tungsten to melt." The two men stared at each other a long time. The silence was broken by a loud pop as Lodon blew into her chewing gum.

"Professor Plummet." Marius maintained eye-contact. "Do you know where we found this numen tester?"

"In the river." Plummet trembled. "Probably."

"Was that what you were doing when General Rocklos was killed?" Marius continued.

"Yes." Plummet bowed his head. Sam's breaths shortened. Why would the professor go so far?

"I assume you know the penalty for lying in a case like this." Marius watched the professor, calm and cold.

"I do." Plummet nodded. "I would give my life for Caerule." Lodon grinned. Marius glared at her.

"Dismissed." Marius leaned back in his chair. The muscles in his brow tensed. "The state calls Major Meg Alumen." Meg rose from her seat before Marius finished his sentence. Sam had never seen her so angry.

"Are you okay?" Meg stopped at Sam's chair and knelt on one knee.

"Major Alumen!" Marius rose from his chair, but Meg ignored him.

"I'm fine," Sam lied. The pain had returned tenfold and his numen was still too weak to heal the injuries. More than anything, Sam was scared.

"Major Alumen!"

"Coming!" Meg glared at Marius before returning her attention to Sam. "This will all be over soon. Trust me."

"Major Alumen!"

"Yes!" Meg took a seat in the wooden chair and crossed her arms.

"Sam never told you about this numen test, did he?"

"Testing errors aren't exactly news."

"Answer the question, Alumen!"

"Fine!" Meg uncrossed her arms. "He did not tell me. I assume he was more worried about the homicidal maniacs that infiltrated Central."

"HA!" Admiral Lodon laughed. Millenavis shook his head.

"Careful, Alumen." Marius spoke soft and slow. "I am still your superior officer; yours and Sam." Meg did not respond, but continued to glare at the Grand Master, unflinching. "At 15:23 today." Marius continued. "We detected a large electrical discharge from the Helena Bridge at your location. Sam was handcuffed to the bridge at that time, was he not?"

"Lakon gave him the key." Meg broke eye-contact. "I'm not sure what time."

"Then you didn't see Sam use his numen while handcuffed?" Marius leaned forward.

"No." Meg looked away.

"I see." Marius smirked. "And have you ever noticed anything strange about Sam's numen?"

"No." Meg answered, but did not meet the Grand Master's gaze. Marius stared at her a long time before leaning back in his chair

"Okay." Marius nodded. "Dismissed." Meg did not look at Sam as she passed. She returned to her seat and stared at the floor in silence. "The state calls its last witness: Detective James Lakon." Meg's head turned with a jerk. Sam peered around the edges of the stone chair. Even Lodon shifted her eyes in mild interest. As Lakon approached, Marius leapt to his feet, toppling his chair in the process.

"What's wrong?" President Millenavis looked at him, concerned.

"Nothing." Marius shook his head, face pale. "Sorry." Lakon rested his arm on the back of Sam's chair.

"And I thought I was the troublemaker." Lakon joked as he scanned the room.

"Lakon." Sam looked up at him. "Please don't do anything stupid."

"No promises." Lakon grinned.

"Detective Lakon." Marius began.

"Yes." Lakon glanced at him.

"Take a seat."

"I'm fine here, thanks." Lakon locked eyes with Marius. Sam couldn't help but crack a smile. It felt good to have Lakon at his side. "What do you want?"

"The truth." Marius demanded.

"Same here." Lakon paced around the courtroom, addressing everyone except Marius. "I was wondering if you could tell me why you're wasting time interrogating a boy who saved your lives today instead of the megalomaniac who killed a quarter million people in our capital city."

"Order!" Marius slammed his fist.

"Don't get me wrong." Lakon ignored him. "I love a good courtroom drama as much as the next guy, but can't this wait until our defendant is old enough to drive?-"

"Order!"

"-or has a lawyer?-"

"Order!"

"-or doesn't have life-threatening wounds bleeding through his shirt?"

"Order!" Marius rose from his chair. "One more word and I'll hold you in contempt."

"No you won't." Lakon countered.

"What was that?"

"You wouldn't have called me unless you needed my testimony. Besides, I don't have much to go back to anyways."

"Are you going to cooperate or not?" Marius closed his eyes. A vein twitched in his forehead.

"I don't know." Lakon shrugged. "We'll see."

"Fine." Marius snarled. "Did you handcuff Sam to the Helena Bridge?"

"I did."

"Did you give Sam a key to those handcuffs to help him escape?"

"I did."

"Did you help Sam escape when he was held captive on the transmission ship?" Marius opened his eyes. Sam held his breath. Lakon stared at Marius a long time before answering.

"I did."

"You're lying." Marius grinned. "All of you." He withdrew a small object from his pocket and held it up for all to see. Sam recognized it immediately. "This key was left on the Helena Bridge. The number confirms that this is the one and only key capable of unlocking those handcuffs. Tungsten is one of the strongest metals known to man, Lakon." Marius picked up a fresh set of tungsten handcuffs and brandished them at Lakon. "Please tell me how you helped Sam escape without this key."

Sam's heart sank. It was over. Marius laid a trap and Lakon walked right into it. No, it was worse. The professor and Meg were caught too. Sam turned to look at her. Meg's eyes widened and the color drained from her face. The professor held his breath. Only Lakon remained unfazed. He continued to watch Marius, unflinching.

Sam began to raise his hand. There was only one thing left to do: confess. If he cooperated, maybe they would spare Meg. Lakon grinned.

In a fluid motion, Lakon drew his revolver and fired. The bullet struck the handcuffs in Marius's hand, splitting the lock. The whole room stared in shock.

"Drop it!" Admiral Lodon rested her sword against Lakon's throat. Sam stared at the Admiral's vacant seat. She was so fast. When had she even moved? Lakon tossed the gun aside.

"It was my last bullet anyways." He shrugged.

"Arrest him!" President Millenavis hid beneath the judicial bench.

"Kill him!" Marius insisted.

"No." Admiral Lodon sheathed her sword. "It was a demonstration, nothing more." Marius stared at the splintered handcuffs. The fire in his eyes had died, replaced by disappointment.

"Then…it's over?" President Millenavis peered over the bench, trembling. "Should we call a vote?" Marius gave a solemn nod. Lodon returned to her seat.

"I don't care about the law." Admiral Lodon spoke first. "Sam saved his country. Not guilty."

"I am thankful for Sam's service." Marius rose to his feet, his unsettling gaze fixed on Lakon. "But I cannot allow the presumption of innocence; not in this case. The Septagon is a threat to all of us, everyone in the world. Even if this trial is inconclusive, the truth will reveal itself in time. Guilty."

"What!" Meg and Lakon shouted in unison. Sam's heart sank. What did Marius mean by that? Sam shifted uncomfortably in his chair. Worse yet, his fate was now in the hands of President Millenavis.

"Err...right...well..." The President began. It was worse than Sam thought. Millenavis did not know enough to judge this case if he had paid attention at all. "My fellow Caeruleans-" He began the judgement the same as his political speeches. President Millenavis stared at the broken Sword of Caerule resting on his podium; the inscription 'Truth, Loyalty, Justice' barely legible through the tarnish.

"My fellow Caeruleans." President Millenavis began again with a faint smile. "Truth, Loyalty and Justice are the pillars of our democracy. No truth has been found in this case. But, Sam's loyalty to Caerule is without question. Therefore, Justice demands a proper verdict. Not guilty."

"Yes!" Meg vaulted over the railing and embraced Sam in a tight hug.

"Ow! Meg. The burns." Sam gasped, but the pain was gone. Sam heaved a sigh of relief. For the first time in four days, he knew everything was going to be alright. Professor Plummet placed a hand on Sam's shoulder, a joyous tear rolling down his cheek. Even Lodon flashed Sam a quick thumbs-up when Marius's back was turned.

Only Lakon remained unmoved. He stood in the center of the courtroom, staring at the floor. He seemed confused by something.

"Lakon, get over here." Sam smiled, but Lakon did not seem to be paying attention. He knelt on one knee and placed his palm on the floor. Lakon's eyes widened.

"Everyone get out of here now!" Lakon yelled.

"What is it?" Meg released Sam.

"I don't know. Just go!" Lakon sprinted to the door. "I'll get Peter." Sam could feel it too: a writhing mass of numen far greater than any he had ever felt.

"Run!" Sam yelled, but it was too late. Pillars of black numen erupted through the floor and the world plunged into darkness.

Chapter 27 – The Pale Raven

Peter Turnus

"Do you believe in God?" Sinon watched Peter with unsettling scrutiny. The earth trembled and Peter glanced at the concrete ceiling, concerned.

"What?" He tried to ignore his former friend, but the broken mirror made things difficult.

"Do you believe in God?" Sinon repeated. "Not that Septem pretender. Do you believe in an actual, real God?"

"No." Peter's heart raced. Something was wrong.

"I'm not surprised." Sinon shook his head. "We've seen horrors few can imagine. What God would allow such cruelty? Then again, why do we?"

"Never thought about it." Peter hoped to end the conversation. It was obviously a distraction, but for what? Peter clenched the tungsten key hanging around his neck, desperate to confirm it was there.

"Neither did I." Sinon continued. "I dismissed religion as frivolous compared to harder science. But, facing the endless mystery of death has an odd way of changing your priorities. I assumed God and entropy were one in the same; random chance; cause and effect; and life nothing more than a chemical reaction in an otherwise arbitrary universe. But..." Sinon smiled upwards. "Fate makes believers of us all."

"What are you talking about?" Peter's breaths shortened. Sinon often used vague double-meanings to confuse opponents. Was the speech the distraction or something else?

"I don't know." Sinon smiled. "And I guess that's the beauty of it." Another tremor shook the room and Peter glanced towards the courthouse. "You're worried about them." Sinon continued. He sounded almost sincere. "So am I. We both know what this county is; what it's done. Truth, loyalty and justice will fail again, as they have countless times before."

"Shut up!" Peter clamped his eyes shut, desperate to clear his mind. Sinon's strategy was clear; a barrage of abstract questions followed by a personalized attack. Still, it made no sense. Sinon was wearing tungsten handcuffs. Peter gripped the key tighter. Was he reading minds or was this a relic of their former friendship?

"That's it?" Sinon's face pained in disbelief. "You swore you'd never lose another comrade."

"Caerule doesn't kill innocents." Peter insisted, desperate to reassure himself.

"They did seven years ago." Sinon's voice remained soft, almost trustworthy.

"Septem wasn't innocent." Peter struggled to shake the thought from his head.

"So you say." Sinon remained firm. "But he's not the only victim of Caerule. What of Ike? They raised him; they used him; they killed him like he was nothing."

"Shut up!" Peter fought the tears welling in his eyes. "That was my fault. No one else."

"You know that's not true." Sinon pleaded. "This world killed him. Now it's happening again and you're doing nothing to stop it." Peter met Sinon's gaze. Even now, he felt the hopeful innocence of his former friend. "Peter. Please." Sinon begged. "It's not too late. We can save them together; like old times. Just give me the key."

Peter's grip slackened. He stared at the tungsten key, imprinted in his open palm. Could reclaiming the past be so simple?

"No." Peter turned away from Sinon. "You'd kill me if you had the chance." He refocused his numen. Again, Peter felt nothing. Only dread remained. A third tremor shook the room. Sinon smiled and began to chant. His rhythm matched the beating of Peter's heart.

The day is here.
We stand as one.
The chains of fear,
Are now undone.

To all mankind;
To every part;
The free of mind;
The free of heart:

Our nations' shame,
Is not our own.
Our only claim,
Is life alone.

The only war,
Is fought within.
The soul is your
One place to win.

We stand with you,

Chapter 27 – The Pale Raven

Extend your hand
To others who
Your heart demand.

Together now,
We heed the call,
We will not bow,
We will not fall,
Again.

The earth trembled. Walls cracked. Black numen erupted from the ground. Peter created a barrier, too late. Concrete slabs fell from the ceiling, striking him in the head. Peter collapsed as rubble thundered around him. Light faded. Darkness reigned. Peter closed his eyes.

"Peter!" A voice called in the distance. "Peter!"

Peter basked in the sun's warm glow. The ides of March were a distant memory and April was all but forgotten. The budding May brought dandelions. Yellow shoots bursting from the hilltop, stretched their feeble stems towards the light.

Peter was young again; maybe seven or eight. He would always come here to relax after a hard day of training. Sinon was there too. Peter grabbed him in a bear hug and they tumbled down the hill, laughing.

"Peter!" Major Patricia Rocklos tried to stifle her amusement as she shook her head. "You shouldn't do that. One of you could get hurt."

"I'm fine." Sinon smiled, brushing the grass from his shirt.

"Nevertheless." Rocklos nodded. "You two are friends. Protect each other, no matter what."

"Peter!" A voice strained. "Help me."

"Sinon?" Peter squinted towards the voice. His vision blurred and refocused. It wasn't Sinon.

"Help…me…lift…this." Lakon threw his weight against the concrete slab trapping Peter's leg.

"Lakon?" Peter breathed. "How-"

"Later." Lakon grit his teeth. Peter pushed with his unbroken arm. The stone did not budge.

"I can't do this." Peter lowered his arm. It was hopeless. His mind and body were shattered. The weight was too heavy.

"Yes you can!" Lakon would not let go. He continued pushing the unmoving stone. "Trust me." Peter blinked. It wasn't his imagination. A faint trickle of numen flowed from Lakon, glowing with soft white light. Peter took a deep breath and pressed against the slab.

The stone shifted. Inch by inch, they pushed together until, at last, Peter wriggled free. Peter examined his crushed leg. Lakon sat against the slab, panting.

"We have to get back to the others." Lakon surveyed the devastation. Peter's eyes adjusted. He and Lakon rested atop a pile of rubble from the toppled building. Beneath them, twisted fragments of a metal table reflected pale moonlight. Peter's face paled. His eyes widened in realization.

"Lakon!" Peter shouted, but it was too late. Sinon smashed Lakon over the head with his tungsten handcuffs. Lakon fell to the ground. Sinon wrapped the chain around Peter's neck and squeezed.

"You underestimated me." Sinon grinned as the chain cut tighter into Peter's throat. "Did you really think I'd risk the future of this world on a numen battle with you? I broke this city. I broke this country. And now." Sinon smirked at the black tendrils of numen erupting from the earth. "The most powerful man in the world is bending to my will."

Peter choked and sputtered as he clawed at the tungsten chain. His face reddened. His arms shook. The fading lights of Aprilis blurred before his eyes.

"It's beautiful isn't it?" Sinon's lip curled as he surveyed the devastation. "So beautiful, we forget how fragile it truly is." Sinon pulled the chain tighter, strangling the final breaths from Peter's lungs. "One change in entropy and everything falls apart, but not you. You remained constant; loyal until the end." Peter's vision darkened. The General's words rang in his mind: *protect each other, no matter what.*

"I'm sorry, Peter." Sinon whispered in Peter's ear. Was it real or a memory? "You always were my closest friend."

Intense heat seared across the chain and the handcuffs disintegrated. Sinon tumbled backwards. Peter gasped for air.

"Enough!" A voice tore through the night. Peter turned towards the noise. His eyes blurred in and out of focus. Above them, a small, pale-faced man lowered his hand. There was no mistaking it. This was Raven.

"We should kill him now!" Sinon snarled. "He'll only get in our way."

"More than you already have?" Raven glared at him. Sinon clenched his fist.

"Everything I did." Sinon rose to his feet. His eyes burned with unrelenting fury. "Was for you." Raven's face darkened. He walked towards Sinon, calm and composed.

"You think I wanted this?" Raven spoke soft and slow. A chill ran down Peter's spine. Raven descended until he stood eye-level with Sinon.

"No." Sinon held his ground. "I know you wanted this." Their eyes locked, cold, hard and unflinching.

"Regroup with the others." Raven turned away. "I'll deal with you later."

"Welcome back to the fight." Sinon turned to leave. Raven remained silent. Sinon walked towards the river and disappeared behind a pile of smoldering rubble. Raven returned his attention to Peter. A shroud of dark numen coated his hand like a blade.

"Do it." Peter lay on his back, staring into the night's sky. He was done fighting. He couldn't win and, even if he could, what was the point? Raven raised the blade.

"Jet?" Lakon raised his head a few inches before passing out. Raven stopped. He stared at Lakon a long time, his face tired, almost sad. He lowered the blade.

"Take care of your friend." Raven said to Peter after a long pause. He walked towards the crystal waters of the Atropa River where the horizon glowed rose fingertips of sunrise.

Chapter 28 – A Change in Entropy

James Lakon

"All stars." Sam placed the final piece on the board. His face remained solemn and sad.

"Great job." Meg congratulated him, but continued staring out the window. In the distance, Lakon heard the shrill blare of trumpets. He shifted his weight, trying to prop himself up in the hospital bed.

"Lakon!" Sam rushed to his bedside. Meg rose from her chair, but remained on the opposite side of the room.

"Welcome back." She flashed Lakon a quick glance, but avoided eye contact.

"Thanks." Lakon rubbed the back of his head. "How long was I out?"

"Not sure." Meg looked back to the window. "Peter brought you back."

"How is he?" Lakon stared at the ceiling. The danger had passed, but something was still wrong. Meg did not respond.

"We were actually hoping you could tell us." Sam glanced at Meg, confused. "He was pretty beat up. What happened to you guys?" Meg remained still, but her eyes glinted with curiosity.

"I don't know." Lakon turned away. All this time, she still didn't trust him. "How are the others?"

"Dead, mostly." Meg answered just as Sam opened his mouth. She turned towards Lakon, but continued to avoid his gaze. "Everyone in the courtroom survived, thanks to you. As for the rest of Central…" Meg sat on the bed and stared out the window.

"I'm sorry." Lakon clenched his fist. The struggle, the sacrifice, the lives had been for nothing. Their loss was clear, brutal and total.

"You want revenge, don't you?" Meg sighed. It was a statement not a question.

"Are you going to stop me?"

"No." Meg withdrew a piece of paper from her pocket. She handed the paper to Lakon. "That is an offer to join Central, signed by Marius, Lodon and President Millenavis, himself. If you accept, you can start training immediately."

"Do you have a pen?" Lakon unfolded the paper and began reading.

"Lakon." Meg held Lakon's arm and looked him in the eye. "Once you sign this, there is no turning back. Please, think about it, at least until the end of the day." The trumpets blared a second time. Meg turned away. She brushed a tear from her eye and left the room. Sam watched until the door closed behind her.

"Thank you for covering for me back there?" Sam smiled.

"What?" Lakon groaned and clutched his chest.

"At the trial, I mean." Sam looked at Lakon, concerned.

"Oh! That." Lakon laughed and winced. "You saved my life. It's the least I could do."

"Lakon?" Sam asked. "Are you feeling alright?"

"Actually." Lakon closed his eyes. "I don't feel so good. Could you get a doctor?"

"Right away." Sam dashed from the room.

As soon as the door closed, Lakon sprang from the bed. He ran to the dresser and put on his clothes. Without bothering to tie his shoelaces, Lakon slipped out the door and walked down the hall, head down. Behind him, Sam and a team of doctors rushed to the now empty room. Lakon timed his walk and slipped through the elevator door just after a nurse swiped her card.

"Lobby." Lakon smiled. The nurse pushed the button without bothering to ask for identification. The nurse left on the fourth floor. As soon as she left, Lakon pushed the button for floor two and exited the elevator. Below, Lakon heard confused shouts and stomping echoes up the elevator shaft. Lakon proceeded to the nearest room, walked past the patients and jumped out the second-story window.

Outside, Lakon slipped into the large crowd marching towards the forum. He weaved through the mob, moving further and further from the hospital. After two or three minutes, Lakon sat on the curb to tie his shoes.

The crowd's excited babbling grew as Lakon neared the forum. There were people from all parts of Caerule, even the island territories. They spoke different accents, laughed different jokes, rambled different politics. It did not matter. Everyone was thrilled, basking in the pride for their shared country.

Lakon left the crowd. He followed a winding path through the remains of new and broken monuments. He was almost at the forum. Just a few more steps and...

Peter emerged from the shadows. His face was solemn but stern.

"Get out of my way, Peter." Lakon turned to face him.

"I hoped you'd sleep through this." Peter sighed.

"I bet you did. Move!"

"I can't do that." Peter remained firm. "I have no choice."

"We always have a choice."

"No. We don't."

"So that's it?" Lakon grit his teeth. "I thought your failure with Sinon would have taught you the importance of getting the right man."

"No." Peter shook his head. "It's taught me the problems of one man do not matter at the expense of a country." The trumpets blared a third time.

"You're wrong, Peter. That is when it matters most. Any country that abandons justice for convenience is doomed to fail." Lakon walked past Peter. There was still time. It was not too late.

"Where are you going?" Peter asked.

"To stop this." A transparent blue barrier formed in Lakon's path. Lakon reached into his coat pocket.

"Drop it!" Meg's finger pressed against the back of Lakon's head. She was ready to kill him. Lakon felt her confusion and fear.

"You too Meg?" A tear rolled down Lakon's cheek. He turned to face her.

"Drop it!" Meg's eyes softened but her voice remained firm. Lakon reached deeper into his pocket and withdrew his Aprilis PD badge.

"Fine." Lakon threw the badge at Meg's feet. The badge split as it struck the ground: the white stallion of Caerule on one side, the blue rose of Aprilis on the other. Meg's face paled. "I never deserved it anyways." Lakon turned away.

"Lakon!" Meg called after him. Lakon kept walking. "Lakon, please!" Meg ran after him.

"What?" Lakon stopped. He could not bear to look at her. "I will have no part in this." Meg looked at the ground.

"If you don't like it." Meg began to cry. "Change it!" Behind them, the crowd resounded a loud cheer.

"You asked me a question on the ship yesterday." Lakon stared into Meg's tearing eyes. He wanted to hurt her. "I've made my decision." He turned away from her.

"Lakon, please-" Meg began.

"Watch what happens here today." Lakon's face darkened. "Because, one day, it will be Sam." Meg did not respond. Lakon continued walking, brushing tears from his eyes as he rejoined the thronging crowd.

Head bowed, Lakon weaved through the sea of joy and exuberance arriving, at last, at the forum. Here, the crowd was thickest. Here, the noise was loudest. Here, the mob was liveliest, dancing about the forum's center where the wooden stage lay, waiting. These were the people Aprilis PD swore to protect. These were the people Miles gave his life to defend. Lakon hated all of them.

The crowd cheered and applauded as President Millenavis walked towards the stage, waving the broken Sword of Caerule. He smiled. He shook hands. He even kissed a baby. The President ran up the stairs two-at-a-time and turned with a flourish to wave at his adoring fans. He grabbed the microphone from the podium and pranced around the stage as Caerule's national anthem blared across the forum.

The ocean waves are rough.
Our enemies are tough.
We continue sailing to;
Our Caerule;
Of the just and true.

And we'll sail on the rising tides;
Till the light of the horizon dies;
Our Caerule Blue will guide us through.
Trust in me.
I will trust in you.

Do not cry, oh my beloved;
We are blessed by God above;
Our flag flew though darkness grew.
Our Caerule;
My crew sails for you.

And we'll sail on the rising tides;
Till the light of the horizon dies;
Our Caerule Blue will guide us through.
Trust in me.
I will trust in you.

Fallen free by land or sea;
Your memory lives in me.
We stay true to all we knew;
Our Caerule;
Honors all of you.

And we'll sail on the rising tides;

Chapter 28 – A Change in Entropy

Till the light of the horizon dies;
Our Caerule Blue will guide us through.
Trust in me.
I will trust in you.

"My fellow Caeruleans!" President Millenavis pointed the microphone towards the crowd so their shouts echoed through the speakers. "Thank you." Millenavis returned the microphone to his mouth. "These past few days have been trying for us all. But, I assure you, Caerule will emerge greater and stronger than before." Lakon bit his lip. "Truth, Loyalty and Justice are the pillars of our democracy." President Millenavis held the sword for everyone to see. "And justice will be served." The crowd roared their approval. Millenavis basked in the applause.

"Our enemy was formidable. Many brave men and women fought for their country, some making the ultimate sacrifice." Millenavis bowed his head. The crowd followed his lead. Lakon looked across sea of people. Only one person was not bowing: Paul Whitney.

"Paul!" Lakon tried to fight through the crowd. The boy met his gaze. Broken and helpless, Paul's eyes ran red with tears. "Paul!" Everyone stood, obscuring him from view. "Paul!" Lakon pressed forward. He forced his way through the crowd. Paul was gone.

"What's the matter with you?"

"God damn it!"

"Show some respect!"

Voices raged around Lakon, spiteful and bloodthirsty. A trumpet blast called their attention back to the stage. Lakon's eyes darkened as he watched Marius drag Neil Whitney towards the stage.

"I'm innocent," Neil pleaded. The crowd did not care. They booed, jeered and threw stones. Blood stained the forum.

Marius pushed Neil up the stairs. Three times, Neil fell. Three times, he was forced back to his feet. The crowd continued cheering. Marius continued shoving. Millenavis continued speaking.

"Not since the end of The Great War have I seen Caerule so united. For our country, I have never been more proud." President Millenavis smiled, handing Marius the broken sword. Marius threw Neil to his knees and glared in Lakon's direction. "Today, we stand together! Today, we declare victory! Today, we show the world who we truly are!" Marius raised the sword. "God bless Caerule!"

The blade fell, the crowd cheered and entropy increased again.

Lodon's Logbook

Introduction

Congratulations, soldier. The fact you're reading this means two things. First, you're alive. Pay attention and maybe we can keep it that way. Second, you have clearance to read this document, meaning you are either a contemptable Central brownnose or someone I trust with my life.

The following documents are excerpts from my personal logbook, selected for their relevance to the Helena Bridge incident and the events that followed. All entries were written prior to these events and will need to be updated accordingly.

Caerule suffered much these past few days. We lost family, friends, comrades and more. The time for mourning has passed. Now, we must rebuild. The soul of our great nation will be defined in the coming months. I expect you to join me in defining it.

To my trusted allies, I assure you, Caerule will emerge from this stronger and prouder than before. And, to any enemies who may be reading this, I warn you, the tides of vengeance are rising.

-Fleet Admiral Margaret Lodon

Numen Overview

I hate numen. When it's not granting unfathomable power to Caerule's enemies, it's being wielded by some of the most arrogant and overrated Generals our country has to offer. I'm not sure which is more dangerous. Nevertheless, it is imperative for commanders to understand all threats present on the battlefield, so I require all naval officers to study numen regardless of their ability to use it.

For better or worse, Caerule and the other Great Nations, have censored information about numen from the general public. This restriction seems to have originated during the Great Schism more than seven hundred years ago. Since studying the Great Schism is also restricted, the reasons for this ban are unknown.

Numen is a form of supernatural energy present in all living and most non-living things. As far as we know, the power existed throughout history and seems to play key roles in most religions. All cultures have different origin myths, but most seem to involve a pantheon of between one and eight gods that gifted their "divine power" to humanity long ago. Trace amounts of numen have since been found in all organic and most non-organic matter (including celestial bodies) casting doubt on these mythical accounts. The history of numen continues to be a debated subject for scientists and anthropologists allowed to study it.

All humans possess numen, but less than five percent have enough to use it effectively. Life isn't fair. Get over it. Thresholds vary between nations but, generally, Caerule will not bother training anyone with a numen count less than eight hundred Wolframs. Those with lower numen counts are less likely to develop a numen "power", one of the main goals of numen training. These powers typically fall into one of seven categories, Creation, Manipulation, Transformation, Observation, Assimilation Adaptation and Augmentation.

Numen Categories

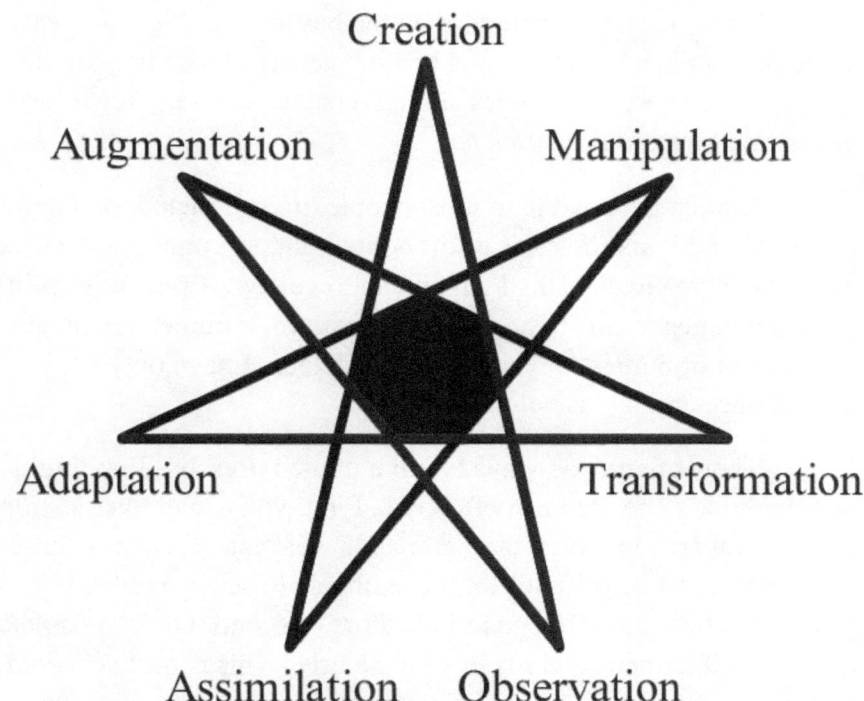

Numen Category	Description	Notable Users
Creation	Create objects or energies, often with unique properties	Peter Turnus Rex Newton Sam Pere
Manipulation	Manipulate objects or forces of nature	Sylvania Birnam
Transformation	Transform objects or materials, often with unique properties	Abraham Panzer
Observation	Use numen as a "sixth sense" to gain information otherwise unobtainable	Sinon Donafer General Patricia Rocklos
Assimilation	Enhance the user's abilities by absorbing numen from others	Marius Sulla Tom Bell
Adaptation	Alter the user's physiology, often with unique abilities	Meg Alumen Leah Penthes
Augmentation	Channel numen into existing objects, imbuing them with unique properties	Artemis Arundo General Jesse Bell

Numen Combat

Numen is a powerful tool on the battlefield. It can increase strength, stamina, durability and healing ability, depending on the user's skill. These advantages are universal to all users, regardless of their numen classification.

Numen is invisible to most people, myself included. I am told it typically manifests as a soft white light, surrounding the user in a protective cloak. This I am unable to verify. A person's ability to sense numen seems to be correlated with their numen count and the amount of numen they are trying to detect. I have only seen numen once and it was colored gold.

There are no bad ways to kill a numen user, but I've found two methods to be the most effective. First, you can deliver a strong attack to an area in which their numen is weakest. Targeting these weaknesses can be difficult for those unable to sense numen, but fighting stances are often good indicators. Second, you can deplete their overall numen reserves in a long battle. This is best achieved by forcing your opponent into situations disadvantageous to their unique numen ability.

The metal tungsten can be a valuable tool in numen combat. It has the lowest numen sensitivity of any known material and, supposedly, cannot be created, transformed or manipulated. From personal experience, I know this assumption to be untrue but am unable to share specifics at this clearance level.

Most weapons, infrastructure and restraints designed to resist numen users will employ tungsten in some form. Tungsten weapons and projectiles are difficult for numen users to block, equivalent to a similar strength numen attack. Tungsten infrastructure cannot be influenced by numen, forcing saboteurs to depend on alternative destruction methods. Tungsten handcuffs and similar restraints have the added benefit of suppressing captives' abilities to utilize or protect themselves with numen.

Great Nations Overview

Great Nation	Description
Caerule	Caerule is the world's dominant naval power and leader of global shipping. Our primary foreign policy objectives are maintaining these monopolies at all costs. Our economy is fourth largest in the world and second largest per capita. Consisting of two water-locked continents and a series of island territories, no land belonging to Caerule has ever been successfully invaded and I intend to keep it that way.
Aquilla	Aquilla is the world's most populous country and Caerule's strongest ally. Their standing army is larger than the other six Great Nations combined, consisting primarily of infantry and powerful numen users. Aquilla is the world's third largest economy, but smallest per capita. Conditions are improving but widespread poverty remains a challenge for the country.
Ferox	Ferox is a brutal country that pursues genetics and eugenics to horrifying extremes. They often initiate wars and are the only country to be invaded by the other six Great Nations simultaneously. We lost. Ferox excels in biological warfare if you could call it that. Their country teems with vicious wildlife, most of which was genetically engineered in secret government laboratories. These experiments, while ethically questionable, have made Ferox an innovator of medical technology.
Nemo	Nemo is the world's preeminent industrial power and largest economy. Experts in military and industrial automation, they frequently invade smaller countries for resources to fuel their insatiable appetite for continued growth.
Ardor	Ardor is the oldest and formerly most powerful nation, being the only country in history to have conquered the entire planet. Ardor maintained this worldwide dominance for approximately five hundred years before the events of the Great Schism fractured their empire. Weakened by centuries of feudalism and civil war, modern Ardor is by far the smallest economy of the Great Nations. They maintain their current power with unparalleled missile stockpiles.
Borea	Borea has emerged as the world's leading air power and primary rival to Caerule's trade monopoly. Their economy is the second smallest, but fastest growing of the Great Nations. Borea's military primarily consists of a strong air force, which boasts the ability to strike any target within thirty minutes.
South Alamus	South Alamus is by far the most technologically advanced of the Great Nations. If they put their minds to it, I am convinced they could conquer the other six Great Nations, easily. However, they always seem to have other objectives. South Alaman weapons are superior in every way, but rarely progress past the prototype phase. Their military scientists seem more interested in research than practical mass production. South Alamus has the second largest economy in the world and are the wealthiest per capita. Their leaders claim to be peaceful, but I do not trust them.